ACCLAIM FOR THE NOVELS OF CHARLENE TEGLIA

"This is great erotic fiction! . . . Fresh, sexy, and humorous."
—*Romantic Times BOOK reviews*

"Action-packed and ferociously seductive."
—*Romance Reviews Today*

"I highly recommend this sensual feast to erotica lovers everywhere."
—*Fallen Angel Reviews*

"A great book full of action and adventure . . . Charlene Teglia has a knack for creating wonderful stories with characters that will keep readers coming back for more."
—*Romance Junkies*

"The dilemma of loving the enemy is devilishly designed in Charlene Teglia's evocative XXX supernatural romance."
—*Genre Go Round Reviews*

"Don't miss out on this incredible new talent."
—*Love Romances*

"A must-read."
—*The Road to Romance*

"Ms. Teglia is a terrific writer who has penned a story of love and magic that left me sighing at the end."
—*Just Erotic Romance Reviews*

"I laughed, then I sighed and had tears in my eyes at the end . . . a book I intend to read again and again!"
—*Joyfully Reviewed*

ALSO BY
CHARLENE TEGLIA

Wicked Hot

Satisfaction Guaranteed

Wild Wild West

ANIMAL ATTRACTION

CHARLENE TEGLIA

ST. MARTIN'S GRIFFIN
NEW YORK

This is a work of fiction. All of the characters, organizations, and events portrayed in this novel are either products of the author's imagination or are used fictitiously.

ANIMAL ATTRACTION. Copyright © 2009 by Charlene Teglia. All rights reserved. Printed in the United States of America. For information, address St. Martin's Press, 175 Fifth Avenue, New York, N.Y. 10010.

www.stmartins.com

Library of Congress Cataloging-in-Publication Data

Teglia, Charlene.
    Animal attraction / Charlene Teglia. — 1st ed.
      p. cm.
   ISBN-13: 978-0-312-53741-8
   ISBN-10: 0-312-53741-7
    1. Werewolves—Fiction. I. Title.
  PS3620.E4357A85   2009
  813'.6—dc22

                                       2008035893

10 9 8 7 6 5 4 3 2

To the fabulous staff of The Human Bean for keeping the espresso brewing

ACKNOWLEDGMENTS

Thanks to my husband for advice and technical help on guns and ammunition, and to the Write Ons for writing on with me.

ANIMAL
ATTRACTION

CHAPTER ONE

IT'S AMAZING HOW MUCH CAN CHANGE IN THE SPACE OF A HEARTBEAT.

One minute, I was alone in the Tysons Corner leather store organizing stock. Rehanging jackets that had been tried on and decided against, or more likely tried on for no better reason than to get me to turn around and reach up to unhook them. It had been that kind of afternoon.

And then the hairs on the back of my neck stood up. My first thought was, *Oh shit, I'm going to be robbed.* In which case I would calmly and quietly open up the register and let the crackheads clean it out. There are some things worth fighting for, but a minimum-wage job in a mall store isn't one of them.

"I want . . . that," a voice said far too close to my ear. The voice was deep, masculine, and sort of growly. The owner of the voice exhaled and warm breath moved over the exposed skin at the nape of my neck. I wished I hadn't cut my hair so short. A strange man's breath on my skin made me feel far too vulnerable.

I turned, putting a little space and the brown leather bomber jacket I was holding between us in the process. Now I could see who I was dealing with. His eyes were dark brown lit with amber. His hair matched his eye color and fell just to the tops of his shoulders, although the natural curl made it look shorter. He had an uncompromising expression on features that looked vaguely Slavic, and while he wasn't much over six feet he managed to give the impression that every inch was formidable. He wore blue jeans and cowboy boots and a white long-sleeved T-shirt with a Harley-Davidson logo that couldn't possibly be warm enough in the dead of winter, even in Virginia.

Maybe he really had just come in for a jacket. The hackles he'd raised coming in didn't lie down, though, so I remained on guard. I have pretty good instincts for trouble, and they've saved me too often for me to ignore them.

"I don't think it's your size," I said, continuing to hold the distressed leather between us. Not that it made much of a barrier, but it was something. "There are more over there." I tilted my head to indicate the rack. My hands stayed right where they were, at about middle height where they could block low or high without having to travel the full distance either way.

He gave me a measuring look and then obligingly moved to the display of bomber jackets. I breathed a little easier when he put a couple of feet between us.

"Chandra," he said, drawing the word out. He lifted a sleeve for closer inspection as he said it. "That's your name?"

"Says so on my name tag," I said. I smiled, but my lips were tight over my teeth. I didn't want to encourage any familiarity. He'd come into my store while I was alone, he'd stood too close, he'd breathed on me, and now he was using my name. That was a good tactic for getting somebody to relax and trust you: use their name. It had the opposite effect on me, coming from him.

"Did you know it means 'the moon shining'?"

"No," I lied. I knew what the books said, but I was pretty sure it really meant my birth parents were liberal arts students with more romantic ideas than money or sense. They'd put me up for adoption and stuck me with the name as part of the adoption requirement. Although part of me had always wondered if that was so I could be tracked down eventually. There aren't a lot of redheaded American women in their early twenties with Sanskrit names.

"Do you dream of us?" He raised his head as he asked the question, his eyes intent on mine.

"I have lots of dreams. Everybody does." I shifted my feet, preparing to fight or run if I needed to. I didn't like anything about this encounter. "One of my dreams involves making sales and staying employed. Do you want to buy that?"

"I haven't tried it on yet." His lips curved in a smile I didn't like, even though I had to admit it looked good on him. He looked like he was laughing at me. Toying with me.

"I'm not sure it fits." He took it off the hanger and put it on. It seemed to me that he drew the motions out deliberately, like he was putting on a show for me.

I watched the way he moved, but not because I was taken in by a nice body. I noted the harnessed power in his movements and mentally upgraded his strength significantly over my initial estimate. If it came to fight or flight, I'd run. I was too likely to lose a physical confrontation, no matter how many dirty tricks I knew. He was solid and graceful and he knew how to use his body to advantage.

"I'm Zach," he said, smoothing the front of the jacket. My eyes followed his hands. The jacket looked good on him. I suspected pretty much anything would.

"Nice to meet you." My tone was flat and unfriendly. The gleam in his eyes told me he wasn't discouraged.

"Now we're on a first-name basis." Zach the stranger took a step forward, and I stepped back to maintain our distance. He quirked a brow at me. "Running away?"

I ignored the question. "Bombers are on sale this week. Twenty percent off. Would you like to wear that out?"

"Yes." He grinned at me. "I suppose you'd like me to buy it and leave now."

"You might also want something to protect the leather." I waved at the counter by the cash register. "You should treat it before it's exposed to rain."

"The cow this came from stood outside and got wet," Zach pointed out, his lips twitching with what looked like a barely contained urge to laugh.

"The cow wasn't a fashion garment." I walked around and behind the register, managing not to turn my back to him in the process.

"Already you're changing how I dress, and we haven't even had our first date." Zach the outrageous flirt took the jacket back off and handed it to me so I could remove the security tag and scan the price. His flirting didn't reassure me at all. Everything about him screamed *stranger danger,* no matter how hot he looked in tight jeans and boots and a leather bomber.

"Then you're getting off lucky, since we aren't going to have a date." I charged him for the leather protector and told him the total.

Zach gave me a gold card that didn't improve my opinion of him in the least. So he had money. That didn't make him safe. It might conceivably make him an even greater threat. Some people thought money would buy anything and enough of it made them exempt from the rules.

According to the card, his full name was Zachary Neuri. I gave him the jacket to wear out of the store and bagged the bottle I didn't think he'd ever use. Which made me even happier about selling it to him.

"You don't trust me." Zach's smile vanished as he donned the garment.

"Mom warned me about guys like you."

"Then you should have expected me." He looked so intent and determined as he said it that I had to fight the urge to take a step back. "I'll be seeing you, Chandra."

After he left I stayed still, focusing on breathing until my heart rate settled down. What was that crack about my mom? I'd meant my adoptive parent, but was he in some way connected with my mysterious all-records-sealed birth mother?

I finally went back to organizing the stock, but I couldn't shake the feeling of being watched. When two other store employees came on and my shift ended, I was glad to leave. I wandered through the large shopping center on a random route just in case I wasn't simply jumpy and paranoid after meeting Mr. I'll-Be-Seeing-You.

Most guys didn't rattle me, not even bullies. Zach had not been most guys. But I didn't see anybody who matched his height and shape, didn't glimpse a brown bomber or curling hair, when I paused and turned to look around me from time to time under the guise of browsing. So I made my way to the entrance nearest my car and headed toward my parking spot. I walked quickly but steadily, head up, eyes forward, the keys ready in my hand.

A trio got out of a car near mine, two men and a woman. I didn't make eye contact, just noted their position and adjusted my angle so that our paths wouldn't intersect.

Except they did, because the trio moved toward me and spread out, making a sort of loose net. They were too close for me to safely get my door unlocked and inside, so I turned to put the side of my car at my back and drew my feet into the cat stance.

The back of my neck was prickling again and goose bumps marched up and down my skin. I ignored the distraction and kept the three of them in my field of vision.

Which is why I saw Zach before they did. He appeared behind them, seemingly out of nowhere, and maneuvered himself in front of me so fast I blinked.

"Rhonda. Wilson. Miguel." Zach nodded at each of them in turn. "Did you want something?"

"Is she your bitch?"

The woman who I guessed must be Rhonda asked the question. I had a sudden vision of Zach and myself in orange prison garb and swallowed a laugh. His bitch? Was she kidding?

"She's my business and none of yours." Zach's answer was flat.

"She's on our territory." This from the big, bald black guy. I wasn't sure if he was Miguel or Wilson. Neither of the men looked Hispanic to me.

"She has a job in the mall."

"She should find another one. It'd be better for her health."

I went cold. Had I stumbled into some sort of gang-related turf struggle? *Thanks, Zach.*

"I take her health very seriously." Zach's tone intensified with threat.

"As seriously as we take the insult of your presence here?" That came from Rhonda, followed by a roundhouse kick that proved she wasn't just a pretty face.

After that, things happened fast, and moments later the three of them were down. Zach grabbed my wrist, plucked the keys from my hand, and unlocked my car, pushing me inside and following me in one uninterrupted move.

I scooted over the gearshift and into the passenger seat, my back to the door, my fingers reaching for the handle to open it to jump out the other side. Zach caught the arm closer to him in a grip that was hard enough to hurt.

"Stop."

I froze. Then I saw blood on his Harley shirt that hadn't been there before. The shirt had a new rip in it. "You didn't zip the jacket," I said, staring. That was dumb. Leather might have protected him. "Which one of them had a knife?"

"Rhonda."

"And she called *me* a bitch." I shook my head and reached out a tentative hand, lifting the shirt to see how badly he was hurt. "Do you need a doctor?"

"No. It wasn't silver."

I frowned, unable to process why the metal the blade was made out of would make any difference to the severity of his wound. My frown deepened when I couldn't find the cut on his perfect six-pack that should have been there to go with the damaged shirt and the blood.

"I'm fine, but feel free to inspect." I looked up and found Zach's eyes on me, full of humor and a heat I didn't think the situation warranted.

I planted my hand on his bare skin and ran it slowly over every inch that wasn't covered by his jeans. Belly, ribs, chest, all of it strong and beautiful and warm to the touch, and none of it marked by any sign of injury.

"I can unzip if you want to keep going." Zach indicated his lap. I took my hand away, let his T-shirt fall back into place, and sat back.

"No, thanks." I didn't know what to think. I still didn't trust him, but he'd defended me, fought for me. Taken a wound for me. And now it had somehow vanished? "Who the hell are you?"

"Zach." He lifted the hand he hadn't released and drew it to his lips. He pressed a warm kiss to the back of my hand. Heat shivered over me. "We have a date."

"No, we don't."

"The moon is waxing." Zach leaned toward me and brought his other hand up to cup my cheek. I didn't pull away. "It'll be full in three more nights. If you don't come to us by then, we'll come for you. It's time."

"What, are you in some sort of gang or cult?" I blurted out the question. "I don't want any trouble."

"Trouble wants you." Zach caressed my cheek, trailed his fingers along my jaw, and touched the racing pulse at my throat. "You'd better find another job. We've been looking out for you, but nobody likes you coming onto panther turf six days a week. Next time there might be more of them, or they might be quicker."

Zach had been unbelievably fast, and he'd still been cut. They could be quicker than that? I mentally kissed my job good-bye and wondered how fast I could find another one. Or maybe I should simply move on. Zach's implication that others were watching me, following me, and planning to move in on me three days from now made greener pastures pretty attractive.

"Don't try to run." Zach frowned at me as if he'd read my mind. "It's dangerous for you to live apart from us, especially now. You need to come home."

"I have a home. You don't belong in it." Not that he'd be unpleasant to wake up to, but he did seem to be up to his neck in complications. Anybody sleeping next to him might be sleeping in a danger zone.

"Maybe you belong in mine." Zach's lips curved, and then his head dipped. It was more the promise of a kiss than the real thing, a brush of lips, a breath of heat. It was enough to send my heart stumbling and make my blood rush. "Come to us, Chandra. You'll find us at the place you see in your dreams."

Before I could think of a comeback, Zach was gone and I was left wondering if I'd imagined the whole thing. Just in case I hadn't and there were more people waiting to spring out at me, I climbed back into the driver's seat and headed for my nice, safe, sane apartment where I hoped there wouldn't be any surprises waiting.

CHAPTER TWO

HOME FELT MARGINALLY SAFER, BUT NOT ENOUGH TO BE MUCH COMfort. I stopped inside the entry hall for my mail, inserting my key into the box for my unit. Habit made me scan the envelopes while I stood there. Sure enough, one was for 2C, not 2B. I set it on top of the boxes, the common tenant exchange for misdelivered mail.

I went upstairs to my second-floor door with an uneasy tension between my shoulder blades. Having my own door closed and locked behind me made me feel a little better. Almost getting jumped in a parking lot could really put a girl on edge.

I dropped the mail on my kitchen counter and after scarfing down a quick dinner to satisfy my increasingly demanding metabolism, I went to feed my goldfish, Ernie and Bert. I'd bought the pair and the glass bowl they lived in the week before I found my current job.

According to a book I'd read on feng shui, goldfish in the wealth corner of your home could ease financial troubles. I wondered if there was a feng shui remedy for finding out your job was in gang territory.

Ernie and Bert came to the surface, mouths open, ready for dinner. I sprinkled a pinch of fish food over the water and watched them nibble.

"I made some new friends today," I told them, thinking of Rhonda, Miguel, and Wilson. And Zach. I wasn't forgetting Zach. Zach who flirted with me while he made the hairs on the back of my neck prickle, who fought off three opponents, at least one of them armed, and told me I should've been expecting him.

I was expecting him now. He said he'd been watching me and if I didn't come to him in three days, he'd come for me. He'd hinted that he knew things about me and my birth family. He was the first lead I'd found in a string of dead ends, and I was curious enough about what he might know to stick around.

"I think one of them wanted to date me," I added, even though Bert hadn't asked. "In a stalkerish sort of way." What kind of guy tells you he's been watching you and kisses the back of your hand?

I looked around the apartment. It was decorated in modern bland. Light gray carpet, beige walls, white blinds over the windows. Matching vertical blinds covered a sliding glass door to a postage-stamp-sized balcony. I kept a stick in the door so it couldn't be opened from the outside if somebody managed to climb to the second floor. Which was unlikely. But meeting my new friends made me nervous enough to go check to make sure the door was still secure.

With the exception of the goldfish, I hadn't done much to personalize the neutral décor. I had a futon in the living room that did double duty as sofa and bed, a bookcase that housed my DVD collection, and a small TV set.

For some reason, the look of the apartment bothered me today. I frowned and looked closer, wondering if something was out of place. If something was, I couldn't tell.

Maybe I was just seeing it the way a stranger would and I didn't like what it said about me. Bland and utilitarian, not much in the way of personality, more of a waiting station than a home.

Of course, it pretty much *was* a waiting station. I'd graduated college a year early, and now I was circulating my résumé in search of a real job. So far I'd had two offers, both of which would have meant relocating to the West Coast. Nice, but I didn't want to leave Virginia.

Fairfax County not only offered easy access to mountains and beaches; it also was home to six Fortune 500 companies. The combination of career and recreation opportunities was hard to beat. Most of all, I hoped that if I stayed where I'd been born and raised, someday I'd find out who my birth parents were. Or at least get the answers to some of my questions.

So, if I was so set on staying, why did everything in my life look so temporary?

"I'm young," I said out loud. "You're not supposed to be settled at my age. You're supposed to dress and live like you just got out of college, where you mortgaged your soul to student loans."

Bert and Ernie swam around agreeably. Fish make such nice roommates. They listen and they don't argue.

The light on my answering machine was blinking, so I hit Play.

"Hi, it's Michelle. I have some of your mail. I'm holding it hostage until you call me. I haven't seen you since your birthday." There was a short pause on the machine before she continued, "I hope you're okay. Your nightmares sound like they're getting worse."

The sound of my friend's voice made my stomach tighten. I'd been avoiding everybody. Apparently Michelle had noticed. She also lived in the apartment below mine. If she was hearing more nocturnal noise, then it wasn't my imagination. The night terrors that had been a recurring problem since adolescence were now nightly.

In pretty much every way, I'd taken a turn for the worse after my twenty-first birthday two weeks earlier. My metabolism was off the charts. Sounds, smells and tastes I'd been sensitive to before were now unbearable. Everything set me off. But what could I say? *Sorry, Michelle, I can't get together because your perfume makes me feel like I'm suffocating from one floor away?*

My mind drifted back to Zach and his odd question. *Do you dream of us?* It'd be nice to have an explanation for my bad nights and the bruises I kept waking up with, but since I'd just met him, Zach couldn't possibly be the cause.

I did wonder what kind of group "us" included. Not the trio he'd fought off in the parking lot. But some group. It wasn't just Zach who was expecting me to show up in three days. It seemed like too much to hope that "us" might mean the family I knew nothing about. But the fragile hope rose anyway, tempered by a deep measure of caution.

I didn't know anything about my heritage. I knew next to nothing about Zach. And given the way we'd met and the things he'd said, I had plenty of reasons to proceed with caution if I did go to meet him.

Although I couldn't imagine where he thought I'd go even if I wanted to. The place in my dreams? Please. That had to be a line. Except he'd seemed serious when he said it.

Tired of my thoughts spinning like a hamster on a wheel, I told myself to forget Zach. Even if he was going to show up here looking for me, it wouldn't be tonight. The moon wasn't full.

When I woke up, I realized three things. I felt a cold draft coming from an open window, I ached in several places, and a strange man was holding me in a sort of bear hug. His hands pinned my wrists crossed in front of my chest and his legs trapped mine.

The hair at the back of my neck stirred and gooseflesh marched over my skin. Zach was my first suspect, but the man behind me didn't match my memory of his build or scent. I closed my eyes and said a silent prayer that it wasn't Miguel or Wilson.

"Hello," I said cautiously. My voice sounded hoarse, as if I'd been yelling. "If you're here to rob me, I'm broke and I don't have any drugs."

"I'm not here to rob you. I'm here to babysit you," the man behind me said. He sounded pissed off about it.

The various aches I felt reminded me of the aftermath of a hard sparring session. I tried to stretch, but Mystery Man held me firmly in place.

"Would you let go, please?" Now that I was awake, I really wanted my personal space. And then I wanted to know who he was and how he'd gotten inside.

"So you can try to break my jaw again? No."

He *was* pissed. But if I'd succeeded he wouldn't be talking, so I didn't think he was hurt. "Were we fighting?" I asked.

"You were fighting. I was defending myself." His grip tightened as if in silent warning that he wasn't about to let up.

I guessed he'd come in during one of my bouts of night terrors and I'd fought with him without waking up. "This is my apartment and I didn't invite you in," I pointed out.

"Good thing I'm not a vampire," my uninvited guest said. "I figured you were screaming because you had a problem, so I didn't wait for permission."

I wanted to ask if Zach had sent him to keep an eye on me. Not that I'd count him as one of the good guys if he said yes, but it would mean he wasn't one of the panthers. Whoever they were. I didn't ask because if he was on the other side, mentioning Zach might make him more pissed off. And tempted to take it out on me.

So I stayed quiet, feeling the tension build until my skin was practically crawling with it. My heart seemed to beat faster every second and I fought to control my breathing, trying to slow it down and pretend a measure of calm.

After what felt like eternity but must've been less than a minute, he let out a growling sound of frustration that would have frozen me if I wasn't paralyzed already. "I'm not going to hurt you."

"Right." My tight voice said plainly what I really thought.

"I'm not going to let go of you, either. You fight dirty."

That sounded like a grudging compliment.

"Kenpō," I said. "The fight is over when your opponent is unable to continue."

"Smart." His approving tone made my brows raise.

I wondered how long we were going to stay like this. It was almost a parody of lovers spooning. I didn't think I could break his hold and get free long enough to call 911, and even if I did, he'd have me at his mercy again before I completed the call, let alone before help arrived.

I hoped he really was there to babysit me. It didn't seem reasonable that he'd just restrain me otherwise. He could have tied me up, stolen my goldfish, murdered me.

Maybe he could be reasoned with. "You can let go of me now. I promise not to hit you." *Unless you deserve it.*

He didn't answer. I tried to wiggle out of his hold, and his grip tightened.

"This has been a very strange day," I said. "Why don't you just tell me what you want from me?"

"What I want?" His low, rough voice had an odd tone to it. His hold didn't change and he didn't move, but something shifted. The word *want* seemed to echo in my head, taking on intent with each repetition.

My heartbeat thumped louder. I wished I'd kept my damn mouth shut.

"Now you're afraid." He seemed to find that funny.

Great. Alone with a sadistic stranger. Who was holding me. On what served as my bed.

"What I want is a kiss." His voice sounded as dark as the night.

I gulped and the sound was far too audible.

"You kissed Zach. Fair's fair." His voice traveled down my spine, leaving a wake of hyperalert tension behind.

"He kissed me," I corrected through frozen lips. And how the hell did he know about that?

Something familiar registered, the distinctive smell of leather. He was wearing a leather jacket. Had he bought it from me? Could I identify him if I saw him?

The leather creaked as he shifted. His lips touched my temple and I stopped breathing. His hands holding mine prisoner suddenly seemed unbearably intimate. If he moved his hands just a little he'd be touching my breasts. The sweats I wore didn't seem like much of a barrier. They were loose and easily pushed aside.

"Turn your face," he said.

If I turned my head toward his, our lips could touch. If I kissed him, would he let me go? Would it distract him and give me an opportunity to get the upper hand, or at least get away?

Thoughts racing faster than my heart, I angled my jaw to bring our mouths within meeting range. Then heat seared my mouth as he claimed it with his.

It wasn't the brief taste of a kiss Zach had given me. It was hard, hot, and hungry. Terror gave it an adrenaline-packed intensity, sending blood thundering through my veins until I thought my heart would explode in my chest. When he tried to deepen the kiss I kept my mouth stubbornly closed while he licked at the seam of my sealed lips. He growled in frustration. "Open."

"No." The denial was automatic, and as stupid as it was useless. His tongue took the opening I gave him as he turned me toward him, pushing my arms behind my back, where he kept them pinned.

The kiss was dominating, devastating, and I had no way to defend against it. I fell into it as something inside me woke up and welcomed the brutal eroticism that was both combative and seductive. His legs kept mine in a tight scissor grip. He wasn't lowering his guard. The respect that implied pleased me. He seriously thought I could give him some difficulty if he gave me an opening?

His body pressed into mine. His scent mingled with leather filled my senses. The gooseflesh marched impossibly under my skin, ran along my nerves, fired an urgent message through muscle and blood until I trembled with the need to respond in some deeper, instinctual way that went beyond my experience. I felt light, as if all the oxygen were leaving my body, and went limp. He raised his head, breaking the kiss. I drew in shuddering, gulping breaths, not caring if I sounded like a marathoner on the twentieth mile while he seemed completely unmoved. I needed air.

"Zach didn't kiss me like that," I muttered. And wondered if it was a complaint. Nobody had ever kissed me like that. It was like being hit by a freight train of carnal intent, sucker punched in the libido. I hadn't asked for it, but I hadn't tried to break free from it, either.

"He will."

The certainty in the stranger's voice made me shiver.

CHAPTER THREE

I RESTED IN THE ARMS OF A MAN WHO'D BROKEN INTO MY APARTMENT, and wondered why I thought I was safe. His mouth alone was a lethal weapon. "I want a light on," I said once I could talk again. "I want to see your face."

It didn't seem right that I'd had the most intense kiss of my life from a man I wouldn't know if I passed him on the street.

"No."

It was the kind of no that didn't lend itself to argument, but I argued anyway.

"Yes."

No answer. The silence dragged out and I gritted my teeth. It was hard to argue with a man who refused to hold up his end. I tried to break free and reach for a light, but he kept me in place easily.

"Dammit."

He kissed the top of my head. "Go to sleep."

"Right. Because I'm having such a restful night between the breaking and entering and being held captive."

If my sour voice bothered him, he didn't give any indication of it.

I let my muscles relax because keeping myself tense would only tire me. It was surprisingly easy to rest my body against a stranger's. My arms weren't at an uncomfortable angle, just held where they couldn't be used as weapons. I didn't want to get a crick in my neck, so I wiggled down a little. He let me get comfortable, but I could feel the readiness in his muscles. He expected me to try something. That made me smile.

"Do I at least get to know your name?"

The silence dragged out so long I thought he wasn't going to answer me. Just when I'd given up, he said, "David."

David, I thought. Well, that fit. I was in a position to know he was hard enough to have been carved out of marble by Michelangelo.

He didn't kiss me again. I fell asleep telling myself it was for the best.

I woke up alone, with a few muscle twinges and slightly swollen lips as evidence that I hadn't dreamed the whole thing. I got up and did my impersonation of a cat burglar, sliding silently around the apartment, looking for a large man in a leather jacket with lips in similar condition to mine.

I nearly gave myself a heart attack whipping the shower curtain open, but the tub was empty. Cupboards, closets, I checked them all. Then I checked the windows, but they were all closed. The one over the kitchen sink wasn't locked, though, and I remembered the cold air I'd felt in the night.

So this was where he'd come in. I opened it and stuck my head out, gauging the distance from my little balcony. A tall person could stand on the rail and reach this window, but you'd have to want in really damn bad to try that on the second story.

I pulled my head back in and closed the window. Then I locked it. The apartment was as secure as I could make it from crazy people and kissing bandits, so I took a shower and got dressed. I wasn't going to work today, but I expected to be busy.

I wasn't ditching my job because Miguel and company intimidated me. Zach and the three amigos showing up where I worked was one thing. Finding a man in my apartment last night was more serious.

Whoever these people were, they weren't fooling around.

I didn't like this pattern of strangers popping up, keeping me on the defensive. Time to stop reacting to events that took me by surprise and do something proactive.

After a phone call to cover my shift, I headed to the library. I had one clue to follow. It was thin, but it was all I had.

Zach had said I'd find them in the place I saw in my dreams. I'd woken up with the memory of a dream fragment that might have been nothing more than my subconscious processing my close encounters with Zach and David. Still, I thought it was worth pursuing. Zach had been there with me, and David. He'd been a faceless presence in the dark, but I'd known it was him with dream logic. And something about the place was familiar, like I'd seen it before and would recognize it again.

Two hours later, I was ready to believe the place I was looking for existed only in my head. But it had seemed so vivid, like the dream incorporated a real place I'd seen, if I could just remember where.

Maybe it was for the best. Even if I found the place and it wasn't just a dream, it might be too risky to go there. Of course, the way things were looking, going to work or staying home was risky.

On impulse, I typed Zach's surname into the web browser's search window. The results surprised me. I'd expected references to local business or society news. Instead, I learned that Neuri was a name for a northern Slavic tribe whose men turned into wolves.

Neuri. Werewolves. Zach's claim that the knife didn't hurt him because it wasn't silver and his full-moon deadline took on a new slant.

My vision blurred and I blinked to clear it. Too much time on the library's computer. I closed the web browser and realized it wasn't just eyestrain. A wave of dizziness hit me and I cursed myself for skipping breakfast in my rush to play detective. Stupid, stupid, stupid.

Fortunately, I had an unopened bottle of Gatorade and some power bars in my car. I'd started keeping snacks handy when my metabolism went nuts. Now I just needed to walk that far without passing out.

A black-haired biker was reading a magazine a few tables away. I'd noticed the motion in my peripheral vision when he came in, but when he ignored me I'd decided it was safe to ignore him. Still, I couldn't help wondering if he'd move when I did. I scooted my chair back, preparing to leave. He stayed seated and turned another page.

There, see, not every guy in a leather jacket is part of some conspiracy to make you crazy. Relieved to only have one problem to cope with, I got to my feet slowly enough that blood wouldn't rush from my head and make things worse. Then I made my way toward the door, pretending to be browsing so my tortoise pace would seem reasonable.

Once I'd made it to the driver's seat, I fumbled in the glove box for a bar and then realized my hands were shaking so much that the simple task of opening the wrapper was a challenge.

That frightened me more than finding David in my apartment last night. It would've been nice if my birth parents had included medical information in the adoption records. For instance, had I inherited a risk for type 1 diabetes?

I dropped the bar and swore. I reached for it, and my hand seemed to swim through fog. *No, please, don't let me black out here,* I prayed. *I'll be good. I'll call my doctor and get a checkup right away.*

My prayers were answered by a knock on the window, right before the car door opened. I turned my head toward the sound and wasn't altogether surprised to see the biker there, crouching down to put himself at eye level with me.

"Stupid, stubborn fool."

I blinked. He didn't sound much like a Good Samaritan. He sounded like my surly babysitter from last night.

"You're not driving in your condition. Scoot over."

Right. Driving was probably a bad idea. I nodded in agreement, and then my face fell toward the steering wheel. A masculine hand intervened, probably saving me from a nasty bruise. I was lifted and settled in the passenger seat, and the biker climbed in. "Here. Drink."

Something touched my lips. I drank obediently. The liquid was sweet and cool, balm to my parched throat. The bottle moved away and I protested. "Thirsty."

"Slow." The masculine voice sounded stern. I heard the sound of paper ripping, and then my rescuer prompted me to eat. He didn't need to tell me twice.

"You're taking pointless risks," he said while I chewed and swallowed. "Come home. We can help you."

My mouth was full, so I couldn't answer, but what could I say? All of a sudden everybody wanted me to be somewhere, but nobody bothered to give me a damn set of directions.

The fog receded as the food and liquid hit my system, and I blinked until I could see the man behind my steering wheel clearly. His lips didn't look like mine felt, but the size and shape and sound of his voice were a match for my late-night visitor.

He was bigger than Zach, as well as older and tougher looking, but the cheekbones and the cast of his features showed a resemblance. He wore his black hair shorter, so I couldn't tell if it curled. His expression was a lot harsher than Zach's had been. He looked coldly furious, in fact, gray eyes glaring at me.

I wondered what he'd look like if he smiled, and why I wanted to find out. He wasn't *that* good a kisser. Okay, yes, he was.

It struck me that he and Zach had something else in common. Neither of them wore any sort of aggravating scent. They were both refreshingly free of cologne, aftershave, or the chemical reek of fabric softener. Considering the harsh combination of strong smells that clung to the average person, the absence came as a relief.

"Hi, David." My voice sounded old and creaky and I grimaced.

"Chandra." He said my name as if he was biting the sound off. All things considered, it didn't surprise me that he knew it.

"Are you mad because I tried to hit you last night?"

"No." David passed the bottle back to me and I drank with greedy haste. "I'm mad because you're going to get somebody killed. Probably yourself."

I finished the Gatorade and the rest of the bar and straightened up. "I skipped breakfast. It's not a crime." Although it was stupid. I wouldn't let it happen again.

I studied him and continued my mental comparison. Zach had the kind of polish that said private school and old money. If David had ever had any polish, life had long since worn it off. If I had to guess, I'd place him as ex-military.

"Finished?"

"No. Be patient. If you'd let me turn the light on last night, I could've looked all I wanted then."

"I meant, are you finished eating?" He gave me an unreadable look. What, he didn't think I'd want an eyeful of the stranger I'd sort of spent the night with?

"You're more interesting than food."

A muscle in his jaw jumped, but he didn't answer. Tension rose in the car and I realized he was really pissed off. My brain finally kicked into gear and it occurred to me that I didn't have to stay in close proximity to a large, hostile male. I reached for the door handle, but David was faster. His hand covered mine and held the door shut. *Déjà vu,* I thought. It was like a replay of being in my car with Zach, and it annoyed me to be slower than both of them.

"Let go." I kept my voice steady and hoped I wasn't still visibly trembling. I didn't want to look weak.

"Idiot."

"Stop calling me names." I felt my eyes narrow as anger pulsed through me.

He looked like he was swallowing glass as he ground out the word, "Sorry."

Anger evaporated as quickly as it had come. Maybe a soft answer really does turn away wrath.

"Let's start over. Hi, my name is Chandra. Strange people keep popping up and acting like I should know what's going on. What the hell is going on?"

For an answer, David let go of my door and turned on the ignition. "I'm taking you home."

Taking me where? Alarm clamored in the back of my head and adrenaline spiked, burning away the sugar in my system in the process. The gray fog returned and I cursed my weakness as I subsided into the passenger seat. "Is Zach there?"

"Yes." His jaw tightened as he stared straight ahead. "I'm taking you to Zach."

"Okay." I had a few questions for Zach. David could save me the time and hassle of finding him. I closed my eyes, just for a minute. I opened them when the engine shut off, shocked to realize I had no idea how much time had passed or where we were. Something was really wrong with me.

I heard booted footsteps on gravel before my door opened and then Zach was there, unbuckling my seat belt, scooping me up as if I were a child. David walked beside him and the three of us went up onto a covered porch and then inside a solarium filled with greenery, rich with the mingled scents of earth and growing things.

The men were arguing. "I wanted her to come of her own free will," Zach was saying.

"You didn't see her passing out at the wheel," David snapped in response. "It's too late for that."

Too late? I didn't like the sound of that, but I didn't seem to have the strength to speak up.

The argument became impossible to follow then, because they stopped speaking English. The foreign syllables didn't bother me. It meant I wasn't distracted by the words and could concentrate on their voices. I liked the sound of them.

"Chandra. Swallow this." That was Zach, coaxing with an underlying tone of command.

"Later," I evaded. I didn't want to be drugged, but I wasn't in any state to fight about it.

"Now."

One of them held me while the other poured something noxious into my mouth. I swallowed convulsively and then gasped as it burned all the way down. My eyes teared as I wheezed. "Water!"

Zach gave me a glass, which meant David was the one holding me. I drank and sighed in relief as it cooled the fire in my esophagus. "What was that?"

"Herbal tea. A family remedy." Zach's voice was calm, his face composed. "Are you feeling better now?"

In fact, I was. The fog was gone and strength pulsed through me. With every heartbeat I felt more alert, more alive. A sense of almost euphoric well-being filled me.

Something that felt this good this fast couldn't be trusted. "Please tell me that wasn't meth."

"No. Just wolfsbane."

Wolfsbane? My mouth opened and shut soundlessly a couple of times before I managed to say, "That's poisonous."

CHAPTER FOUR

MY HEAD WAS NOW CLEAR ENOUGH TO PANIC. I WAS GOD ONLY KNEW where, in the hands of a man whose last name made his interests in silver and moon cycles suspicious to say the least. And he hadn't hesitated to pour a known poison down my throat.

"It has medicinal uses." Zach frowned at me. "Foxglove is poisonous, too, unless you have a heart condition. Then digitalis can save your life."

"Thanks, but I don't want a botany lecture. I want an antidote." My voice rose in both pitch and volume. David's hold on me tightened as if he thought I might be planning to lunge at Zach.

"Easy." David's voice was low and gruff behind me. "It helps with the transition, that's all."

"Transition?" I practiced deep breathing and tried to calm down. Panic wouldn't help me. I needed to think. Starting with paying attention to my surroundings.

A look around told me we were still in the solarium. Now that I wasn't fainting, the room took my breath away. Terra-cotta tile floor, trees and flowers in decorative pots and planters, deep-cushioned chairs and sofas scattered around in the sort of inviting casual arrangement that takes a professional to create.

It was like sitting in a magazine spread. If this was Zach's house, I'd been right. He did have money. I felt a twist of envy, not so much for his bank account but for this room. It was exactly what I'd want if money were no object.

It was what I'd dreamed of. Last night.

I blinked and turned my head, half-hoping I wouldn't see blue tiles in a series that showed the phases of the moon making a staggered path along the floor. I did. My heart thudded and my skin prickled in recognition while my brain scrambled for a rational explanation.

One came almost instantly and I clung to it in relief. I probably *was* sitting in a magazine spread. This was the kind of house that got featured in *Architectural Digest* and *Better Homes and Gardens*. Some time in the past, I'd seen a picture of this room, and the image had stuck in my head. Zach asking me if I dreamed of them had combined with the odd moon tiles to trigger last night's episode.

"Do you like it?" Zach asked. "I like to start the day in here."

I loved it. I coveted it. Out loud I said, "It's nice. Unusual design on the tile." Then I waited to see what he'd do with the opening I'd given him.

He didn't mention the moon motif. Instead, he stood up and extended a hand toward me. "Would you like to see the gardens? You're dressed for it."

Sure, why not? I could have a nice tour of the grounds before I keeled over. Except I didn't feel unwell. I felt like I could run a marathon. Had he lied about giving me wolfsbane?

My jeans, fleece pullover, and cross-trainers were warm enough for the sunny day and comfortable for walking. I put my hand in Zach's for an answer, and David let me go.

It was an odd feeling, as if I'd been passed between them. Then again, I hadn't exactly been invited over for lunch. They probably wanted to keep ahold of me in case I decided to bolt for my car. It might be awkward for Zach if I turned up at an emergency room claiming he'd given me a deadly dose.

Zach's grip was warm and strong. He led me through the solarium to the door that opened out into a garden that looked spectacular even in winter. A fountain decorated with stone figures stood in front of us. We took a gravel path that led around it. Zach's stride was energetic, and I realized I had no trouble matching him. David kept pace behind us. We passed low benches, arbors, and what looked like an honest-to-God hedge maze, and then there was an open field ahead of us with woods on the far side.

"Want to race?" Zach asked me, challenge gleaming in his amber eyes.

"So the poison can go through my system and kill me faster?"

"I didn't poison you. Do you feel poisoned?"

"No." I didn't want to admit it to either of them, but I hadn't felt this good all month. Energy sang in my veins and my muscles quivered with the urge to move.

"Run with us." Zach dropped my hand and waited to see what I'd do. David came up to stand on my other side, so the three of us formed a loose starting line.

I turned to look at David. He wanted me to run; I could see it in his face. He was almost smiling. If I had to describe his stance, I'd call it playfully competitive.

It didn't add up. They didn't act like kidnappers or killers. They didn't feel like a threat, either. That warning instinct that made my skin prickle from their proximity had shifted to a bubbling sense of eagerness to race between them.

"Why did you bring me here?" I asked David.

"You needed help." He didn't hesitate over the words, and his eyes met mine without blinking.

"With the transition." I repeated what he'd said in the solarium. He didn't answer.

I looked back at Zach. "Why did you say I should've expected you? Why did you think I'd know where to go when you told me to come to you?"

"Well, for starters, we sent you a certified letter the day after your twenty-first birthday." Zach frowned at me. "Somebody signed for it."

I blinked, thinking back over the past couple of weeks. I'd gotten a lot of mail, most of it thanking me for sending my résumé and promising to keep it on file should another opening come up. Bills. And the stuff that went straight into the trash, sweepstakes and free vacation offers that were anything but.

A real, personal letter would've stood out. So it had gotten delivered to the wrong apartment, and that was probably what Michelle's message was about.

"I haven't been myself since my birthday," I said, figuring that was answer enough.

"Oh, you've been yourself," Zach said. "Just more yourself than you're used to."

The two of them looked at each other over my head, and I hated the sense that they were on the same page when I didn't even have the right book.

"Then you weren't refusing to come," David said. "I thought you were being stubborn."

"It would be nice if somebody would just come out and say whatever you have to say. I take it this is about me being adopted?" I prompted.

"Yes." Zach reached out to touch my cheek. "The short version is, this is your family home. The longer version is that you have a rare genetic condition."

"Oh. Is that all." I reeled inwardly. Good news: I might have visiting rights to that gorgeous solarium. Bad news: It meant my genes were plotting against me. "Am I dying?"

"No." Zach stepped closer, warm reassurance in his touch, concern in his eyes. "No, not at all. It's just that the condition presents fully in adulthood."

" 'Presents,' what the hell does that mean?" I heard the edge of panic in my voice, and didn't care.

"It means you're like us." David reached out to touch me, too, the three of us forming a circuit I could swear an electrical impulse flowed through. Touching them made me feel strong, connected, on the verge of some unknown potential. "Neuri."

"Werewolves." I said it out loud and waited for one of them to laugh and tell me I'd been had.

"Yes," Zach said. "Would you like to race now?"

I thought about my active night episodes I couldn't remember the next day, my extreme sensitivity to sounds and smells in the past weeks, my roller-coaster metabolism. The allergy to silver I'd discovered on my first and last attempt at piercing. David's claim that he'd heard me outside my apartment, impossible for human ears.

"I would like you to prove it," I said.

Zach looked at David, who stepped away from us and started to strip silently. I decided there was no reason not to look if he insisted on showing off, so I watched as he discarded shirt, shoes, and then everything else. He wore boxer briefs and managed to make them look sexy. His chest and shoulders looked more powerful naked, muscles lean and sculpted, his belly hard, and flat, athletic legs. He had the kind of muscle development that came from use, not the kind built in the gym just for show.

He would have kicked my ass in a race.

I looked away when he peeled the briefs down his hips. I didn't want to embarrass myself. Beside me, Zach stood focused and intent, and it wasn't because he wanted to compare equipment. Command radiated from him and something else that made my skin prickle.

Naked, David dropped into what looked like a sprinter's crouch. I had to fight an almost overwhelming urge to join him, as if he was triggering some reflex. I made myself stay upright and kept still with an effort as an alien energy surged through my body, seeking an outlet it didn't find.

David's spine rippled. Muscles and tendons stretched, moved, the way my own seemed to want to move. Fur sprouted. And then somehow a huge black wolf looked up at me with David's gray eyes.

"Jesus." I staggered and might have fallen over my own feet if

Zach hadn't caught my elbow in a supporting grip. "I frenched that?"

"You what?" Zach pulled me closer, his eyes narrowed.

I shrugged. "He broke into my apartment. We kissed. There was tongue involved." A lot of tongue. Very involved.

The wolf grinned. He padded toward me and I swear, he was planning on nuzzling my crotch. I blocked his muzzle with a swift raised knee, and the wolf's jaw dropped in what looked like a silent laugh. He butted my hand, and I wove my fingers into the thick fur at the base of one ear. If seeing was believing, touching made it even more real. He felt warm, soft, alive. Then he took off, powerful legs flying over the field.

Neuri. I shivered and wondered what it felt like. The buried remnant of a dream stirred, and I fell into a flash of memory. *Running on four feet. Other wolves around me. The joy and sense of rightness in our unity, the sound of the triumphant round we sang together echoing in the night.*

"Am I going to change like that?" I asked Zach, my voice faint. I wondered if the alien impulse I'd fought while David changed was my own wolf trying to get out of a body that didn't know how to let it.

"Yes. Tomorrow night. But the closer it gets to the full moon, the closer you are to the transition and the worse your symptoms will feel."

I swallowed and nodded. Suddenly I didn't feel like running. I wanted to sit down and put my head between my knees. I must've looked like I felt, because Zach made a low sound of concern and scooped me up in his arms. I didn't object.

"You should have more tea."

I nodded and then tentatively rested my head on his shoulder. I was turning into a werewolf. Drinking wolfsbane couldn't make things any worse.

I saw the others as Zach carried me back the way we'd come. Men ranging in age from about my own to late thirties, and every one of them eye-catching. It wasn't just the very attractive way they were put together; it was the way they moved, the ripple of muscle and sinew, the confidence, that indefinable something that made women stare. *Animal attraction,* I thought, and resisted the urge to laugh.

Some were taller than others; some had dark hair and some were blond. There was even one redhead to match me. He caught my eye and grinned. His eyes crinkled in the corners, like he smiled often. I wondered if we'd both be dark auburn-coated wolves, since David's hair color matched his wolf pelt.

They fell in behind us, all of them openly curious about me. I noticed none of them looked surprised. So Zach had been telling the truth: They were expecting me.

I waved over Zach's shoulder, and if I hadn't already been faint, their reaction would've done me in. In perfect unison, they each dropped to one knee, head bowed, one arm folded over each chest to touch a closed fist over the heart.

"Princess."

The chorus of masculine voices shocked me more than the sight of David sprouting fur. I burrowed into Zach and whispered, "I think you have the wrong girl."

"No mistake." Zach continued on without pausing, "We know who you are."

"Be serious," I hissed. "There's like twenty of them and they're all deluded. If you told them I'm a princess, they're going to be pissed off when they find out they got on their knees for the wrong person."

Zach opened the door to the solarium and brought me inside. "There's only nine. Eleven including my cousin David and myself. The pack isn't what it used to be, but that's enough to give you fair choice."

"Fair choice for what?"

I let Zach settle me onto a fat chair and give me another cup of herbal death. He watched while I drank it. "For a mate," he said, his expression unreadable.

I burst out laughing.

Zach didn't crack a smile and my laughter took on a sharp edge. "That's ridiculous," I said. "In the first place, I'm not about to get married. I don't even have a real job yet. In the second place, if I was going to pick a guy to hook up with, who are you to tell me I only get to pick from the eleven of you?"

"Who am I? I'm the pack alpha," Zach answered. "The acting head, until you choose a different king. And if you think you aren't in need of a mate yet, wait until tomorrow. You'll have needs no human male can meet. Without us, you'd suffer."

Us? Plural? Tension knotted my stomach. "I am starting to get a very bad feeling about this. Please tell me you aren't planning some kind of orgy."

Zach sat back, his eyes knowing. "Was kissing David unpleasant?"

"Well, no." "Unpleasant" was hardly the word I'd use to describe that kiss.

"Did you dislike kissing me?"

I squirmed in my chair. "It was fine." It had been the mere promise of more to come and it had stolen my breath.

"It would be easier for you if you'd come when we sent the letter. I'm sorry you didn't have more time to come to terms with this, but you can't hide from what you are. You won't have to do anything you don't want to do."

Sincerity vibrated in his voice and concern showed in his eyes. Funny, but that didn't make me feel any better.

The door opened and I heard footsteps on the tile. The men, or Neuri I guessed I should think of them as, came in and formed a ring around us. That also didn't fill me with warm fuzzies. Although it did fill me with a prickling of energy, like getting close to a transformer. I almost expected the air to hum.

"Welcome home, Chandra," Zach said in more formal tones. "Tonight we'll celebrate the return of our princess. Tomorrow night, you will take your place as our queen and choose your king."

Nerveless fingers lost their grip on my cup. It shattered on the tile.

CHAPTER FIVE

"WHAT? NO. I MEAN, I THINK YOU'RE ALL EXTREMELY HOT, BUT NO. Look, I'm sorry, but I'm not going to be your princess or your queen," I croaked into the silence. "I have other plans. You'll have to get another girl."

Finding out I might grow fangs and fur under the next full moon was bad enough, but being told I had to pick a life partner from their group was a bit much.

"There aren't any others." Zach spoke in a soft voice, but there was a steely sound to it.

"Bullshit." I stared at him, narrow eyed. "You can't tell me all werewolves are members of the Y chromosome group."

"Not all. Just most." Zach gestured and the redhead who'd smiled at me went away. He came back a few seconds later with a dustpan and whisk broom and went to work cleaning up the breakage.

"Lycanthropy is like color blindness," said a blond with blue eyes and a nice baritone. "Sex-linked. It affects more men than women."

Biology class wasn't so far in the past that I couldn't follow him. Something like 12 percent of men were color blind. But it affected less than one-half of 1 percent of women.

I scrunched into my chair as understanding hit me, and tried not to feel like a target.

"You're scaring her," the redhead said. He swept up the last shard and winked at me. "We won't bite you. Unless you're into that."

"Gee, how reassuring." But despite my sarcasm, his humor did make my tension recede. Just a little. They weren't falling on me like, well, a pack of wolves. Still, that didn't mean I wanted to date them, singly or together, much less marry one.

En masse they made a stunning selection of gorgeous manhood. Healthy, young, virile. Some woman would appreciate them. Hell, I appreciated them. But it was hard not to lose sight of the fact that they wanted me for what I was, not who I was. Even if I did want to go wild with one of them and supposing I lost my head utterly and made a commitment, I wanted a man who wanted me for *me*.

Although if they all kissed like Zach and David, it might be tempting to overlook that while I explored my options. I blinked the thought away and focused on more immediate concerns. "Nice to meet all of you, but I would really like to talk to Zach alone right now. I have questions. Lots of them."

Zach nodded and the rest of the pack organized themselves to exit, but not back the way they'd come. They went through the door on the far end of the solarium into the main part of the house.

"Do they all live here?" I figured I might as well start with the more innocuous questions.

"All of us live together, yes."

Onward. "Are you all related?" A nice way to ask if they expected me to date my own cousin.

"In most cases, only very loosely." Zach smiled a little as if guessing one of my sources of discomfort. "We stick together and intermarry, for obvious reasons. The family tree crosses branches, but there's no close enough blood relative to you for consanguinity to be an issue."

I didn't know whether I should feel disappointed or not. "What about my parents?"

"I'm sorry." Zach's face sobered and he moved closer, taking my hand between both of his in an unexpected gesture of comfort. "We're not immortal. Your mother was killed in a car accident, and your father . . . lost heart. He was challenged by a wolf who disputed his ability to lead in his grieving state. He won, but died of injuries sustained in the fight."

"Fights to the death, forced marriages, you make it all sound so appealing." My voice came out flat. I tried not to picture wolves tearing at each other, the horror of knowing there were people inside the fur. "What happened after that? Why was I adopted? Why did you let me think I was human all this time?"

Out of all the day's revelations, that one hit hardest. The knowledge that my entire life was a lie.

"My father was his second in command, so leadership fell to him until you were ready to choose a new king. Given the dispute, he thought you'd be safer growing up outside the pack. Ray, the challenger who lost, or one of his followers might have tried to prevent your free choice."

I shivered at what Zach didn't say. "So not everybody's happy to have the lost princess restored."

"No. Not everybody." He admitted the truth, and I appreciated that even while I wanted to scream about the rest of it.

"Can I at least hope that none of those followers are among my prospective dates?" I couldn't bring myself to say "mates." Even the word was too permanent, too real, and I really wasn't ready. But damned if I'd kiss my father's killer or any wolf who'd supported his challenge.

"Rest easy, Princess." The corner of Zach's mouth turned up, just a little. "Ray split the pack after the challenge fight. He'd defied the alpha and lost. That made him outcast. When he left, his men went with him. You're safe here with us."

"Good to know." Although he was still out there, somewhere, wasn't he? Well, one problem at a time. I needed to make something clear. "Zach, you have to understand I can't be what you want. Even if all this is true, even if I am about to turn into a wolf, that doesn't mean I'm ready to just give up my life."

"Nobody's asking you to do that." His grip tightened around my hand. "But you have to understand that you need us. You might not realize it yet, but you will tomorrow."

Dread turned my mouth metallic and my muscles into lead. "Are you talking about estrus?" *Pop quiz*, I thought on the edge of hysteria. *What's worse than turning into a werewolf without warning? Turning into a werewolf in heat.*

He nodded. My throat tightened, making it hard to swallow. I forced out my next question anyway. "Will it happen in human form or animal?"

"Human." He went still, as if he thought any move he made might be interpreted as aggression.

"Will there . . ." I licked my lips and tried to think of how to ask about their man parts, but there was no delicate way and I had to know. Lupines had an extra at the base of the penis. The bulbus glandis swelled into a rounded knot after penetration, tying a pair together until mating was complete. How wolflike were these men? "Do you have . . . oh, hell, Zach, do you have knots?"

"Yes."

I appreciated the way he answered me, just straightforward. No avoiding the issue or making fun of my concerns. But he'd raised a new question. "Doesn't that cause some social problems for you guys?"

I imagined the parade of prime masculine specimens I'd just seen staying forcibly celibate because they couldn't explain their bonus features to human girlfriends. All that pent-up sexual frustration looking for an outlet.

"The knot only forms during sex with a female werewolf. To human women, we just seem wider at the base."

Lucky me. I felt faint and it must have shown, because he was quick to add, "Remember, you're made like we are."

I remembered. I remembered the knot could lock a couple together for more than half an hour and there were eleven of them. My heart rate kicked up, and adrenaline fueled my muscles into action. Before I'd even formed the thought of escape I was flipping over the back of the chair. I hit the ground running and I made it out the door, then to my car.

"Keys, keys," I whispered the chant like a prayer as I threw myself inside and reached for the ignition. My hand found empty space. Had David taken them? I felt frantically on the floor by the driver's side, anywhere he might have left them, and then it was too late. Zach was there, reaching in for me on the driver's side, and three other Neuri guarded the passenger side.

"No, I didn't do anything!" Zach was yelling at one of them as his hands closed on me in a gentle but implacable hold. "She had questions. She asked about the knots and then she ran." He drew me out of the car, into his arms, very slowly. "Chandra, Chandra. We won't hurt you; I promise."

The other three came around and pressed close. I recognized the lean redhead and muscular blond who'd spoken to me inside, and another brown-haired man who looked like the youngest of the bunch. Their proximity caused a mixed reaction, as if I saw them with two sets of eyes. Part of me registered their nearness as comfort and protection. The other part saw three strange men as a potential threat. The divided perception paralyzed me.

I let them lead me back inside. This time Zach directed me to a formal living room and pressed me down into a soft leather couch. He took one side of me, and the redhead took my other side. The other two claimed places down the length of the couch.

"Chandra, this is Will. Matt and Jack are brothers." Zach pointed to each in turn as he made the introductions. Knowing their names didn't make me feel any better about the possibility of having sex in the throes of estrus with virtual strangers, but it did make them seem less, well, strange.

Will was the young brown-haired man. He had chocolate brown eyes that seemed kind. Matt was the buff blond, and Jack the red-head. They had matching blue eyes but otherwise couldn't look less alike.

"All of us are happy to meet you," Jack said, not smiling now. "Please don't run off without hearing Zach out."

"I want to talk to David," I said through lips that felt stiff. Or maybe it was just the way I was clamping my jaw to keep from screaming. "Is he back?"

I had a question for him, and a horrible suspicion that I already knew the answer.

Zach made a gesture at Will, who stood in response. "I'll go get him."

Zach really was the alpha. All the others looked to him, listened to him. What would happen to the group if I didn't want to choose a mate, or if I didn't want Zach? I stuffed that concern down and decided to worry about myself first, then decide what responsibility, if any, I had to the wolves.

It didn't take long for Will to reappear with David, who was human again. He'd put his jeans on but hadn't bothered with a shirt or jacket, and I wondered if they tended to have higher body temperatures than humans.

"Can we talk for a minute?" I aimed the question at Zach, figuring the rest would go along with whatever he said, so I might as well ask the one in charge.

Zach motioned to Jack and Matt. They collected Will and trooped out. David stood looking at me, hands on his hips. "You wanted me?"

The wording combined with the sight of his bare torso made

my mouth go dry. I had to swallow before I could ask my question. "Yes. Last night, you said you wouldn't let me go because you didn't want me to try to break your jaw again."

He raised a hand to rub his chin. "It healed almost instantly. Nothing to worry about."

I felt ill. "I broke your jaw. In my sleep." Because my night terrors weren't what I'd always believed they were. They were periods when the wolf hidden inside me started to assert itself.

"Like I said, you fight dirty." David's gray eyes were hard to read, so for all I knew he was holding a grudge. It didn't matter. He'd told me the truth.

He was stronger than any human, and even for a human male he was big, fast, and built. And I'd hurt him. What could I do to a normal person, under the influence of my transformation? I was trained in martial arts. I knew the body's strike zones, where and how to do damage with maximum efficiency.

"I hurt you," I whispered. Saying it out loud made it more real.

David tilted his head as he considered me. "You kissed me and made it better."

Like that made it all right.

I'd also driven my car to the library, and less than two hours later I'd been incapable of driving home. I'd blacked out. What if that fog had swallowed me while I was on the freeway?

The conclusion was inescapable. I was a danger to myself and others in this state. I didn't know what all the physical implications were, but I was changing. I might be ignorant of the risks those changes involved now, but I didn't have to stay that way. There was a wolf pack right in front of me, ready and willing to help me cope.

"I'm sorry." My voice sounded small in the large room. David moved to close the space between us, taking the empty seat next to me on the couch, so I was bracketed between the two of them.

"For kissing me?" David took one of my hands. I realized with a start that Zach was holding the other and wondered when that had happened.

"No." That drew one corner of my mouth up in a tiny half smile. There was nothing about that kiss I was sorry for, except maybe that it had ended.

"We understand that you don't have control, Chandra," Zach said, and the sincere note in his voice made me turn toward him. "You'll learn. We'll help."

And just how many ways would I be out of control? My eyes teared and I blinked the moisture away. "What about sex? Zach, you said I wouldn't be expected to do anything I didn't want to do, but am I going to be unable to stop myself?"

I found myself folded into a twin embrace, as each man wrapped an arm around me, nestling me between them. Zach's arm curved behind me, while David's hugged around my belly. It felt warm and safe, not sexual or aggressive.

"We'll help," Zach said, which wasn't quite an answer. "And instinct will guide you. Wolves are monogamous; they seek one mate and mate for life."

"Nice evasion," I sighed. "You've already implied I'll be kissing my way through the rank and file under the influence of going into heat. Just tell me what's going to happen."

"What will happen will be what you want," Zach promised. "We'll compete for your favor. You'll choose who you want and how."

"Define 'compete for my favor.'" The sensation of being

sandwiched between two men, with the memory of kissing both of them fresh in my mind, was starting to make me feel warmer and interested in something beyond pure comfort. That did not bode well.

"Sexual competition." Zach's voice was matter-of-fact, but his hand traced the back of mine as he spoke, and that small touch felt dizzying. "I know the knots scared you, but sexual contact isn't limited to intercourse. There are lots of options. Kissing. Touching. Oral sex, manual stimulation, massage."

I licked dry lips. "So I'll be expected to get physical with all of you, but not necessarily get . . . knotted."

"Right." From the sound of it, the topic of conversation combined with our nearness was starting to get to Zach, too. But I gave him points for not making any moves.

"And whoever I do it with is my mate?" This seemed like the most unfair part of the whole deal, that I'd be driven by biological urges to have sex and tied for life to whoever I had it with. Maybe I could avoid that by getting relief from nonintercourse sexual contact.

"You may accept more than one partner," Zach said, his voice carefully neutral. "But after the first full moon, you'd be expected to name your choice."

Talk about a lot to come to terms with, and very little time to do it in. I drew a shaky breath in and let it out slowly. "And whoever I choose is the new wolf king."

"I'll abide by your choice, whatever it is." Zach seemed to miss my meaning, but he brought up something I hadn't considered. That I might choose somebody else, and he'd oppose it.

So, I had Zach's word that he wouldn't force me into any particular choice and wouldn't fight it if I chose somebody other than him. That still left me with ten men who would be king competing for my body. Given what I could see of the palace, there was considerable incentive. I didn't kid myself that my heart would rank in equal importance. And my body was turning against me.

I turned to David. "Are you still up for a run?"

David looked to Zach before he answered me. "Sure. I'll take you."

CHAPTER SIX

ONCE OUTSIDE, I FELT A LITTLE LESS TRAPPED. BUT I DIDN'T REALLY think I had the energy to run. Dread of the unknown future sapped my strength. "Can we just walk?" I asked David, waving toward the hedge maze. "Maybe in there. As long as we don't get lost."

"Sure."

"A wolf of few words." I headed toward the entrance and he kept pace with me, shortening his stride to match it to mine.

"Didn't think you wanted to come out here for small talk."

We entered the maze, and I stopped to inhale the fragrance of living things. Even in winter, the garden held the promise of green springtime. David paused beside me, waiting and watchful.

"No," I agreed. "I wanted to come out here because I wanted to think and I'd like a military perspective. Unless I'm very wrong, you have one."

He nodded, confirming my guess. I wasn't surprised. It was in his bearing, his manner. He had a disciplined watchfulness that said "noncivilian."

"Army? Navy? Air Force?"

"Marines."

"Figures. Marines, first to fight." I forged ahead with my feet and my words. "I'm missing pieces of the big picture. For instance, those panthers I met at the mall. Am I right in guessing that they are actual panthers? Cat people?"

"Yes."

With that one word my world expanded even further past the borders of the mental map I'd always known. I'd voyaged well off the charts and into dragon territory. Not just werewolves but other shape-shifters existed.

"Are they a problem?"

"They've been increasingly aggressive," David said. "More incidents of individual and small-group conflicts. Maneuvering against our territory. I think they're positioned to challenge us in an organized attack if they perceive a weakness."

"As in, a change of leadership." I kicked at the ground, hating the feeling of being pushed into a corner. Not that I had anything against Zach. Just the opposite, the more I saw of him the more he impressed me. His pack trusted him and respected him. That alone spoke volumes. Then there was the state of the estate we were on. If Zach was in charge of the money, appearances said he was very smart about managing it.

David gave a noncommittal grunt but didn't disagree.

"Do you think Zach is the best leader?" I asked for his opinion not sure he'd give it.

"Yes."

"Why?"

"He thinks first, acts second. Looks at the big picture. Acts for the good of the pack." We walked on in silence before David added, "That's not an endorsement of him as a mate. I'm not qualified to judge."

"Didn't ask you to." We wound through the maze, and David took a subtle lead, directing us along the right route. We took a final turn and then we were in the center, a circle inside the hedges with a bench under a rose arbor facing a small fountain. The fountain had two levels, an upper level filled by a figure of a maiden pouring water from a pitcher, and the lower filled from a wolf's head with an open mouth. How appropriate.

Between the height of the hedges and the arbor, this spot would provide an oasis of shade in the summer, when the humidity pressed down and turned the air into hot molasses. "Pretty," I said out loud.

I contemplated the peaceful scene while I digested David's statements. If I chose Zach, the general order of things in the pack would be sustained. That was probably best for all concerned, no matter how I might feel about it personally. And how I felt about it wasn't really possible to gauge just now. Too many shocks, too many revelations, too much to process.

"Will I be expected to live here?" I crossed over and took a seat on the bench, drew my feet up on the stone platform, and rested my chin on my knees.

"Do you have to be told it's the safest option?" David sat beside me, his gaze level and his face serious.

"No. I get that." Not that I expected waking up to coffee in the solarium to be a hardship. And given my intense reaction to perfumes and colognes and chemical smells, life on an estate with extensive private grounds inhabited by people who wouldn't assault my airways was a real bonus.

Luxury aside, safety came first. If I was the lone female werewolf in the area, I wasn't just a target to prospective mates. I was also a target for pack enemies, and that included the rogue wolves who'd split off. Even if I knew how to handle the transition of shifting from human to wolf form and mastered the instincts and abilities that went along with that, even if I could trust myself not to hurt somebody, it would be dumb to rob myself of twelve devoted bodyguards.

My life as I'd known it was well and truly over. My plans for the future, well, at least I'd achieved one goal. I knew who my real parents were.

I absorbed that while my stomach sank and my head went light. "You know, I had that whole secret-princess fantasy as a kid," I told David. "That someday my real family would show up and I'd be some sort of princess. My fantasy did not include growing fangs and fur under the full moon."

I hadn't dreamed of a prince who howled, either. Orgies had also not made the list. My imagination seemed woefully inadequate.

He didn't answer. Probably he guessed, correctly, that there was no good response. After a while, my butt started to notice how cold and hard stone could feel. I got stiffly to my feet. I waited for my babysitter to take the lead, and I followed him out of the maze in silence.

When we returned to open ground, I took a good look at the house. It was a sprawling brick structure, more than adequate housing for twelve. It could probably hold twice that number without anybody feeling crowded. I made a silent bet with myself that whatever bedroom I was assigned to could hold my apartment two times over.

The lines of the building were graceful, classic. Whoever had designed the place had an eye for beauty and the skill to execute his or her vision. It had a sense of stability, and I guessed it was over a hundred years old.

This house had stood the test of time. The pack had endured since very early history, if my Internet search results could be believed. Slavic mythology went back to Neolithic times, possibly earlier. Which made sense, if humans and shape-shifters had evolved together.

I'd wanted to discover my roots, I reminded myself. Too late now to whine that ignorance was bliss. Besides, in my case ignorance was dangerous.

"David." He stopped when I spoke, and turned back toward me. "Do you want to be the pack leader?"

"Not particularly." His voice and face were neutral, giving nothing away, but I thought I detected tension in his body.

"Then why did you kiss me?"

His gray eyes took on heat. "I didn't say I don't want you."

Oh. I tried not to trip over my own feet while I absorbed that one, and told myself not to make too much of it. Of course he wanted me. He was a male werewolf and I was a female approaching heat. Naturally he'd be willing to take advantage of proximity, and the upcoming sexual competition allowed a certain freedom to indulge.

Still, it was nice to hear that he just wanted me, no strings.

We went back inside without another word exchanged. My head buzzed with facts and speculation. Overload. I found myself longing for a bath and a nap. My stomach growled and I added a meal to the list, preferably one loaded with nutrients and something, anything, that would stabilize my metabolism.

The red-haired werewolf, Jack, met us in the solarium and fell in behind me as David led the way into the house. Jack was a little taller than me, but not so much that he loomed. His lean muscled frame made him seem less physically imposing than his broad-shouldered brother. "Where's Zach?" I asked Jack.

"He has a meeting. Videoconference. The rest of the team is on a tight project delivery schedule, so you get me for company." Jack grinned at me, obviously pleased with the arrangement, and I found myself relaxing in the face of his good humor.

"Project?"

"Yep." Between them, they walked me through hallways and into a large, sunny kitchen. "This is the main campus of Neuri Enterprises, a web programming, design, and implementation collaborative."

Werewolves with day jobs. I wanted to laugh, but really, they had to earn a living like everybody else. The taxes and upkeep on this place probably didn't come cheap, either. "I guess you guys aren't cut out for office life, what with your night hours and the inability to work around the full moon."

"Corporate America is a bit too rigid to suit our lifestyle," Jack said with a wink. "Most of our clients are at a distance, in New York, California, or at international locations. With phone-

and videoconferencing, there's not much need for travel or face-to-face meetings."

Huh. The kind of business that could use a technical writer. "Maybe I should give Zach a copy of my résumé."

"He has it. You're hired." Jack didn't miss a beat as he pulled out a chair for me.

I blinked. "Do I get medical and dental?"

"With your natural ability to heal and resistance to disease, you won't need them. We're all disgustingly healthy."

Jack put a plate of something unidentifiable in front of me, and David poured a glass that probably contained more wolfsbane. He gave me a look I took as silent warning not to screw around with my changing body's needs. Like I needed to be told. I picked up the glass and waved it at him in a mock salute before I drank. I was starting to get used to the stuff. It wasn't so bad once I got past the horrible taste and the acid way it burned my throat.

"You won't be expected to start immediately," Jack went on. "After your first change, you'll need about three days to adjust." He waited until I'd put my glass down before he named my salary, adding, "Room, board, and company car included."

Good thing he waited. I might've dropped my drink again, and he'd already cleaned up after me once.

"I have a car," I said, because I didn't know what else to say. I'd just been offered twice my best hope for starting salary, with the added bonus of flexibility for my special needs. Plus housing. Of course, the catch was that I shared the job and house with eleven men who could tear my throat out, but everything had its downside.

"Yes, but we would all feel better if you drove a Volvo," Jack returned deadpan.

The safest car on the market. Message received, I thought. I started eating my glop. It was as tasteless as it looked. "Do I want to know what I'm eating?"

"No," David and Jack answered together.

Great. I tried not to think about the possibilities as I swallowed. I was tired of feeling like crap and still frightened by my blackout, so I did what the experienced wolves thought was good for me. The stuff was easy to get down, at least.

Jack and David had a quiet conversation about some deliverable schedule while I ate, and it was nice to hear something so normal. So human.

Something none of us would be tomorrow night. We'd be driven by animal needs, animal instincts, and revealed for what we were in animal form.

I put my fork down and stared at my plate. "Will it hurt?" My quiet question came during a lull in the business talk. David was the one who answered, and he didn't have to ask what I meant.

"Some. It's uncomfortable when your body shifts from one form to another. Like growing pains."

I nodded, then pushed my chair back. "Do I have a room?" I wanted quiet, space, and maybe a pillow to vent my emotions on.

"You do." The two of them shepherded me up two flights of stairs to the top floor and around a hall to my doorway. I turned the knob and walked in, wondering what my chamber in Wolf Manor would hold.

The door opened into a big sitting room, with a bedroom off to one side and a smaller room that held a desk on the other. My first impression was one of space and light. I was right about the size. My postage stamp apartment would be lost in here.

Hardwood floors throughout gleamed as if newly polished and gauzy drapes softened the windows. The sitting room had a brown leather couch and matching high-backed chair, convenient end tables, and a colorful Persian rug I knew my toes would sink deep into.

It was a comfortable room, not girly or frilly, just beautiful and elegant. A vase with a subtle arrangement of greenery and blossoms on one table lent a light fragrance to the air. I wondered who had put fresh flowers in here when I'd just arrived and if they'd come from the solarium.

I wandered into the bedroom and discovered it had a cedar walk-in closet with skylight, a tiled bathroom with a jetted tub to soak in, and French doors that opened onto a small balcony that looked out over the garden and hedge maze below. Two chairs with a bistro table nestled between them, and a potted tree made the balcony a temptation even in cold weather.

The bedroom also held a wrought-iron king-sized bed that loomed overly large in my imagination even though it suited the room's proportions. Matching tables with little brass lamps went on either side, and deep white rugs that looked like sheepskin lay on the floor. No matter which side of the bed I got up on, my feet wouldn't get cold.

A thick satin comforter in a shade somewhere between purple and midnight blue covered the bed. It would feel cool and smooth against bare skin. I tried not to think about who or what else would be touching me on that bed.

"Is it okay?"

I turned around and caught Jack's worried look. I'd stared at the bed a beat too long, and I'd already bolted once. *Try not to make the nice werewolf nervous.* "Fine. Everything is fine."

With the room, at least. It was beautiful and the furniture alone probably cost more than my last year's tuition. My life was in shambles, but my private suite was gorgeous. I tried to smile at Jack. It didn't quite form.

"I'll get her settled," David said. Jack took the hint and left, closing the door behind him.

David closed the distance between us and slid an arm around my waist, guiding me toward the couch. We sat and I didn't resist when he drew me onto his lap crosswise, my legs resting on the cushions, his arms bracing me, his shoulder providing a convenient resting place for my head.

"Zach won't be long," he said, his voice a soothing rumble in my ear. "I'll stay with you until he's free, if you want."

I nodded in silence. I did want. I'd thought I wanted privacy and solitude to come to grips with things, but now I realized I wanted exactly what he'd given me. I wanted to be held.

"I'm scared," I said in a voice just above a whisper.

"Of us?"

I gave a slight shake of negation. "Not exactly. Of me. Of what I might do. Of what I am."

He didn't tell me I was dumb to be scared. Instead, he gave me a slight squeeze. "You'll get through it."

I liked his confidence, even if I didn't share it. I tried to absorb it into my pores along with the warmth of his body. He was still bare from the waist up but didn't seem cold. "Do you run a higher temperature than normal?" I asked, curious. "And are you leaving your shirt off because it's more comfortable, or because you want me to admire your manly chest?"

"Yes, yes, and if you do, it's a fringe benefit." He answered my questions in order, then lifted my hand and placed my palm against the wall of his chest. I liked the feel of his skin and couldn't help contrasting it with the touch of fur.

"This is weird," I said, but I didn't let that stop me from running my hand down to his belly, exploring the muscle and sinew. David was a mouthwatering specimen of male flesh, to all appearances no different from any other man. The differences were under the skin, I thought, and shivered.

"That I'm not wearing a shirt?"

I smiled and shook my head. "No. Weird is sitting in a were-wolf's lap. Weird is knowing I petted you on the head in one form and had your tongue in my mouth in another. If I hadn't seen you change, I wouldn't believe it."

I let my hand glide back up to explore the slope of his shoulder and the heavy muscle of his upper arm. He didn't stop me, so I took silence as permission. Touching him made me feel safer in some odd way. As if I was taking control. Would I have any tomorrow night? Or would I be reduced to blind need?

"I wish it didn't have to be like this," I whispered. My throat felt tight and I swallowed convulsively against the pressure. "If I touch you tomorrow, I won't know if it's what I want or if it's just what the wolf inside me wants."

"You *are* the wolf." The assurance in his voice made me raise my head and search out his eyes with mine. "You want what you need."

"You make it sound so simple."

"It is." David's head bent toward mine in a slow descent, allowing me plenty of time to decide if I wanted to accept the kiss or reject it. I moved into it, meeting him halfway.

CHAPTER SEVEN

HIS MOUTH MOVED OVER MINE WITH HEATED ASSURANCE, AS IF IT WAS inevitable that my lips would soften and open. When they did just that under the pressure he exerted, he deepened the kiss, tasting the inner curves of my parted lips with the tip of his tongue before sweeping inside to claim that space. He made a series of slow in and out movements, gradually growing deeper and bolder.

He made a low, growling sound when I sent my tongue to twine and mate with his. His arms tightened around me, and I realized dimly that I was digging my fingers into his biceps. It didn't seem to bother him.

The sound of the door opening and closing registered on some dim level but didn't intrude until the couch dipped. I tried to break away, and David brought his hand up to cup my jaw and hold me in place while he finished kissing me with thorough attention that refused to be rushed to an unsatisfactory conclusion.

By the time he ended the kiss and released my mouth, I felt dazed and breathless. I turned to look at Zach, already knowing it was him, wondering how I looked to him with my face flushed and my lips swollen from kissing another man.

Zach's brown eyes were darker than I remembered as they met mine, and unreadable. I met his gaze in silence, wondering if he found this little preview of things to come as uncomfortable as I did. He'd see me doing a lot more than kissing other men tomorrow night. And he'd be among them. My stomach tightened at the thought, even while my curiosity stirred. Before all the revelations, kissing Zach again would've been high on my list. Now everything had gotten complicated.

"Practicing for tomorrow?" Zach asked.

I shook my head. "Kind of the opposite. I just wanted something . . . human." A small thing. A kiss, a touch, not driven by a biological state or a profound physiological transformation or desire for gain. Just a human yearning for contact.

"You wanted him to make you feel human." Zach held my gaze and I felt something stir in the air, like an undercurrent. "Maybe I should show you what it feels like to embrace your beast."

My heart thumped painfully in my chest. I remembered that frustrated urge to do something while David transformed. "What if I can't?" I didn't know how to be a wolf, how to shift, how to live with their rules.

"You can." David sounded sure as he gathered me up and planted me in Zach's lap. Talk about passing the buck. "Don't fight it, or you'll make it harder on yourself than it needs to be."

Then he left, and I had to bite my lip to keep from asking him to stay. *He has things to do besides babysit you,* I told myself. And what kind of wimp did it make me if I wanted him to stay as a buffer between me and the pack alpha? So Zach wanted to demonstrate something. Was I really afraid to face the beast inside myself?

"You look like you're bracing yourself for a dose of nasty medicine," Zach murmured. He sounded amused rather than offended. He ignored the tension in my body as I held myself stiff and still while he wound his arms around me in a loose embrace. "You've kissed me before."

"That was before." Before I knew what he was. Before I knew what I was, and why he was interested in me. Before he told me what was in store for me. At the thought of finding myself helpless at the center of lusty male attention, every remnant of the warm, sensual response David had drawn from me evaporated.

"Before David." There was a hard note in Zach's voice that made me angry.

"No, you ass. Before you told me you planned to put me at the center of an orgy to determine who gets the honor of knotting me on a regular basis while running the pack." To my horror my voice cracked and tears leaked from the corners of my eyes. I brushed them away and went on, "I don't want a mate. I don't want to be the door prize at your sex party. I don't want to give up everybody I care about for fear I'll do something to hurt them myself, or just manage to make them targets for pissed-off werepanthers and rogue werewolves. I don't want—"

The litany of things I didn't want got cut off when Zach laid a finger against my lips. "Shh."

I fell silent, shaking with the rush of emotion I'd unbottled and had nowhere to put. Then his lips replaced his finger, and I had an outlet, after all.

At first, the angry mix of frustration and fear and feeling trapped boiled up, finding expression in the crush of flesh to flesh. Then slowly, subtly, it transformed into something no less fierce but tinted with the realization that there was at least one thing I did want, after all. And that curious want became a key Zach knew how to turn.

Desire. For something hot and wild and unknown. For something pent up and feral burning in my blood. For something unnamed and unknown just under the skin, hungry for contact and unassauged by the kiss that had grown openmouthed and deep. With every thrust of his tongue, Zach fed the awakening creature inside me. I felt the animal buried within come closer to the surface, straining to get closer to him.

I ran my hands over his chest, needing more. His shirt felt like silk, and the texture delighted my fingers while the warmth that was Zach lured me to discover the expanse of skin and muscle underneath. I fumbled with buttons, dimly aware that his hands were moving under my fleece, up the sides of my waist, and that was good but not enough.

A primal hunger rose from some deep inner reservoir. I poured it into the kiss as I pulled his shirt open, my fingers moving over the skin I'd bared in a plea and a demand.

Zach shifted to spill me from his lap onto the couch and moved over me, pressing me down into the cushions, his body a welcome weight. Still, I burned to be closer. Frustrated need thundered inside me. Too many barriers between us, too many clothes, and he was at the wrong damn angle. . . .

I froze, realizing where I'd gone and how quickly I'd gone

there. I wanted him naked and inside me, and I didn't even know him.

"What's the matter? Afraid of the big, bad wolf?" Zach teased my lips with his, soft kisses that brushed and clung and ended only to start all over again.

"I'm not afraid of you." I moved my mouth with his in a vain attempt to keep the addictive pressure of his lips on mine, and he laughed softly.

"No? It must be something else, then." His hands tugged at my fleece shirt, sliding it up. I held my breath for a minute, wondering if he'd raise it until my breasts were exposed, and cursed myself for wearing a sports bra that morning instead of something lacy and sheer that would make his mouth water. "Maybe you're afraid I'll be lousy in bed."

The teasing note in his voice made me want to kick him in his masculine self-confidence, except that would be self-defeating. I didn't want to hinder his performance. Did I? "Who says I'll ever want to find out if you're good or not?"

That would have sounded more convincing if I wasn't panting and shuddering under him, fighting the urge to claw his pants off.

"I plan to tempt you until you can't resist finding out for yourself," Zach said. He drew my shirt higher and teased the lower edge of my bra with a fingertip. "But right now I have a different objective."

That did it. I *was* going to kick him. Then his finger slid under my bra and sent a wave of hot delight over my breast and I changed my mind. "Objective?" I managed to get the word out before I lost the power of speech.

"Mmm." He slid his hands around behind me, lifted me up enough to undo the catch, and lowered me back down with my bra a defeated barrier. "I want to show you what you are, and that it's nothing to be afraid of."

If he had an objective, I decided, it was driving me over the edge of sanity. Why didn't he strip my shirt off, tear my bra away, fill his hands with the flesh that ached to be touched?

But Zach seemed determined to move slow. One part of my brain acknowledged that as a good thing, given how uncharacteristically fast I wanted to go. And that sent a chill of trepidation down my spine. Was this what I wanted to be? A mindless creature of need, heedless of consequences?

"No," I whispered.

"Yes." Zach kissed me again, light, soft, slow, as if he had all the time in the world and was content to spend it doing nothing more. "You can trust the wolf in you, Chandra. You have sound instincts."

"Then why didn't my Spidey sense warn me about you?" I grumbled against his mouth.

"It did. You knew I was something to watch when I came into your store." He kissed me again, harder this time. "You were planning ways to take me down if I tried anything."

That surprised a rueful half laugh, half sigh from me. "No, I wasn't. I figured you could take me, so I was planning my escape."

"What does your Spidey sense say now?" Zach licked at the corner of my lip while he slid a hand up my rib cage, teasing me, tempting me.

"It says you won't mean to hurt me," I said, the unaccustomed mix of fear and desire making me more blunt than I intended. "But I think you will, anyway."

"Harsh." Zach drew back, sat up, and pulled my shirt over my head. He left the bra just covering me, but it was loose and open and we both knew how easily he could push that aside when he wanted what was underneath.

"I don't think so." I stared up at him, confused by the swirl of emotions he stirred. "I think your intentions are good, just not necessarily good for me."

"You are what you are, Chandra." Zach held my eyes while his hands moved up, under my bra, cupping and shaping my breasts with his palms. "I didn't make you this way, but I plan to make you accept it. You can't fight yourself, not when the change comes."

"I love it when you talk dirty." I narrowed my eyes at him, pissed that he was touching me so intimately, caressing my breasts and brushing his thumbs over my nipples as if he had the right to make me squirm and respond, when he had his own agenda and his own vision of where I fit in it.

"You think I want to talk about this now?" His eyes darkened almost to black and his hands on me turned hard, demanding. "You think I don't just want to peel you out of your pants and get your naked body under mine?"

"Uh . . ." I wet my lower lip, suddenly afraid I was going to get what I'd asked for, and his gaze zeroed in on that little movement. Then his mouth was on mine again, devouring, ravaging, his tongue driving inside, hot and sweet with an edge of dark, sexual threat. He could take me if he wanted to, right here, right now, and I wouldn't fight him.

But I wasn't ready even if my body thought I was, and he knew it, and he eased back by degrees, gentling his hands and lips until he was just holding me intimately. I lay still except for the tremors of desire and alarm that ran through me, my breath coming in pants, my heartbeat so loud I thought it echoed in the room.

"That's what I'm afraid of," I said finally into the silence. "I would have let you inside me, even though I don't know you and don't want a mate and don't know if I could accept the consequences."

"You know me better than you think." Zach teased my nipples, a light, sure touch, pleasurable, undemanding. "You knew I wouldn't take this further than you wanted me to."

I shrugged, and the movement made his hands do distracting things to me. "Maybe not, but you're still on top of me."

"We can change that if it makes you uncomfortable." He slid his hands away, a disappointment and a relief, levered himself up, and then pulled me back into his lap. I noticed he didn't offer to put my shirt back on. Instead, he stripped my dangling bra all the way off, baring my breasts to his sight. And he took a good, long look while his hands explored my torso, stroking, touching.

I missed the weight of his body crushing into mine, and that alone meant we'd done the right thing by changing position. If he'd slid his hand into my pants instead of into my bra, he'd know exactly how much he affected me. Of course, he could probably tell anyway. I squirmed in discomfort at the thought. How did you hide anything from a werewolf? Heightened senses, acute observation, he could probably see the flush of arousal on my skin and smell it in the air.

"Stop that," Zach murmured. "If you keep wiggling around on my lap, you may have to deal with the consequences. My control only goes so far."

"Ah. Sorry." I stilled, more concerned about causing him pain than causing him to lose control. "Nervous," I added, by way of explanation.

"Nobody will interrupt." Zach kissed my temple and nestled me closer, so that my skin touched his, his open shirt allowing the soft curves of my naked breasts to meet the hard, hot wall of his chest.

"That's another thing." I kissed the curve of his shoulder since it was within reach. "Are they all going to watch? Am I going to be a complete slut with all of you, spreading my legs for anybody who wants a turn? Maybe in the throes of heat I won't care, but how am I going to live with myself the day after? How will any of you live with each other, knowing every other male has carnal knowledge of his mate?"

Zach cupped my chin and tilted it up until he could look into my face. "How can we make you understand? I want you. David wants you, too. We all do. We're all pack, Chandra, all one. And you're ours. We're drawn to you because you belong to us, drawn to protect you and care for you, and yes, to pleasure you however you'll allow it."

"I'm betting I'm going to allow plenty," I sighed. "Look at me already. You come in and I'm trading tonsils with David. Now I'm half-naked on your lap, and I wasn't thinking about hurting David's feelings when I was under you."

He gave me a little squeeze. "Are you worried about jealousy? What you do when your wolf emerges for the first time isn't a matter for judgment. The heat makes the transition easier. I won't hold what you do with the others against you if you choose me afterward. It's what you need and it's only fair. We all want a chance to be the one you choose."

Not all, I thought, remembering David's words. He'd said he didn't want to be the new wolf king, and I believed him. He had the lone-wolf vibe. A wife would cramp his style. So would taking on responsibility for the whole pack. "You sounded jealous earlier," I pointed out.

"I'm not perfect." Zach rubbed my back in slow up-and-down strokes that relaxed me despite the topic of conversation. "But it wasn't you kissing David that got me. It was the way you pulled away from me. And that wasn't about him at all, was it?"

"It's not a foregone conclusion that I'll pick you," I muttered. "I don't want to give you the wrong impression about something like that."

"As long as you keep an open mind, that's all any of us ask."

How fair that sounded. How unfair it felt.

CHAPTER EIGHT

I HUDDLED IN ZACH'S LAP, WONDERING WHY I COULDN'T JUST LET GO and enjoy the moment.

What's not to enjoy? You have your own harem, I told myself. It didn't cheer me. For some reason I felt less like they were mine to play with and more like I was theirs to pass around.

I heaved an unhappy sigh. "Some girls would love this," I told Zach.

"You might love it, too, if you'd stop being afraid of it." Zach shifted me more sideways on his lap, tilting me back on the couch's armrest.

The change in position arched my upper torso, making a display of my breasts. He seemed to enjoy the effect, content to study the picture I made without touching for a long pause. Which of course began a rising heat of anticipation that grew as the moment dragged out, until my skin felt tight and flushed and my nipples budded into aching points, as if begging for attention. "Maybe you love it a little," Zach added, giving me a knowing look.

"This part doesn't suck," I mumbled. And then the word vibrated in my head, making me flash onto a fantasy of Zach's mouth closed over my nipple, licking and sucking. Desire curled low in my belly. Bad choice of words. Or good, depending on how I wanted to look at it.

I shook my head to clear the haze of lust that was forming there and covered myself with my hands. "Can we take a time-out? I'm losing track of the conversation."

"Time-out implies you want the clock to pick up again later." Zach gave me a very slow, sexy grin that made its way to his eyes and made them gleam with amber light.

"You like that idea?" I didn't have to ask, but I did anyway. Although flirting with a werewolf I didn't intend to sleep with yet probably meant the heat flaring between us had fried a few of my mental circuits.

"Yes. I'm not done with those. I've barely seen them." He stared pointedly at my hands doing an inadequate job of hiding my breasts.

"We just met," I pointed out. "You shouldn't have seen them at all."

"And yet, I've seen and touched." He placed his hands over mine, touching my breasts again by proxy. "If that bothered you, I wonder why you were squirming under me and making those little moaning noises. None of which sounded like 'no.'"

I blushed dark red, all the way down the way redheads do. I started searching around in vain for my shirt to hide both my breasts and the scarlet wave of embarrassment engulfing my skin. "Fine, I have no self-control. What happened to my shirt?"

"I took it off." Zach's lazy good humor irritated me, especially since it made him sound sexier.

I scrambled out of his lap and turned my back to him while I found my fleece pullover and slid into it. My nipples felt tight and puckered against the fabric, my breasts loose and accessible without my bra.

I turned back around and folded my arms over my chest. My eyes fixed on Zach, specifically the very attractive picture he made sitting with his legs slightly apart and his silk shirt open so it made a frame for his mouthwatering chest and abs. "Could you button up, please?"

"Am I distracting you?" He quirked a brow at me, clearly already sure of the answer. Fine, he could make me say it out loud, I didn't care, but I needed him to cover up or my mouth was going to be too busy to talk and I doubted I'd hear anything he said over the hot blood roaring in my ears.

"*Yes.*" It came out a lot more emphatic than I meant it to. Zach started to refasten the buttons, but he didn't rush. I gritted my teeth and waited until he was finished. "Thank you."

He patted his lap in silent invitation. I shook my head and took the chair. Safer. He frowned, and his obvious displeasure bothered me a lot more than I expected.

"Sit with me. I won't attack you."

The tone of command in his voice resonated as if triggering a hardwired response. I got back up and sat beside him. I kept a little space between us, but the fact that I'd obeyed him shook me. It showed in my face and my voice.

"So alpha isn't just a title."

"No. And you already knew that."

I nodded. "You could make me choose you," I said, putting one fear into words.

"That wouldn't be much of a choice, would it?" Zach scowled at me and leaned over to cup the side of my face with one hand. "I could've persuaded you to let me take you on this couch, even though we both knew you weren't ready, but coaxing you out of your pants wouldn't make me your mate."

I blinked, thinking I was missing something. Zach caught it and explained, "It's a choice of your heart, not your hormones. The act of mating doesn't make you mated. Not that it isn't a nice start, but sex doesn't determine your choice. You could sleep with all of us and choose none of us."

I blinked again and gave him a look of open disbelief. "All of you? How much stamina do you think I have?"

A grin twisted his face. "I didn't say you would, but you could."

I cleared my throat. "Moving on. So sex doesn't force my choice. If I can't say no to you, or a few of you, it doesn't mean I have to live with the results for the rest of my life."

"Well, you'd have to live with the memories." Zach's fingers threaded into my hair and gave a playful tug. "I'd do my best to make sure you didn't forget it."

"Fine, okay, memories are results, and hopefully they'd be happy ones." A thought hit me. "What about other consequences? I'm on the pill, but does that work for werewolves?"

Zach stilled. "It hasn't come up in previous generations. And other shifters haven't exactly shared information. I can tell you condoms are ineffective because of the way we're built. Not usually a problem since we're immune to human disease."

No condoms. My face registered my reaction to that bit of

news. Zach stroked his hand through my hair as he asked, "Is it really so awful to consider?"

I blew out a breath. "I stick to dating one guy at a time, and I don't sleep around."

Or at all, really. One less than satisfying experiment in college had cured me of the belief that I was missing out by saying no all through high school. I hadn't been waiting for marriage, just something. *Something with teeth,* I speculated, looking at Zach.

"It isn't cheating when you haven't made a choice or a commitment, and it's not like we won't all know. You wouldn't be doing anything behind anybody's back."

I groaned and buried my face in his shirt. "I'm not a performance artist. I hate the thought of you all watching while I'm doing intimate things with each of you."

"Do you really?" His voice softened as his hands stroked along my spine in reassurance. "It doesn't turn you on, even a little bit, to picture yourself as the center of attention? To imagine me kissing and touching you while David goes down on you?"

My whole body clutched and I think my heart stopped as I flashed on that scenario. Zach's wicked mouth claiming mine while David staked an oral claim. Zach's skillful tongue sliding between my lips in tandem with David's sliding into the slick folds of my sex. I might've whimpered.

"Maybe a little bit." My voice sounded ragged.

"There's nothing wrong with enjoying what you need." He spoke quietly, but the firm acceptance came through loud and clear. "And you will need us."

I bit my lip. "Will I? Or will it just be about my body?"

Zach shifted us, moving until we lay facing each other on our sides. He put my back to the couch so that he closed me in with his body. It felt safe, secure, like he was protecting me and not trapping me.

"You aren't separate from your body." His brown eyes had a troubled light as they searched mine. "Either of your bodies. Are you planning to try to split your mind and emotions from what your body does? Because that's not healthy. Sex isn't supposed to be something traumatic you have to protect your inner self from."

That surprised me. "You're not just a pretty face."

He touched my mouth with his, once, light and soft before repeating what was probably the pack motto. "Alpha isn't just a title."

I moved against him a little, inviting more pressure, more closeness. Zach slid his knee between mine, and I relaxed into the intimate press of his thigh parting mine. Maybe I could trust myself, trust my body. Both of my bodies, the one I knew and the one I was about to discover. "I get that."

I snuggled into him and admitted to myself that I liked the way it felt to press our bodies together, and it wasn't about sex. Well, maybe a little about sex. But mostly it was about warmth and closeness and safety and feeling good. Feeling as if I belonged. As if I'd come home. That took me by surprise, and Zach felt the change in my body.

"Problem?"

"No. Just surprised." I slid my arms around his waist and hugged him, feeling like I was taking a daring step. "This feels right."

"Good," Zach said in a voice thick with masculine satisfaction.

"No, I mean really right." I searched for the words to explain. "It never felt right before. Being close. It felt right with David, too."

"We're pack." Zach nuzzled me. "It *is* right. You belong with us. Your senses recognize us, even if your human mind doesn't understand the message."

Pack, I mused. *Another word for home?*

"Trust yourself," he whispered, kissing me just below my ear in a sensitive spot that made me shiver. "Trust yourself to know what's right, to have good instincts. Go with your gut and do what makes you feel good. Your gut will never lie to you."

"Next you'll tell me to trust you," I muttered.

Zach shook his head. "Words won't help. This will." He sat up and stripped off his shirt. Then he undressed me. I let him, my heart racing and my mouth dry, feeling his intent in every movement he made. When he started to tug my panties down, I panicked and grabbed at the fabric to keep them in place.

"I can make you come with them on," Zach said, his hands on the thin material that was all that stood between me and total nudity.

I didn't know what to say to that, so I searched out his lips with mine, and then neither of us said anything for a while. He crushed me into the sofa cushions. His bare chest covered my breasts and the weight and heat of him thrilled me. He worked his leg between mine, then slid his hand into my panties. I gasped at that intimate contact. He swallowed the sound and searched out the tight bud of my clit. The sensation of his fingertip gliding over that point would have stolen my breath if his kiss weren't already accomplishing that.

Zach's tongue twined with mine. His body rocked into the cradle I made for him as his finger moved lower, parted me, found my flesh slick and welcoming as he pushed inside.

It was a clear prelude of what was to come. Tomorrow I'd have him on me again with no clothing between us. When his hand came between my legs, it would be guiding his cock. The knowledge made my breath come in pants. He pushed a second finger into me, then a third, and rubbed my clit with his thumb.

The pressure applied to that point combined with the sensation of his fingers filling me, working in and out of me, felt indescribable. My hips moved, urging him on. His chest rubbed against my breasts, stimulating my nipples as he moved over me.

I felt my spine bow as tension coiled and shot free. I peaked in a frenzied rush while his mouth devoured mine and his hand inside my panties proved how easily he could make me come with them on.

I didn't resist when he stripped them off and moved down, pushing my thighs apart to lap at my bared sex with his tongue. He tasted me, suckled my clit until my hips bucked in a silent plea for more, then buried his tongue inside me, thrusting it in and out. My flesh felt sensitized rather than satisfied from orgasm, and the oral stimulation pushed me toward a second peak.

"Zach." I dug my fingers into his hair and strained to spread wider for him. He cupped one hand over my breast and placed the other just above my mound so his thumb could press against my clit. He ravished my sex with his mouth and tongue, played my body with his hands, and didn't stop until he'd wrung every last ounce of response from me I could give.

Afterward we rested on our sides, facing each other, legs tangled together. I entwined my fingers with his and focused on slowing my racing heart.

"I like that," Zach murmured, tightening his hand on mine.

Me, too, I thought, bemused. Holding hands. Next I'd be drawing hearts next to his name.

"Zach."

"Mmm."

"I have questions."

He rocked his body into mine. "I don't suppose one of them has to do with how fast I can cover the distance from this couch to your bed."

I resisted the urge to laugh. "No."

He tugged our joined hands up and kissed my knuckles. I tried not to get giddy and weak-kneed over that, but it melted me. "Ask me anything."

"How did you become alpha?" I held my breath, hoping I wasn't opening a painful topic, but I had something of a personal stake in the answer. I wanted to know just how dangerous it was to be the wolf king.

"My dad didn't think it was right to tie somebody half his age to him for life. He thought a new queen needed a new king. He held the pack together until I was old enough to take over. Then he formally stepped down and went to enjoy his retirement."

So the role of wolf king didn't necessarily come with a death sentence. Good to know. "I have friends and family outside the pack. How am I going to make that work?"

"For starters, don't make plans with them around the full moon," Zach said. "Avoid it; suggest alternate times; tell them you're Wiccan and those are important religious days if you have to give an explanation."

I thought about telling my adoptive parents I'd joined an all-male coven and decided to put that off as long as possible.

"So you think it can work?"

"Anything can work if you need it to."

He sounded so sure, I almost believed him.

CHAPTER NINE

A FEW HOURS LATER, I STOOD LOOKING AT MYSELF IN THE FULL-LENGTH mirror mounted on the walk-in closet door. Cinderella was going to the ball, and the fairy godmother had delivered.

In this case "the fairy godmother" meant Internet shopping and delivery by messenger. Dinner was a formal occasion, my official welcome and introduction to the pack. Zach had told me to dress appropriately and handed me a gold card of my own before leaving to attend to other business.

I'd selected a forest green velvet sheath that left my arms and shoulders bare and hugged my body all the way down to the ankles, with a split in back up to the knees so I could walk.

Flats had struck me as the practical choice since you never know when you'll need to move fast and heels throw me off-balance. Sheer flesh-toned hose and silk tap pants in the same green as the dress rounded things out. The dress was fitted tightly enough in the bodice to provide support, so I hadn't tried to find a strapless bra that wouldn't show underneath. "Formal" means not flashing tacky glimpses of undergarments.

I'd used the shower in the bathroom and found it stocked with an array of natural soaps, shampoos, and conditioners that wouldn't irritate my nose. I left the conditioner in extra long to turn my dark red hair sleek and silky. Brushed smooth, it made a shining cap. The short hairstyle and sleeveless sheath seemed to emphasize the vulnerable hollows of my collarbone and the back of my neck. Or maybe I was just nervous about exposing my throat to a wolf pack.

I looked as good as I was going to look. I admitted to myself I was stalling as I smoothed the velvet over my hips. *Be brave. It's just dinner.*

Right. I squared my shoulders and left my suite, retracing my steps to the stairs and down to the main level. Except once down there I realized I didn't know where the dining room was. I couldn't remember if I'd passed it on the way to the kitchen coming in from the solarium, so I decided to follow my nose and ears.

A murmur of voices ahead told me I was heading in the right direction. I found the open doorway and looked in before I entered the room. And then I wanted to just stand there and take in the picture they made.

The guys cleaned up well. I'd never seen so many tuxedoes outside of a prom or a wedding party. They all looked good in black suits, crisp white shirts, and black bow ties. Even David. Maybe especially David, who looked the least civilized despite the formal tux he wore as correctly as if he were in uniform.

All of them looked a little uncivilized, in fact, despite their outer polish. There was something in the air that made me wonder if they were planning a skirmish instead of seating arrangements.

Zach looked as good in formal wear as I'd expected him to, the James Bond of werewolves, urbane and sophisticated. He seemed as comfortable in his suit as he had in the Harley T-shirt and jeans I'd first seen him in. He'd probably be equally comfortable in his skin.

I realized I was imagining him naked just when he looked up and caught me watching him. I felt my face burn as if he could read my mind. Of course, with the way I blushed, he wouldn't need to.

He crossed the room to offer me his arm. I raised a brow at him as I took it. The last time I'd seen him, he'd gotten me naked and gone down on me. Now he wanted to be all proper?

He murmured for my ears alone, "Nice dress."

"Thank you." I made my tone sedate.

At a more public volume, Zach said, "Thank you for joining us, Chandra."

I smiled around and said something inane like *happy to be here.* Zach walked me around the room and made formal introductions, beginning with David. David took my hand and kissed it with grave propriety. His gray eyes fixed on mine with an expression that told me he wanted to do something very different.

I swallowed hard as we stood there for what felt like eternity with his lips barely touching the back of my hand, and wondered how in hell a simple look and a polite public gesture could be so infused with carnal intent. He released me and stepped back before I started breathing hard.

I'm toast, I thought, and kept smiling while Zach made his way through pack hierarchy. Redheaded Jack and blond Matt I already knew. They each gave me a devilish smile and turned my hand over to kiss my palm and the pulse point at my wrist.

The brush of lips there felt surprisingly intimate and I blinked at the unexpected zing it sent along my nerve endings. Jack grinned and winked at me over my hand, and I grinned back because it was impossible not to. The parade continued, greetings and welcomes and names I tried to fit to the right faces while they all subtly seduced me with their best manners.

Last was Will, the youngest, and I wondered if he was the omega wolf. If so, he didn't seem picked on. In fact, I thought the others were a little protective of him, and Zach gave him an approving look when he kissed my hand with practiced flair.

He straightened and smiled at me. A lock of brown hair fell over his forehead in a disarming contrast to the masculine intent in his chocolate eyes. That look made me wonder what part of me Will was planning to kiss next. The wayward thought sent a rush of heat to color my cheeks. Will's smile widened when he saw it, but he let me go and stepped back.

Zach led me to the table and I did my best not to stumble over my own feet. My heart was stumbling enough, erratic and beating too hard. The room almost hummed with electric expectation, or maybe that was the feel of a pack gathered close together. I felt an answering hum inside myself, and knew the wolf was looking forward to coming out to play.

Zach seated me at one end of the table and took his place at the head. The others filled in the space between us. David claimed my right. I didn't think the significance of our seating arrangements was lost on anybody. I wondered how I'd make it through the first course without losing my composure if our eyes met too often. *Make a note. Keep your eyes to yourself.*

Male voices flowed around me in a continuation of various conversations. They were all comfortable with one another, with themselves, and with me being here, I thought. Posture and tone of voice, the unguarded eyes and easy smiles, all said so.

I felt intensely aware of David beside me. My lips tingled with the memory of the last kiss he'd given me, devastating my mouth while Zach watched, ending it only to place me in Zach's lap.

Then there were the rest of them. I let my eyes wander over the table and replayed the formal introductions and how I hadn't hesitated to touch any of them. Hadn't wanted to hold my hand back, hadn't tensed as each of them took it to kiss.

Maybe it was just because I'd never been around my kind before and now I'd gone from famine to feast, but I liked them. I responded positively to them, all of them.

Yes, and maybe you're just going into heat and looking to rationalize it.

I stopped toying with my water glass and picked up the wineglass. Since Zach no doubt bought the good stuff, I tipped the glass a bit to one side. Sure enough, the red had legs. The bouquet burst in my nose, a delicious prelude, and when I tasted the wine I almost closed my eyes and sighed with pleasure.

"Like it?" Nathan, the wolf to my left, asked the question.

"I'm having dinner with eleven gorgeous guys. What's not to like?"

"You think we're gorgeous?" He grinned at me, a teasing light in his eyes.

"Yes. You guys raise the bar pretty high. I had to spend half my new salary on this dress so I could blend in." I waved my hand to encompass the group of them in stunning formal attire.

"It was worth it. And you can afford it now," Zach said from the opposite end of the table. His eyes glowed with amber heat and open admiration.

"Now that I have a better job than the one you told me to quit," I said. I gave a faint shake of my head, feeling played. But then again, if the mall put me in panther territory and David was right about them gearing up to challenge the entrenched wolf pack, I couldn't quit fast enough.

"Maybe if you're not on their turf, the panthers will settle down," Nathan said.

I risked a look at David. "Do you think I was causing the escalation?"

"No. You've only worked there for the last few months. It goes back further than that."

"What about the wolves who left the pack?" I sipped my wine to fend off the chill I got from thinking about my birth father's killer.

"They've kept their distance, but we know they didn't leave the area. Ray's been seen from time to time." David spoke in a flat tone that told me just how much he disliked the situation.

I didn't like it, either. Rogue werewolves on one side, aggressive werepanthers on the other. And Ray letting himself be seen struck me as a taunt or a warning.

Talking about pack history made me wonder about David's personal history. "Did you grow up here?" I asked, waving a hand to indicate the house.

"No. I grew up with my mom. My father was Neuri. They split before I was born. He didn't know about me, and she didn't know what he was."

That explained why he and Zach seemed to come from such different worlds. "Why'd you join the Marines?"

He bared his teeth in a grim parody of a smile. "I had a lot of aggression."

"You must've been a recruiter's dream," I murmured. "How'd you manage to stay undiscovered in the military?"

"I enlisted early. Lied about my age, then finished my four years about the time Zach tracked me down and I found out I couldn't keep passing for human around the full moon."

"You didn't know what you were until adulthood, either." The implications struck me. "I had no idea we had so much in common."

For an answer, David reached over and caressed my cheek. My heart almost stopped. I met his eyes again. The heat in them could turn Antarctica into a desert. It leaped from his eyes to mine, spread through me, starting low in my belly and rippling out, a slow burn that turned my muscles languid and left me feeling voluptuous. Ripe.

My lids lowered, my lips parted, and my breath came a little faster as I leaned toward him by a fraction. Inviting. He stroked his thumb along my cheekbone, followed a line down to my mouth, touched the pad to the full curve of my lower lip. I nipped at his thumb with the edge of my teeth.

"What big teeth you have."

His backward fairytale reference made me blink and diffused the sensual burn building between us. "The better to eat dinner with," I answered, and gave the food the attention it deserved.

CHAPTER TEN

NATHAN KEPT MY WINEGLASS FULL, AND THE EVENING BEGAN TO TAKE
on a very pleasant glow.

During a lull in the conversation, Zach stood and all eyes
turned to him. Including mine. Of course, my eyes had been wandering his way all through dinner. There was something really interesting about meeting the eyes of a man you'd kissed intimately
with the length of a formal table and a group of people between
you.

Zach met and held my eyes now. A hint of a smile played around
his lips that made me wonder what he was up to. "Time," he said.

Which made sense to everybody but me. The group rose to
their feet. I followed a beat behind. I wanted to ask David what this
was about, but interrupting Zach might be more than bad manners
in this context. He was the alpha. So I waited for enlightenment.

Zach came around to stand beside me. He crooked his arm in

invitation. I took it and let him lead me along. Good thing I'd worn flat shoes, given the bottomless glass of wine I'd been enjoying. I'd hate to trip in front of the rest of the pack, who'd fallen into file behind us.

Being close to Zach stoked up the embers he'd left glowing earlier, and I liked having an excuse to touch him. A small thing, my hand on his arm, but it reminded me of my hands on his bare skin. His on mine. I pushed that image away so I wouldn't fall over my own feet, flats or no flats.

"Where are we going?" I asked.

"Out."

"Could you be more specific?"

"Outside." I heard a hint of laughter in his voice. "You can wear my jacket."

"It's dark out there." What were we going to do, stumble around and fall over shrubbery?

"That happens at night." He dipped his head toward mine. "Scared?"

"Of being blind in the dark with a pack of wolves? Nah." Although I was, just a little, and that made my pulse leap.

We reached the solarium and Zach paused to remove his jacket and settle it around my shoulders. He took his time, smoothing the fabric over my arms, brushing my breasts as he drew the edges of the jacket together.

The stolen caress, done in front of the others but hidden from any eyes, public but still our secret, sent my heart skidding sideways. There was a little thrill in knowing we could get caught. Although I really didn't know how I'd feel about it if it was David who caught us fooling around.

And how would he react? I didn't know. Couldn't guess. I was in over my head. Too bad this situation didn't come with a rule book.

"You are scared." Zach paused, his hands still on the front of the jacket.

"Not of the dark." Just the dark thing inside me that wanted out.

"Afraid of me?" Zach's face turned serious, his eyes darkening.

"No." I stepped a little closer to him and rubbed the top of my head against his chin. "Maybe a little. I liked that too much."

"What, this?" His hands skated over the swells of my breasts again and my breathing hitched.

"Stop that." But the way my body shuddered into his said just the opposite.

"I'll behave," Zach said, sliding an arm around my waist to guide me out the door. We walked out into the night lit by a chandelier of stars and the almost full moon. The pack spread out in a loose group.

"If we're taking a walk, we're all overdressed," I pointed out.

"We're not walking far."

We made our way to the big fountain and I realized it had been turned on at some point. It was also lit, an effect that couldn't be appreciated during the day. The soft glow and the murmur of falling water created a romantic, fanciful atmosphere. Music from hidden speakers added to the mood.

"Dance?" Zach turned me to face him.

"Here?" I made a small hand gesture to indicate our position.

"Yes, here." He slipped his hands behind my back, putting light pressure on the lower curve of my spine, urging me to move closer.

I stepped into his arms and we shifted into a slow dance. I laid my cheek on his shoulder and surrendered to the moment. I'd never been romanced like this before. Moonlight and music, cool night air chasing away the soporific influence of wine, the seductive brush of Zach's body against mine.

The song ended. Zach's lips brushed the top of my head. "Thank you."

Then he handed me off to David, and my head spun as I found myself in his arms. His hands settled on my waist, possessive, sure, strong. I moved my feet in a daze as I struggled to adjust to the change in partners. He was graceful and controlled, but there was an edge to his movements that thrilled me, as if only a thin layer of civilization hid a savage hunger.

Dancing with him brought out an answering hunger in me. I let my body sway into his, felt his hands move down to mold my hips and pull me closer. My breath came faster through parted lips, and just when I thought he might kiss me, he let me go instead. I found myself with a new partner.

They were all trying to drive me crazy, I decided. But Jack wanted to whirl and dip me, making me laugh with his antics.

Matt surprised me with a tango and, when I protested that I didn't know how, said, "Just follow your partner," and then I could, after all. He led me through the steps and ended with my back against his chest, his arms holding me lightly, loosely, but so seductively I almost swallowed my tongue.

By the time I'd danced my way down to Will, I was grateful for a simple clutch and sway. And as we moved together, it occurred to me that this was one way to subtly break down barriers, allowing touch in socially acceptable public ways, getting me accustomed to the scent and feel of each of them in a nonthreatening manner. It was only dancing, after all. But tomorrow night it would be more, and it would be easier because I'd talked and laughed and eaten and danced with all of them.

I didn't know if I should be grateful or if I should feel manipulated. Thinking about it divided my concentration and I stepped on Will's toes.

"Sorry." I stopped and stood in the circle of his arms. "I think I'm all danced out."

"Want to sit?" Will indicated a bench by the fountain.

"Sure." I made my way to it and perched. The pack had drifted off, and I saw an opportunity to have a moment to myself. "Would you mind getting me a glass of juice or something? I'm feeling a little low on energy."

"Did you overdo it?"

"I'm fine. I just need to rest for a minute." I gave him a reassuring smile. He hurried off. I rested my arms on my legs and leaned forward with a sigh. Now that I'd stopped, I did feel a little lightheaded. I peered at a blade of grass near my foot that appeared to be growing and shrinking, blinked hard, and hoped I wasn't going to faint again. *Hurry back, Will.*

I looked around to see where the others were. They had to be close by, but I couldn't spot any dim shapes moving in the night. A sound to my side made me turn my head, my hand already moving to reach for the glass Will was bringing me even if it held wolfsbane. But it wasn't Will moving toward me. Even in the dark I recognized the big man who'd been in the mall parking lot, Wilson or Miguel. He hadn't introduced himself.

I checked my motion, but too late. He'd caught me with my

guard down and was taking the opening I'd given him, catching my arm in a hold that forced me down. Sitting off-balance was a lousy position to fight from, but I aimed the heel of my foot at his knee and kicked hard. Five pounds of pressure to collapse a knee. Go for the vulnerable spots; aim to disable.

My free elbow was already heading for his groin, but he blocked me, then levered my body lower. If he got me on the ground, I'd have a hard time breaking his hold. I threw my head back into his jaw and connected with a solid thunk. His hold loosened. I twisted free and brought my hands together, making a double hammer fist to smash the side of his jaw. Even a badass werepanther might stop for a minute if I dislocated the joint.

He blocked me again, moving so fast he blurred, and then his fist caught my temple before I could block or parry and the lights went out.

I opened my eyes to a jolting sensation and realized I was upside down, draped over my abductor's shoulder in a fireman's carry. We were still outside, and I saw filtered starlight through the canopy of tree limbs. He'd run with me to the woods visible from the gardens. I thought I may have only been out for a few minutes. We were still on wolf territory. And they'd be coming. But how fast? Did anybody know I was missing yet?

I knew one move that would probably stop the werepanther, a move that could too easily be fatal to a human. Unfortunately, I'd have to reach his throat to do it and my angle was wrong. In fact, short of punching his kidneys, my options were pretty limited back here. Which meant I needed to give myself better options.

Don't think about it; just do it. I rose up and threw my weight backward, catching him off-guard, making him fight to hang on to me and recover his balance. And in that moment, I had my angle and my chance. The side of my hand struck his windpipe and I didn't try to soften the blow. *Aim through the target.*

He dropped me and went to his knees. I kicked his temple as hard as I could, and he went all the way down. No waiting to see if my opponent was disabled. David had healed a broken jaw almost instantly. I took off running, but where to? I didn't know the woods, didn't know the way back to the house.

I listened for other sounds, like a werewolf rescue party, but it was hard to hear over the blood pounding in my ears and my shoes striking sticks and rocks as I ran as fast as my dress would allow.

Running blind was only good for putting distance between me and recapture. I'd have to find a safe spot to get my bearings. But before I could find one, a man stepped out into my path and I ran full tilt into him.

The force of impact didn't knock him back, but I bounced a little and that put a couple of inches between us. I stared at him, trying to make sense of what I saw. A hunter? On private land, at night? He looked like the woodsman from "Little Red Riding Hood."

"You didn't give me a chance to rescue you." He sounded equal parts accusing and disappointed as he plucked me off my feet and swung me up to cradle me against his chest. "I was going to be dashing and impressive. You might have swooned at the sight."

I blinked. Friend? Foe? Not wolf, whatever he was. But he didn't feel human, either. He smelled green, like the forest.

"He hit you a good one. I didn't change fast enough to prevent that. Sorry." He held me with one arm and with gentle fingers touched the side of my head that had taken the blow.

"Change?"

"I was the entrancing blade of grass you were looking at when our party got crashed."

The one that had gotten taller and smaller, making me think I was on the verge of passing out again. "So you're, what, the lawn?"

He laughed, a bright, ringing sound. "I'm a Leshii. Forest lord and friend to wolves. I can be as small as a blade of grass or as large as you see me now."

"Must be hell on your wardrobe." I felt dazed and winded, shaky and spent. Maybe this was all a hallucination and I'd wake up on the garden bench with Will pouring wolfsbane down my throat and David swearing at me for overdoing it.

"It's fun," the Leshii said in a cheerful voice. "And now I'm rescuing you after all. You were getting lost."

"Thanks."

The motion was making me dizzy. I shut my eyes, just for a minute. When I opened them again I was back on the bench, Will bending over me looking worried, lots of yelling in the background. I looked around but saw no signs of the lord of the forest or whatever he was. Maybe he'd gone back to blending in with the lawn.

"Panther grabbed me," I told Will. "Left him in the woods. Didn't see any others."

He nodded and called something I didn't understand to the others. "They'll find him," Will said. "Can you stand?"

How bad did I look? Maybe I didn't want to know. I nodded yes and was immediately sorry when dark sparkles swam in my vision and my head pounded. "With help," I amended, and leaned on him as he got me on my feet.

We hobbled inside, or rather I did, and he was nice enough to shuffle along with me.

A white-faced Jack met us and took my other arm. His touch sent a welcome rush of warmth through me. "You don't look so good," he said.

"You should see the other guy." Nausea roiled in my belly. What if I'd killed him?

"I hope to." Jack sounded grim. "Coming here. Taking you. Will went nuts when he came back and found you gone with panther scent all around."

The whole thing couldn't have taken long, I thought muzzily. Then again, I'd blacked out twice. And talked to a blade of grass. Had I dreamed that? My head ached and I gave up thinking. It was enough to put one foot in front of the other, down the hall, up the stairs, to my room.

Jack lifted me onto the couch. He stroked my forehead and I noticed his hand felt hot, but it soothed my headache, so I didn't complain. Then the two of them prowled the rooms, probably checking to make sure nobody was here but us. When they came back, I saw that Will had a soft knitted throw in hand.

"Are you going to cover me up and tuck me in?"

"Yep." He shook it out and spread it over me, then slipped off my shoes and covered my feet, too. "Room's clear. You can close your eyes if you want to."

Like I could take a nap while chaos reigned around me. But my eye drooped and I realized I was that tired. I couldn't relax if I had to stay on guard, though. "One of you stay until Zach's back?"

"Try to get rid of us."

Wouldn't dream of it. The gray fog of exhaustion rolled over me. When it let me back up, Zach was there. I was fiercely, wholly, shockingly glad to see him, as if his presence made everything right again. And I acted without thinking, reaching for him, fastening my mouth on his.

CHAPTER ELEVEN

I'D LIKE TO SAY I CAME TO MY SENSES AFTER HALF-CLIMBING HIS BODY and locking lips until oxygen deprivation was a real threat, but it was Zach who drew back far enough to let our eyes meet.

"How do you feel?"

I took inventory. "Headache. Sore muscles. Shaky."

"Up to talking?"

I nodded and my head didn't throb in protest, so I took that as a sign of progress.

Jack and Will had left, probably while Zach and I were busy. Zach sat on the couch with me in his lap, running his hands over me as if reassuring himself that I was all in one piece. "Tell me what happened."

I told him about the werepanther attack, but hesitated before mentioning the Leshii. Would I sound crazy? No crazier than a werepanther bent on kidnapping, I decided, and plunged ahead.

"Then a guy dressed like some kind of hunter who called himself the lord of the forest said I was lost and brought me back here. That's it."

"That's it," Zach echoed, his tone flat. "The Leshii hasn't been seen since your father died and Ray split the pack. Now he shows up for you, and all you say is 'that's it'?"

I shrugged. "I kind of expected you to tell me I was hallucinating. Who is he?"

"A friend and ally. The lord of the forest, like he told you. We're his pack. Or at least we were. When he disappeared, we thought he might be allied with the rogue wolves. Maybe he was just waiting for you."

"Maybe he's just been busy," I said. "Forest lord doesn't sound like the kind of job with a lot of downtime. What about the panther? Did you find him?"

"No. We found the spot where he hit the ground, signs of struggle, but his footprints went on to the edge of the woods. Then we lost his trail."

I let out a breath I hadn't known I was holding as I exhaled relief. I wasn't a killer. "He came by himself?"

"Yes." Zach smoothed his hands along my ribs and settled them at my waist. "You make very tempting bait, apparently."

"Do I tempt you?" I wanted to think of something besides danger. Not that flirting with Zach was all that safe.

Zach slid a hand down my hip and thigh. "I'm beyond tempted. I want to tear this dress apart, but I don't think now is the time. You've had a traumatic experience and you're exhausted."

"So you're going to be noble."

"Yes."

"Will you sleep with me tonight anyway?" I tried not to sound needy, but I felt safe with him and I didn't want to be alone.

"If you hadn't asked, I was going to insist." He smiled at me, but it didn't reach his eyes. They still showed a shadow of concern. "I want you where I can see you and feel you."

"It's a big bed," I said. "You might lose me."

"I'm an excellent tracker." Zach shifted me forward until my feet touched the floor. "Can you walk?"

"I'd better, or I'll be stiff tomorrow." I eased my weight onto my feet and stood. We made our way to the bedroom together. He removed his jacket and tie. I remembered deciding I didn't need a bra with this dress and dithered about it for a minute.

"Problem?" Zach asked, noticing my lack of progress.

"There's not much under this dress," I said. "And I don't have pajamas here."

I didn't have a lot of things here, now that I thought about it. I'd have to get my stuff from my apartment. Along with Bert and Ernie. I'd left Michelle a voice mail asking her to feed them for me, but I'd retrieve them after the full moon.

"Not a problem from where I stand." He gave me a heated look.

Well, okay then. I reached back to unzip the dress, slithered out of it, and tried not to blush at the thought of Zach's eyes resting on the breasts I'd just bared. I didn't look at him, pretending the task of peeling off my hose took heavy concentration. That left me wearing nothing but silk tap pants. The flimsy fabric didn't make much of a barrier. Feeling exposed, I practically dove under the covers and pulled them up to my chin.

Zach was down to underwear by that point. I looked. My eyes widened in appreciation.

The bed dipped as he joined me. He scooted to the center of the mattress and wrapped an arm around me, pulling me closer. "Come here."

"I'm pretty much naked," I blurted.

"I know." He reached down to tease the ruffle of fabric that more or less covered my ass. "These are nice."

His hand slid under the loose tap pants, squeezing, stroking. This was getting interesting. He ran a fingertip along the lower curve of my ass, tracing a path to my inner thighs. I held my breath as he teased me.

"Thought you said you were being noble tonight," I said, my voice gone thick.

"I am."

Damn. Second night in a row I was sleeping with a sexy man, and we were just going to sleep. Since they were two different men, though, that was probably for the best. I wasn't sure my brain could handle the reality of two lovers.

"You're getting tense again."

"David," I said, figuring I might as well open that can of worms. "I slept with him last night."

Zach's hand stilled. "Meaning?"

"Meaning I feel a little weird climbing under the covers with you now. Not that I want you to leave. Don't leave." Sudden panic made me turn over and clutch at him.

"I'm not going anywhere." Zach bent his head to me and kissed the curve of my cheek before settling his lips on mine in a slow, deep exploration that left me breathless and wordless. His hand traveled down my body in a slow line, giving me plenty of time to guess his destination and signal him to stop. But I didn't. I let his hand settle over my sex with only a thin layer of silk keeping him from touching naked flesh. Telltale moisture dampened the silk and Zach made a low sound of triumph. "You want me."

"I want you both." I swallowed and fought the urge to rock into his hand. It felt so good to have him cupping my sex. I wanted more. "That confuses me."

"You're awakening." Zach's hand moved, a gentle slide, up and down, petting me, urging me to part my legs and give him more access. "You're seeking a mate. You want to find what you're looking for."

"And I can only do this by being sexual with all of you," I said, disbelief plain in my voice.

"Yes." He kissed me again, hard and fierce. "I'd love to keep you all to myself. But you wouldn't thank me for it tomorrow."

His hand moved in a soft circle, pressing into my flesh, massaging my clit, and I decided that this, at least, was easy. I shifted my legs apart and shivered at the savage sound of satisfaction he made. He moved his hand up to my belly, found the waistband of the silk pants, and pulled them down. My breath caught as his fingertips traced the outline of my labia with no barrier between us. Nothing to prevent him from pushing inside . . .

I clutched at him and he moved to half-cover me with his body. His hand stroked and explored as his mouth claimed mine again. Deep, hot, wet kisses that made my head spin and my heart race. Knowledgeable, sure, enticing caresses between my legs until my hips were moving in a silent plea for more. Heat spiraled through my body. I shuddered with the force of the need he aroused. If he didn't do something to satisfy it, my body was going to break apart.

But he did, opening me and sliding two fingers into my sheath, penetrating me with his hand while his tongue drove in and out of my mouth in an erotic echo. He found my clit with his thumb and stroked it as he pressed deeper inside me, fingertips finding a spot that made me arch up under him and groan out loud.

He built a rhythm that I caught and rode. His fingers teased me, took me. His kisses seduced me. The press of his body into mine made me ache with rising need, and all the while he fed my body's hunger until it reached a point of no return.

I spasmed in pleasure, waves of it breaking over me, making the muscles of my sex grip around Zach's fingers as I rocked into his hand in an attempt to gain more pressure where I needed it. The ripples went on and on, and his hand coaxed more response from me until I thought I'd break if he didn't stop. And I did, finally, heart stopping, grinding myself against his hand as the force of the final orgasm broke me.

I drifted in a daze as his kiss ended and he withdrew his hand. I made a soft sound of protest at the loss.

"No more," Zach said in a harsh voice. "I won't take you the first time when you're feeling like this, reacting to stress and crashed from adrenaline."

"No, you'll just do it while I'm reacting to estrus and turning into a monster," I said. "Thanks for waiting to fuck me in front of an audience while I can't say no." Helpless waves of frustration washed through me, drowning out desire, leaving a bitter taste in my mouth.

"Chandra." He rested his forehead on mine. "It's not like that. You can say no. It's all your choice. And is that what you think we are, monsters?"

I sighed. "No, I just want you to want me. Not to preserve

the pack's power structure. Not to demonstrate a point to the pack when we have sex in front of them. If we do it now, it's just about us."

"I want you. Right now. I don't want to wait." Zach rocked his body into mine, the hard ridge of his cock pressing into me with only the fabric of his Jockeys separating us. "But are you forgetting the knot? You're not up to it tonight, and I won't do that to you if you can't handle it."

Oh. I had forgotten. "I didn't think of that," I admitted. "You're right; now is not a good time."

I was pleasantly tired from manual stimulation, unpleasantly spent from the night's exertions, and the combination left me boneless and tired. If I was going to indulge my lust for Zach, I wanted the whole experience. Not a quick screw before we rolled over and went to sleep.

Especially since it might only be once or twice, then never again.

"I should still do something for you," I said, touching the waistband of his underwear.

"If you want to do something for me, go to sleep so you'll be up to finishing this tomorrow."

There was a thought guaranteed to keep me up all night.

CHAPTER TWELVE

A DEEP FEELING OF WELL-BEING WAS THE FIRST THING I NOTICED WHEN I woke up the next morning. A sense of pleasurable expectation hummed through my body, and I felt utterly relaxed and at peace.

The empty space beside me was the second thing I noticed. No Zach. I pouted when my exploring hand found nothing but cool sheets where Zach had been. I listened but didn't hear him moving around the suite. That dimmed a little of my happiness in the new day. I wanted a good morning kiss.

Don't be greedy, I told myself. I'd gotten plenty last night. Almost more than I could handle.

I stretched and rolled over, enjoying the slide of the sheets and faint scent of Zach they still held. Sun streamed in through the windows, which meant I'd probably overslept. My muscles stood the stretch test without protesting, so I rolled to the edge of the bed and sat up, letting the covers fall away. Cool air on my naked body felt surprisingly good, waking me up all over.

I stood, sinking my toes deep into the sheepskin rug beside the bed. *Mmm.* I closed my eyes to fully enjoy the sensation. There were some advantages to my new digs. Like the soaking tub. I padded off to the bathroom, noticing how smooth polished wood floor gave way to cool tile under my bare feet.

The tub was easy to figure out. I adjusted the water temperature and let it fill while I looked for some kind of bath oil. The cabinet held a bottle of rose oil, and I poured a small amount into the tub. A little perfume went a long ways.

While the tub filled, I turned in front of the mirror. I looked better than I expected this morning. No sign of a bruise on the side of my face. Good color. In fact, I looked kind of flushed. Lips redder and fuller than usual. Well, I'd given them a workout last night, and I was probably still floating from the afterglow.

That led to a bemused curiosity. If Zach could give me orgasms that good with his hands and mouth, what would the real deal be like? My inner muscles clenched at the thought, as if a nerve ran from my heated imagination straight to my sex.

I grinned at my reflection, noting the swell of my breasts, the peaked nipples from the cool air, the light flush on my skin. "You look like you finally got some," I said. "And liked it."

Well, I had. But before I went looking for more, I should clean up. Wash away the evidence of my late-night adventure and make myself smell like something more attractive than day-old sweat.

I stepped into the tub and sank up to my chin in fragrant, silky water. I used my foot to shut off the tap, rising up a little in the process, and that made rivulets of water run down my body, leaving a light sheen of rose oil on my breasts.

"Huh." I'd never really noticed the effect of bath oil on bare skin, other than the way it softened and moisturized. I touched the curve of my breast with a curious hand, feeling the lubrication that made my palm glide over my nipple. Sort of like massage oil. Reducing friction.

I blinked when I realized I was feeling myself up and stopped, ducking under the water again to focus on getting clean. But the slide of water and the light scent of rose distracted me, making me roll and stretch in the tub.

Like a dog rolling in something.

I froze. "What is wrong with you this morning?" I whispered it out loud, but I was already afraid I knew the answer.

Flushed skin that felt even more sensitive than usual. Body visibly aroused. And despite last night's drama, possible future werepanther incursions had been the furthest thing from my mind. Instead, I'd been wondering where Zach went and thinking lustful thoughts.

"Heat" wasn't just a word anymore. Now it was a fever, a feeling of ripeness and readiness, a physical shift that told me nature's on-switch was tripped but good.

As I washed, my hands lingered everywhere they touched. Gliding over calves and thighs, smoothing the curves of my hips, running up my rib cage to explore the swells of my breasts. I cupped a hand over my sex and flashed on Zach's hand there. The way his fingers had worked in and out of me, pressed deep inside me, his thumb stroking my clit. I almost came on the spot, just from the muscle memory.

"Holy crap." My whisper seemed to echo in the tiny room. My sex throbbed from remembered pleasure, ached for more.

This had to stop.

I climbed out of the tub as fast as my languorous limbs would allow and grabbed a towel. My usual brisk rubbing made me wince and stop almost as fast as I started. Toweling made my skin feel raw. So I wrapped it around me instead, blotting water with careful pats. The towel still scraped against my skin even though I knew it was thick and plush and shouldn't have irritated me at all.

Fine. I could air-dry the rest of the way. I rehung the towel and drained the bath, trying to be neat, but every sensation distracted me and made me clumsy. Frustrated with myself, I padded back into the bedroom and retrieved yesterday's clothes. I pulled the fleece over my head, skipping the bra, and still had to fight the urge to claw it back off as soon as it settled against my skin.

This was bad.

The silk tap pants would look ridiculous with the sporty fleece pullover, but I figured they were softer and looser than the regular panties I'd worn when I left for the library yesterday. So I put them back on, and tried to ignore the way the silk rubbed against the seam of my sex. Of course, walking made that impossible, so by the time I'd reached the hallway door I wanted to scream, rip them off, and finger myself to relief.

But I needed to do something else instead. What? Oh, yeah. Find David, Zach, somebody. Get help.

I made my way out into the hall and halted in confusion. What was faster, get downstairs to the main living area or try doors on this floor? Was anybody up here?

No. The wolf inside me was impatient and disappointed to sense this floor empty. Instinct pulled me to the stairs. Help lay that way.

I made it almost all the way down before I had to stop and sit, breath coming in pants, the slide of silk between my legs a sensual torture.

A sound below made my heart hitch. *Look up here,* I wanted to yell, but couldn't seem to coordinate my lips and voice. But Jack's red head appeared anyway. "Chandra?"

I waved a hand at him and tried not to wince as the inside of my shirt rasped over my nipples.

"Need a hand?" He came up the stairs and halted about a foot away from me. "Oh. I see. Ahead of schedule, are we?"

I licked my lips. Relief that help was here restored my speech. "Dunno. Am I?"

"A bit." He smiled at me, but his eyes darkened to a midnight shade of blue. Reacting to my state? "You may be in for a long day. It ends with the moonrise."

That long? "Hell."

"We'll do our best to make it heaven." He gave me a teasing wink and held his hand out to me. I took it, and let him help me back up.

"Clothes hurt," I muttered. "Makes it hard to walk."

"I could carry you." Jack made the offer and waited for me to vote yes or no. I debated for a minute. I might do something embarrassingly wanton if he picked me up. On the other hand, I might have to get naked to walk any farther on my own. And I wanted to keep some sort of barrier to hide behind as long as possible.

"Carry me, please." My voice sounded throaty, like I was inviting Jack to do something more intimate. Maybe I was. Maybe I
wasn't ready to encounter wolves en masse after all. "Wait."

"When you're ready." Jack's voice was steady, soothing.

"Can you keep me up here?" I stared at him, a helpless plea
written on my face. "Keep me from the rest until it's over?"

He looked shocked. "No. First of all, I can't satisfy you by myself. You'd suffer. Second, you have to let all the pack touch you. It's
how you'll know your mate. And if you reject any of us by refusing our touch, you aren't just rejecting a potential mate. You're rejecting a packmate."

"Rejecting?"

Jack nodded, looking almost stern. It made me wonder if the
playful clown was a mask he wore. "Which of us do you want
kicked out because you wouldn't accept us?"

My mouth opened and closed, as I remembered all of them kissing my hand, dancing with me, welcoming me. Going after the intruder who'd taken me. David breaking into my apartment when he
thought I was in trouble. Zach taking a knife for me. The way they
worked together, a unit. Making space for me as if I belonged, too.
"Nobody."

"Then accept us."

I fought the urge to cry. "How?"

"However you want." Jack stroked the side of my face and I
turned into that touch, pressing a kiss into the palm of his hand before I realized what I was doing.

He felt good, right. Pack. I liked his touch and wanted to recip-
rocate. Maybe it would all be that easy. I closed my eyes and nodded. "Okay."

"That's my girl." Jack lifted me with careful hands until he held me cradled against his chest.

I let out a short laugh. "Yours and everybody else's."

He pressed a swift kiss on my surprised lips. "That works both ways, Princess. We're all yours."

While he carried me the rest of the way down, I wound my arms around his neck and nuzzled the spot below his ear. I wanted to lick it but pushed the impulse down. I didn't want him to trip and fall.

"That tickles." Jack's voice sounded soft and pleased, an invitation to continue.

"Mmm." I waited until he reached level ground before I ran the tip of my tongue along the outside edge of his ear, tracing the shape. "Does this?"

"Yeah." His arms tightened around me. "In a very good way."

I nipped at his earlobe and felt almost ridiculously pleased when he checked his forward motion to recapture his balance.

"Hold that thought," Jack muttered, and strode off again at a faster pace. He carried me past the kitchen and dining room, turning to bring me into what looked like a library. Built-in bookshelves lined the walls on two sides. The other two held windows and a fireplace respectively, opposite each other. In the center of the room I saw another plush sheepskin rug like the pair in my bedroom, an assortment of deep chairs with ottomans, and a backless fainting couch. Cushions piled in front of the fireplace made an inviting nest.

So many places to sit, lie, drape myself over . . . I blinked as the sexual possibilities the furniture presented marched through my fevered brain.

"Here?" I croaked.

"Here." Jack let me slide down his body until my feet touched the floor, keeping his arms around me so that I stood in a close embrace. He put one hand to the small of my back and slid the other down to cup the curve of my ass, urging me closer. I went without resistance, liking the feel of him pressed against me. "Big enough for all of us. Neutral ground, nobody's bedroom. Accommodating furniture."

"Ah." I rubbed my breasts against his chest, filled with excited anticipation at the thought of how accommodating the furniture might prove. He squeezed my butt in response and bent his head to steal another kiss. I parted my lips and he wasted no time accepting the invitation I offered, tasting the inner recesses of my mouth with his probing tongue.

He ended the kiss with obvious reluctance. "I need to call the others."

"Oh. Right." I took a few deep breaths, hoping they'd steady me. Instead they just seemed to inflate my breasts and push my nipples harder into Jack's lean, muscled chest. Which made me rub against him to maximize the sensation. "Sorry. Distracted," I muttered. "It's like the nymphomaniac version of ADD."

"Don't be sorry. I'm not complaining." He ran his hand just under the loose silk of my tap pants, teasing the bare curve of my butt. "But we can't get started without waiting for the rest."

"Because that wouldn't be fair," I gritted out, annoyed that I'd have to let go of him when I needed to be touched.

"Not very." Jack grinned at me and turned me loose. "Now I'm going to keep my hands to myself and let you find a place to sit or lay, however you feel comfortable."

"Like I can get comfortable right now." I gave him a disgruntled look.

"I'll be quick." He sped out of the room to prove it.

I tugged at the confining, scratching fleece pullover. I wanted to swear. Instead, I made my way to the fainting couch and fell onto it face-first in a loose-limbed sprawl.

Multiple footsteps sounded outside the hall, then inside the room, and I breathed into the upholstery, torn between relief and dismay as my suitors arrived.

Eleven men. One female werewolf in heat. Time to celebrate my first full moon after turning twenty-one.

Happy birthday to me.

CHAPTER THIRTEEN

A FAMILIAR HAND TOUCHED MY ANKLE, TRAILED UP MY BARE LEG TO stop midway between the silk edge of my tap pants and the hollow at the back of my knee. David. I knew him without looking, but I lifted and turned my head to search out his gray eyes, half-afraid of what I'd find there. Stark lust? Disgust?

Neither. Just hunger and a close regard. "How do you feel?"

I shifted on the couch, rocking my hips and making the muscles in my butt tighten and release in the process. "Like you should move your hand a few inches higher."

"Aside from that." He continued the caress up until he just touched the crease where the tap pants ended, his fingertips brushing the sensitive skin of my inner thighs and making me long to wiggle until I got them to brush my sex. Except that wouldn't be enough, either.

My breath came a little faster and made my voice unsteady. "Nervous. Are you going to hate me for this?"

"Hate you?" He stared at me in unguarded surprise. "For what?"

"For getting naked in front of your closest friends. For being the center in a circle jerk. For playing hide the salami with eleven men." I bit my lip, hating myself for loving the word picture I painted, seeing myself in the center of all that masculine attention, allowing hands and mouths and cocks to lavish pleasure on me any way I wanted it.

From the look of him, David liked it, too. His eyes darkened to the color of a stormy sky. His hand caressed me just under the edge of my tap pants, stroking, teasing. "Does that mean you want to play hide the salami with me?"

"Oh, yeah." I wet my lips with the tip of my tongue and arched my lower back, pushing my ass up in invitation. "I want that." I half-sobbed when his palm followed the curve of my butt until fingertips brushed the curls between my legs. "And that's not all I want."

I rolled over, done with hiding from him, ready to face him. Because we needed to talk before action carried me away. "How will you really feel? Will you still want me after I've had sex with Zach? Or somebody else?"

David hitched a hip onto the couch beside mine and leaned over me to brush a kiss across my lips. "I'll want you. Before. After. During. I'll watch you and I'll want you, and when it's my turn, I'll show you how much I still want you, no matter how many others there've been."

My heart skipped and my sex clenched. "Sure?"

"Maybe you need convincing." He put his hands to my waist, searched out my bare flesh under the shirt I wore, gathered the fabric of my shirt and slid it up, baring my belly, ribs, then breasts before he pulled it up and over my head. He took in the picture I made, a half-naked offering in a wanton sprawl, nipples forming tight buds that drew attention to my needy state.

"Beautiful."

I warmed to the approval in his voice. As if I needed to be any warmer. He bent his head to draw one peak into his mouth and my eyes almost rolled back in my head.

Sensation washed over me. The moist heat of his mouth on my bare skin. Tongue flicking at my nipple, hard enough to make me squirm and gasp. Suction drawing on my breast, sending a wave of reaction to my womb. Just when I thought I might embarrass myself from my response, he released my nipple. Then he blew against the dampened skin and it hardened even more while I let out a shuddering breath.

He turned his attention to my other breast, giving it the same treatment, and I whimpered, hips bucking in reaction as he suckled my aureole and tongued the turgid bud that swelled even tighter from his ministrations. This time when he blew air across my heated flesh, moistened from his mouth, my breath sounded as labored as if I'd been running.

"Sweet." His eyes met mine, all heated intent. He leaned over me, all dominant male. "You taste ripe and sweet and your nipples look like berries, all red from sucking."

I didn't answer. I just stared at him, wondering what he'd do next. And I didn't care what it was or who was watching.

"I bet you taste sweet everywhere."

Oh. I caught his meaning as he lowered his head and his wicked, wonderful mouth slid down as he scooted back, kissing my belly, licking at my navel, and then his hands were catching the sides of my tap pants and peeling them down to my thighs. He kissed my mound, moved lower, searched out the aching bud of my clit with his mouth, and drew on it the way he'd suckled my nipples. My hips came off the couch, and he made a dark sound of animal satisfaction at the response he drew from me.

He tugged my tap pants down farther, past my knees, until his hands could slide up the insides of my thighs and push them apart, and then he was kissing me between my legs, eating at my sex, while I gasped and groaned and spread wider for him.

His tongue explored my folds, thrust inside me, licked up to flick at my clit. He alternately suckled and licked and tongued deep into me, and all I could do was feel.

Tension curled in my belly and my body arched with the force of my reaction. I needed to move. I needed more. I needed him to stop. I needed him to never stop.

"David." I shaped his name with my lips but lacked air to give it voice. My hands wove into his hair, cupping his head, urging him on. Pressure built in sharp spikes. My breath came faster and faster. Pleasure spiraled, fierce, wild, building to an inescapable conclusion.

His mouth closed hard over my sex as his tongue plunged deep inside, and I came with a harsh cry in a rush of release that wracked me with endless shudders as his tongue lapped and licked and wrested every last ounce of response from me.

Only then did I become aware of the male faces over me, of Zach standing to my side, all of them watching.

Scalding color washed over me and I tried vainly to cover myself with my hands. Ridiculous, with David's face between my thighs, still drawing his tongue over my slick, swollen folds, what he was doing to me impossible to hide.

"Don't chicken out now," Zach chided. "You're doing fine." He knelt beside me and ran a possessive hand over one breast, rolling my nipple on his palm, then squeezing it lightly between thumb and forefinger. The pinching sensation sent a surge of lust straight to my womb, making me rock into David's mouth.

"Fine? I've had sex once in my entire life," I whispered. "Talk about zero to sixty-nine."

Zach's eyes turned to heated amber, almost glowing. "Only once?" He palmed my other breast, as if testing the weight. "You're about to make up for it."

"That's what I'm afraid of." I drew a shaky breath and looked around, meeting the eyes that watched the erotic display I was making of myself.

Jack winked at me. Matt wiggled his eyebrows. Will blew me a kiss. Nathan just smiled.

"I am in so far over my head," I sighed.

"We won't let you drown," Zach promised. He bent down to kiss me, and then it was exactly how I'd imagined it would be, Zach's tongue filling my mouth while David's filled my sheath, the twin oral ministrations making me mindless. Except I hadn't taken into account the added dimension of an audience, making me overly aware of the sexual invitation I presented. I felt naked and exposed, and helpless to hide the effect they had on me. I had two male mouths on me, and heaven help me, I wanted more.

I caught Jack's eye and arched my ribs, thrusting my breasts up.

My eye slid to Matt and I waited, unable to breathe, as they moved closer and took positions on each side of me. Zach made a space and kept on kissing me, drawing me further into his sensual spell with every press of his lips, every thrust of his tongue as he claimed and conquered my mouth. And then two hot, male mouths closed over my breasts, licking, suckling, biting softly, the tandem stimulation sending me into a delirium of heated desire.

David licked his way to my clit and suctioned the nerve-rich nub of flesh while he brought his hand up to replace his mouth at my entrance. He pushed first one, then two, then a third finger into my sheath, stretching my sex, filling me, readying me. His fingers worked in and out, deep and slow, until I burned to be taken harder. Faster. Fully.

Matt and Jack drew on my nipples, hands joining in to caress the sensitive undersides of my breasts, to squeeze and knead and stroke.

Zach's mouth grew gentle, kisses turning coaxing and seductive, his tongue twining with mine, tasting my parted lips, drawing me deeper into a world of feeling and need.

Then he raised his head and looked into my eyes, reading the wild depth of my arousal. "What now?"

I knew what he wanted. I wanted it, too. I couldn't bring myself to ask for it. So I closed my eyes and tried to hold on while David's mouth and fingers drove me higher. But before I could tumble over the cliff of passion the four of them had raised me to, David ground his hand against me in a final caress and withdrew his hand. His mouth released my clit. And I fought to keep from screaming.

"What now?" Zach asked the question again. Patient. Relentless.

I avoided the question, looked for Will. "Kiss me," I said through lips swollen from Zach's mouth, my voice hoarse.

Will complied, coming to me and taking a place opposite Zach. I didn't know what I expected. A butterfly kiss, lighting softly. A sober kiss, serious and earnest. What I got was a bruising kiss, a grinding of mouths and wild mating of tongues. It was hot and crazed and brutal, and it only made me wrenchingly aware of the aching emptiness I was desperate to have filled.

Will drew away and then kissed me again as if unable to resist the pull of my lips. I writhed as his mouth crushed down on mine, Matt and Jack still working my breasts and sending shock waves from the nerves in my aureoles to my sex.

And it wasn't enough.

Will ended the kiss and moved away. Matt and Jack released my nipples, moving back in tandem. I shuddered at the cessation of stimulation and closed my eyes.

What now? I could hear the echo in my mind. I knew it was inevitable, but I would postpone that step as long as I could bear. "I want all of you to touch me. One at a time."

Since David already had, he came around to my head and let me taste myself on his lips while his hands played my breasts with sure expertise. I kissed him back as I sprawled with legs splayed. My tap pants were now completely gone, stripped away at some point unnoticed, my sex exposed and glistening from the attention lavished by David's mouth and my own lubrication. The picture of abandon.

And one by one, all the men moved between my thighs and sank fingers into my hungry sheath, sent fingertips gliding over my swollen clit or pinched it lightly, bent to taste me. Not restricting themselves to genital contact, but caressing my hips and legs, my belly, my arms, leaving no part of me ignored. Arousing me by turns until I rushed toward the edge of orgasm, then stopping. The last one palmed my sex and massaged in a slow circle until I moaned into David's mouth and tilted my pelvis up, offering myself. Then he gave me penetration, but only one finger, teasing, twisting inside me, withdrawing, returning, toying with me.

Zach. I knew without looking.

That finger slid out, stroked over the puckered opening of my anus, and I stopped breathing. The lubrication coating his fingertip made it glide across without resistance, surprising me as unexpected nerve endings clamored to life. The caress was unprecedented, taboo, but then, why leave any forbidden act unexplored?

I surrendered to the dark pleasure as Zach pressed the tip of his finger into that virginal opening, slowly pushing farther in, withdrawing, pushing back a little farther than before. And when another hand began to stroke and pet my sex while David caressed my breasts and Zach worked a second finger into my anal opening, stretching the delicate tissues and widening them with an erotic scissoring movement, I found myself teetering on the brink.

I raised heavy eyelids halfway to see whose hand was between my legs. Nathan. He smiled at me and teased the slick, ready folds of my sex with one fingertip, stroking and exploring my plumped labia while Zach thrust his fingers deeper into my ass. Nathan plunged one finger abruptly into my vaginal opening, hard and fast, then withdrew.

I made a low sound in my throat, and David raised his mouth

from mine, looking first into my eyes, then down at what they were doing to me, penetrating me in tandem.

His eyes returned to mine, sure and steady. "Every man here has had a taste of you. Zach and Nathan are filling your soft pussy and your tight ass with their hands while I watch. And I still want you."

I trembled with the need for release and a swell of some un-named emotion.

"Fuck him." David bent his head to mine again and whispered the words against my lips. "I know you want to fuck Zach. You're ready. We've prepared you, and we'll prepare you for more when he's finished and the fire inside you burns all over again."

My heart stumbled and my breathing staggered as he went on, "Fuck him, fuck them all, as many and as often as you have to. Give yourself what you need and give yourself to us until you're sated and you've tried us all enough to be sure. You have to be sure."

His lips moved on mine in a kiss so gentle it wrung my heart as he breathed a promise. "Through it all, no matter what, I'll want you."

I kissed him back, helpless to do anything else, while two other men drew a willing response from my fevered body.

David ended the kiss. He stroked my hair before he framed the sides of my face in his hands. His eyes burned into mine for a long moment. Then he touched his lips to my forehead and moved away.

What now? Zach's question repeated in my head, followed by David's answer.

Fuck him.

In front of an audience.

Fuck him, while David watched another man guide his engorged cock between my legs and plunge it into my yearning flesh, knowing the act would lock us together until he was spent enough for the knot to release.

Fuck him. Point of no return. No changing my mind, no crying out, *Stop, wait,* after that male organ penetrated my waiting sheath.

I closed my eyes again, arching and twisting my hips at the joint sensations that fed my desire but weren't enough to satisfy it. Only one act could quiet the thundering demand of my transforming body.

I opened my eyes again, reached down to touch Nathan's hand between my legs. "Stop."

He twisted the finger buried inside me, then slowly drew it out. And then, while I watched, slid it into his mouth to taste me on his tongue.

My sex clenched involuntarily, and Zach felt those inner muscles spasm as he eased a third finger into my anus, the sensation of fullness in that untried chamber a pleasurable prelude to more to come.

"Zach." I said his name like a guttural invitation. "It isn't enough."

"I know." His voice was low and rough, his amber eyes glowing so hot I thought I could see the wolf within the man. He withdrew his fingers, one at a time, leaving me empty and aching to be filled.

"It has to be you. The first time." I tilted my head up, exposing the vulnerable curve of my throat to the pack's alpha, acknowledging him for what he was, inviting his dominance, submitting to him. "Fuck me, Zach."

CHAPTER FOURTEEN

I'M NOT SURE WHAT I EXPECTED. FOR HIM TO FALL ON ME AND HAMMER home without further preliminaries, maybe. But he made me wait, my body screaming to be taken, while he cleaned his hand and put aside the lubricant he'd picked up from somewhere to ease the entry of those additional fingers into my anus.

The guys had come in with supplies, it seemed. Thoughtful of them. I might be really grateful for lube by the end of the day.

Jack came around to my head holding a glass with a straw. "Drink this."

Crap. "More wolfsbane?"

"Protein shake." He guided the straw between my lips and I sipped obediently even while every cell in my body protested the delay. If I had to spend the day mindless with lust, at least I was spending it with men who were looking out for me. Left to myself,

I'd probably end up dehydrated and weak, because it wasn't food I hungered for.

When Jack was satisfied that I'd swallowed enough, he took the glass away. And then the pack surrounded me, spreading kisses and caresses everywhere, while the beast inside me gloried in their homage. Zach came to push my thighs wider apart with his hands and kneel between them, and I noticed he'd gotten naked.

Had anybody else? I looked around and saw bare chests and feet, pants with top buttons undone, various signs of total group nudity in progress.

Good. If everybody was seeing mine, I should get to see theirs. And it would make skin-to-skin contact so much easier without any annoying fabric in the way. I liked them touching me. I wanted to touch them back. I wondered why I'd resisted this. They were mine, and I was theirs, and it was right that they should all witness and participate.

They stepped back as Zach lowered his body over mine and exultation pulsed through me. This was what I wanted. This was what I needed. I tilted my pelvis up and wrapped my legs around Zach's waist, making myself as open and accessible to him as I could.

He let the broad head of his cock nudge against the slick, swollen folds of my sex but didn't rush to enter me.

"Zach," I groaned, writhing under him. "Please."

He rocked his body into mine and pressed forward, just a little, just enough to make my softened flesh give as if he was testing my readiness. "Sure?"

I clawed at his back. "I have to. I need to. Please, I need you inside me."

"They're watching." Zach murmured the words for my ears

only. "Are you sure? Because once we start, there's no stopping until it's over."

"They can take notes, take pictures, rate our performance on scorecards, I don't care." One thought struggled through my lust-soaked haze and I called over Zach's shoulder, "If any of you put pictures or video on the Internet, I'll have you killed."

Jack laughed. "No recording devices of any kind present. Although it'd make one hell of a private viewing if you want to change that."

"No."

I turned my attention back to Zach. "I'm sorry about what I said last night. I could say no. I could send them away. I don't want to. I want to have sex with you while they watch. They're part of this. They belong."

Zach groaned at my words and I felt the tension cording his muscles. "Don't be sorry later."

That was my only warning, and then he drove his cock into my waiting sheath, hard and fast and deep, and then it was done. I felt the knot swelling inside me as Zach filled the tight clasp of my body with the length and width of his shaft, stretching me. The unaccustomed sensation of full penetration was enough to make me gasp without the added singular feature of that knot.

"Zach." I panted his name and clung to him, struggling to adjust. He gave me a minute to grow accustomed to the weight of his body on mine and the intimate invasion of my flesh.

"All right?" He asked the question against my lips, kissing me, gentling me before he began to move on me.

"Umm." I kissed him back, falling into the moment, tasting the unique flavor that was Zach, delighting in the press of his body on mine and his possession of me. There was melting sweetness and tenderness in his kisses, and dizzying lust in the short, hard thrusts his cock made into my channel. "I like this."

Weak, inadequate words. I loved this. I was insane for more. Only this could cool the fever that burned in my body; only this could give me release and relief.

"In the mall," Zach gritted out as he abruptly rammed his cock so deep I felt the head press against the opening to my womb. He ground his groin against my folds as if he wanted to go even deeper than the limits of flesh allowed. "I wanted to put you up on the counter and get inside you. Right there, in the store."

I made an inarticulate sound of pleasure and felt my sex react to the graphic picture he painted.

"You were right," he went on in a harsh whisper. "I wanted to fuck you in front of an audience. I want them to hear you moaning for me, see you naked and spread wide for me. I want them to know it's my cock cramming you so full you can't move."

He moved in a shifting pattern of short, shallow, then long and deep thrusts so I couldn't anticipate his rhythm. I could only submit and accept each stroke, taking whatever he gave me.

"They're watching now," I murmured back. "Watching you nail me on this sofa." And knowing that sent a thrill through me. I felt powerful and sexy. Hot. My sex gripped and squeezed Zach's thick shaft in a precursor of orgasm.

"I'm going to nail you hard," Zach said, suiting action to words. "Fuck you until I'm good and finished. Come in you until I'm empty and you've taken it all."

Oh, God, yes. I whimpered and worked my hips under him, writhing, twisting, bucking, straining. He drove into me over and over, finally settling into a steady, measured cadence he refused to speed up or deepen even when I sobbed and pleaded.

When I tried to fight him, desperate for relief, he held me down and rode me with relentless force. My world narrowed until it held only heat and need and Zach, feeding but not slaking my desire, making it build with each decisive thrust of his cock.

His name became a litany in my head, repeating with each stroke. *Zach. Zach.* I clung to him, wound myself around him, rocked with him, and he claimed more of me every time he drove home until I thought he might own me completely.

"Please, let me come. Please, I need to," I begged. Tremors wracked my body.

"Tell me you want me," he answered in a fierce snarl. "Tell me you want me to come inside you."

"Oh, God, Zach, yes." I clutched at him, shaking with the force of what I wanted. "I want you. I want you to come in me."

He let out a low growl and let go of the iron control he'd exerted over both of us. He took me fast and ferociously deep. He used my sex with feral abandon and I loved it, loved his voracious cock, loved taking every hard inch he rammed into my soft flesh. He wasn't gentle or restrained, and I didn't want him to be. I wanted this.

"Zach. Yes." I murmured my acceptance and permission, showing him with my body what I had no words for.

"I'm going to come." Zach slammed into me, his cock going deep and fast, all the way to my cervix. "I'm going to empty my balls into you, pump you full of come."

I made a soft sound of need and greed, my body rising up to meet his, my inner muscles spasming as my long-delayed orgasm began to take me. I felt his shaft swell, felt his cock jerk inside me as he started to come in hot, wet spurts. His fluids bathed my vaginal walls, sensitized from sex, and that intimate internal stimulation pushed me to the peak.

"Zach." I didn't know if I whispered his name or screamed it, but I was coming violently and endlessly, hips bucking, my inner muscles milking his cock. It went on and on, the two of us locked together, riding the tidal wave of release, until it finally subsided into eddying ripples.

I lay panting and spent under him. He sprawled on top of me, his shaft buried fully inside me. While we rested with our bodies still joined, I held him to me and wondered if I could contain the emotion of the experience. I couldn't, and it leaked out of the corners of my eyes.

"Chandra." Zach roused himself to nuzzle my cheek and brought his hands up to frame my face, brushing the tears away with his thumbs. "Sweetheart. Don't cry. The knot will release."

Yes, it would. But I wouldn't be free.

"I'm okay," I managed in a shaky whisper. I wasn't, but he hadn't meant to hurt me. I knew that. I'd known it before I said the words that would make the wound in my heart inevitable.

I'd asked him to fuck me. I'd begged him to take me. He'd given me every opportunity to change my mind. I hadn't. More tears slid out, following the first.

"Tell me what you need." Zach slid his arms under me, wrapping around me, cradling me close. "Anything you need, say the word and it's yours."

I needed to own a piece of his soul, the way he now owned a piece of mine. But he couldn't give it to me for the asking. So I just shook my head and burrowed into his comforting strength. Inside me, I felt the knot dissolving. Our bodies could separate, but I wasn't ready to let him go.

"Hold me," I said, my voice raw. "Hold me, just a little longer."

"As long as you want me to." He stayed planted inside me, his arms tight around me, his body weighting mine down and anchoring me, solid and real and warm.

His lips searched out mine. Our mouths met and clung in a deep, sweet kiss that made my heart ache. When he raised his head, his eyes looked like clouded gold. "Don't be sorry. Please don't be sorry you gave yourself to me."

I reached up to touch my fingers to his lips. "I'm not."

Zach rested his forehead against mine. "Then what is it? Something's wrong. Do you think I'm a monster now?"

I shook my head, genuinely puzzled. "What do you mean?"

"I fucked you like an animal. I knotted you. I did it in front of a group."

I slid my hand to the side of his face and stroked it. "I'm not upset about the audience thing. I thought I would be. I'm not."

He lifted his head, and something fierce showed in his expression. "You didn't answer the other part."

I shrugged. "If you're a monster, I am, too."

"You wanted something human."

He would remember that. I wished I could go back in time and kick myself. "I wanted you." That was true, and it could stand for all the rest I couldn't say. I stroked his hair, kissed his shoulder, tightened my legs around him. "I still want you."

Zach levered himself up. "Speaking of that, you'd better take advantage of this breather."

I caught his meaning. The fever in my blood had lowered, but it still burned in me. The respite wouldn't last. I'd need more and I'd probably need it soon.

"Right." I reluctantly loosened my grip on him. He pulled out of my body and moved off to sit beside me. His hands reached for mine and he helped me sit up, too, drawing me close so I could lean into him for support.

Jack brought me another drink. I tugged a hand free, took the glass, and drained it without question, not even flinching at the taste of wolfsbane.

"Thank you." I tried to smile at him as I passed the empty glass back, but I could feel that it didn't quite reach my eyes.

"You're welcome." He leaned in to give me a kiss that zinged in a pleasant way. Zach's hand tightened on mine, and I wondered if he was feeling territorial. If so, too bad for him. I had to deal with this. He could, too.

When the kiss ended, Zach scooped me into his lap and stood with me in his arms. "Let's get cleaned up."

"Right." I rested my head on his shoulder and went along with his plan, although it seemed pointless. He'd marked me and nothing could ever wash that away.

He carried me into a bathroom off the library, sponged us both off, his hands so gentle on me that it made my throat ache. When he finished, he circled my waist and pulled me toward him until our bodies touched. I swayed closer until I rested against him, content to stand there in his loose embrace.

"This is nice," I said softly, rubbing my cheek against his chest.

"Just the two of us." Zach nuzzled my hair and then bent to kiss my temple. "I wanted you to myself for a minute."

"I think we're entitled to a minute." I smiled against his skin as I spoke.

His arms tightened around me. "At the risk of ruining the moment, I need to ask you something."

"Anything," I said in a light, agreeable tone. And depending on what he asked, I might even tell the truth.

"David."

"That's a question?" I cuddled closer and realized I was feeling more aware of the pressure that created against the swell of my breasts, the sensual ache there, the swollen buds of my nipples. Another wave of heat building.

"You didn't ask me what you asked him."

"Still not a question."

"I didn't think I had to spell it out."

No. He didn't. I sighed and let my hands wander over him for the sheer tactile pleasure of it. "I didn't have to ask you. You won't hate me for having sex with him. I wasn't sure the reverse was true."

Zach's fingers dug into me, hard. Possessive. "What if he'd said yes?"

I lifted my head to meet his eyes with mine. "I still would have fucked you first. I just would've tried not to fuck him afterward."

"Tried." Zach's eyes burned with an amber flame.

"That's right. Tried." I didn't blink under the force of his gaze. "I might have done it anyway." Admitting out loud that even if I knew David hated me, I'd still want him.

Zach brought his mouth down to mine and kissed me with bruising force, leaving my lips swollen and stinging. That didn't help my body's rising need for more. My breathing grew ragged, a sweet tension building low in my body. My skin hungered for touch, and my sex clenched in protest at the emptiness that would have to be filled again.

"Zach." I shuddered into him. "I think time's up."

"Not yet." He turned me around so that he held me with my back supported by his chest, the round swell of my naked ass cushioning his groin. He cupped one hand over my breast and ran the other down to cover my sex. His palm massaged my clit, fingertips pressing against my folds. The intimate caress made me groan and shift my feet apart, making just enough space between my thighs to invite more of his touch.

Zach answered the silent invitation, sliding his hand down farther, pushing his fingers into my slick, ready flesh. He squeezed my breast, kissed the side of my neck, stroked in and out of me in a shallow penetration. "You're going to have his cock here."

"Yes." I closed my eyes and rocked into his hand. "Do you want to watch that?"

"I want you to take me in your mouth while he does it. I want you to wrap your lips around me while you wrap your legs around him." His voice was low and rough, his hand working me with deliberate skill.

"Not sure I can," I said as my breath hitched in reaction to both his words and his manipulation of my body. "Limited attention span. Hot idea, though."

"If you can, I want you to."

"Zach." Emotion welled, clogged my throat.

"I'm not trying to make it harder for you." He rubbed his chin against the top of my head as he spoke. "I want you to know I'll still want you when he has you. You didn't ask, but I thought I could show you."

"Oh." He was still willing to share me. I swallowed hard, not sure if knowing that made it better or worse.

CHAPTER FIFTEEN

BY THE TIME ZACH CARRIED ME BACK OUT, I FELT FLUSHED AND URGENT. My body thrummed with need. Sex had sated me for a little while, but not for long.

The room had undergone a subtle change during our brief absence. A cart with snacks and drinks stood in a corner. Convenient. All items of clothing had been discarded, and I felt for a dizzy minute like I was peeking into the men's locker room. All those beautiful, bare, athletic male bodies, comfortable in their group nudity as if the setting made it appropriate.

The locker-room analogy made me tense a little, and Zach noticed. "What?"

"Locker-room talk," I said, my voice pitched for him alone. "I can hear it now. You guys comparing me."

"If anybody says a less than complimentary word about you, it had better not be in my hearing." Zach sounded grim. "That would be grounds for a challenge."

Challenge? I blinked, startled. Seemed like overkill, but if it was that serious, then I didn't have to worry about the guys swapping comments about my performance after the fact.

It still felt kind of odd to face them all again after they'd all taken turns giving me foreplay, watched me come when David went down on me, and then come again underneath Zach.

I felt the blush burning my cheeks just thinking about that. It had felt right and good in the moment, but now I felt self-conscious and awkward.

"You belong to us," Zach whispered, setting me on my feet. He kissed my forehead and put a bracing arm around my waist. "Go let them show you what that means." He urged me forward. I went with reluctant steps, but to my surprise they came to meet me.

"Missed you," Jack said, spanning my waist and pulling me to him for a quick kiss that still managed to pack a wallop. My libido leaped in response. He handed me off to Matt, who nuzzled my neck and caressed my bare ass with obvious enjoyment.

Nathan took me from him and frenched me while he ran his hands over my breasts. His touch made my nipples tighten as if pouting for more. From behind me, another pair of hands cupped and squeezed my butt, and then I was turning into Will, who bumped his erection into my belly with cheerful lust and rubbed his nose against mine, surprising a laugh from me.

Daniel. Sean. Cam. Aidan. Roman. Not just a list of names I'd worked to match to faces last night at dinner. Now they were real to me, touching me with affection and acceptance. Words could be false, but bodies didn't lie. One by one, they showed me I was

theirs and all of them were mine, giving me heated kisses and setting me on fire as my naked body slid against each of theirs in turn.

Sean and I were the same height, and that gave him the right angle to dare the greatest intimacy. When our lips met and our tongues
touched, he guided his engorged penis between my thighs and
rocked forward so that his shaft glided along my labia.

I shuddered at the contact, wanting more, aroused by the realization that I could let them all push between my thighs without
danger of real penetration locking us together.

"My turn," David said behind me, and Sean pulled back, the reverse movement dragging the ridge of his head against the slick
folds of my sex that parted from the pressure. He groaned into my
mouth, and I echoed the feeling. So close, so good, not enough.

Then David was holding me, and my knees went weak with relief because it felt like coming home. The fear that sex with Zach
had changed the fragile bond between me and David evaporated.
He'd promised not to hate me, given me permission by stripping
me naked for all of them, and prepared me to give myself to another man with oral sex. And still some deep part of me had been
afraid that David wouldn't want me now.

A twin fear that I couldn't respond to him after Zach had
claimed me melted away, too. I clung to David, glad to the depths
of my heart that I hadn't robbed either of us of this opportunity to
satiate our mutual hunger.

Maybe tomorrow it would be different. When the heat ended and
my choice was made, I might find that I looked at David and didn't
feel compelled to touch him, didn't yearn for him to touch me. The
intense chemistry between us might burn out from surrendering to
it, or simply go away when I formally accepted Zach as my mate.

For now, though, David and I had this. I wanted to savor every stolen moment. We stood together, not touching except for the press of our bodies, arms tight around each other. He rested his face against the silky cap of my hair. He breathed me in, and I did the same with my face tucked into the hollow of his throat, luxuriating in the unbroken expanse of his skin against mine.

My hands explored the planes of his back, enthralled with the harnessed male strength evident in his body, knowing magic lay under the skin in his blood and bones that the full moon would reveal. I'd seen the transformation with my own eyes, touched the fur. I knew what he was. I could feel what I was. The same. An animal in human form waiting for the moment of release.

"How do you want me?" I asked the question in a soft voice. I figured it went without saying that I wanted him next.

"On your knees," David answered. The muscles under my hands bunched as his hold on me tightened. "I want to mount you from behind and take you on your knees."

I closed my eyes, picturing it. My bare ass upturned, thighs apart, glistening sex exposed. Submissive. Receptive. David behind me, thick cock jutting forward. His hands on my hips, holding me in position. The long slide of that male flesh into mine, and the forming of the knot inside me that would lock us together, making me his until it released.

I realized I was breathing fast and my head felt light.

"I don't want your arms to get tired." He bent his head to kiss the curve of my neck, moving his lips along the sensitive cord that ran up the side in a slow caress that made me shiver with need. "I'll bend you over an ottoman to give you support while you kneel for me. That's how I want you."

"Okay." I felt dazed with lust, crazed with need. "Now?"

"Not now." David nipped at my earlobe with the sharp edge of his teeth and gave it a tiny tug. "Foreplay first. Give the others a chance to pleasure you, make you soft and swollen and slick for me so I don't have to hold back when I'm fucking you."

I gulped, stricken with heat from his proximity, his graphic words, the image of other hands and tongues readying me to be taken with urgent force.

"I can't stand up anymore," I whispered, feeling my bones turn to water.

"You don't have to."

David lifted me up and carried me over to one of the ottoman and chair pairs. With the two parts pushed together, the chair made a half bed for him to lay me on. It'd be easy to turn me over and slide me down until I knelt on the floor, supported by the cushion, when the time came. My nipples ached in anticipation of the way the fabric would rasp on them as my body rocked back and forth from the strength of his thrusts.

He pulled me down until my hips rested on the edge of the ottoman, and gripped my inner thighs to pull them apart. That left me perfectly positioned for oral pleasure. Delicious expectation pulsed between my legs.

"Who do you want to go down on you?" David ran his hand over my sex, petting and stroking but not opening me. "Who do you want to make you come?"

I knew who I wanted without thinking. My body shivered with the memory of Matt and that wicked tango. He'd seduced me with a dance. Now I wanted his tongue to dance between the soft folds of my flesh.

"Matt." I said it out loud, and the throaty sound of my voice made that one word speak volumes.

"Really?" His blond head appeared over mine, looking down into my face from behind the chair. His eyes danced with devilment and I grinned up at him.

"Really."

He gave me a slow, sexy smile. "It was the tango, wasn't it?"

"Yep."

Matt leaned closer until his lips brushed my forehead. "Do you need anything first? Drink, snack?"

I gave a tiny shake of my head. "Not hungry for food."

"Sure?" He reached over the chair's back to tease my nipples, just barely brushing the palms of his hands over them. I arched up into him, eager for more.

"Sure."

His hands vanished, leaving me bereft of touch until he came around to kneel between my open thighs. "Well, I want a snack."

His meaning wasn't lost on me. My toes curled and my pelvis tilted up. "Do you, now?" My voice sounded breathy.

"I do. Now." Matt's hands stroked up the outside of my legs from ankles to hips, an unhurried caress. I liked the implication that he intended to take his time. His head dipped down, but he surprised me by settling his cheek against my belly while his hands explored the hollows of my hips, the curve of my waist. "You feel like hot silk," he said.

A smile curved my lips. "Flatterer."

"Careful." He shifted forward and raked his teeth over the tender skin of my breast, drawing a gasp from me. "If you call me a liar, I'll have to punish you."

"Mmm." The sound came out as a purring laugh. "How will you do that?"

"Many ways." He ran his hands up my ribs, cupped them over my breasts, squeezed, then released them to capture my nipples in a pinching hold. "Like this, to start."

Matt tugged at first one nipple, then the other, not letting up the constant pressure he kept on them. The combination made my inner muscles convulse, and I wondered if he could bring me to orgasm from stimulating my breasts alone in my present state.

"Oh." I licked my lips and stared at him from under heavy-lidded eyes. "What would you do next?"

He released my breast and placed a hand over my mound. "Next, I might have to do this." He squeezed my mound, and then caught my clit between his thumb and forefinger, pinching until it reached that point where pleasure and pain blurred. He took one of my nipples into his mouth and sucked hard, let it slide free, then gave the same treatment to its twin.

My breath came in pants and I made a low sound of need. He repeated the erotic torture, the pressure on my clit making my sex throb, the hard suction on my nipples stimulating hidden nerves inside me, and it was too much. "Matt."

He eased the pinch hold by degrees, a gradual lessening, then rested his hand on my sex, cupping, squeezing, giving me less direct stimulation. He kept his mouth on my breast but lightened that, too, until it was just a hot, wet caress. He licked and laved his way over each rounded swell, then ended with a kiss in the cleft between.

"Be good, and I won't have to punish you," he said, raising his head. He leaned forward to give me a nip on my lower lip.

I had the worst urge to be bad I'd ever felt in my life. And he knew it. He pushed a finger into me and slid his tongue inside my mouth at the same time.

I opened my lips wider for him, welcoming the deep kiss and the tantalizing tease of that finger moving in and out between my legs. It felt so good, it almost hurt. I ached to be filled. I shuddered, and he raised his head to look into my flushed face.

"That close?" Matt sounded surprised.

"Hurts." My eyes stared into his, my whole body pleading for relief.

"I'll kiss you and make it all better," he promised. He shifted position, and then his mouth replaced his hand. The first touch of his tongue to my swollen sex made me groan. He licked my labia, a soothing caress, then thrust between the folds to taste me deeply. He settled the palm of one hand over the curve of my belly and cupped it there, warm and reassuring, moving in a circle to gently massage.

I closed my eyes against the sweetness of the moment. There was so much more here than lust. There was tenderness and caring and consideration. There was desire, a deep well of it, and heat and need and something else. A sense of belonging, of connection.

Rejecting their touch meant rejecting them from the pack, Jack had said. Was that a two-way street? The way Matt made love to me with his mouth said yes. All of them showing me they were willing to accept me as a mate, or as their alpha female.

My legs curled around him, my feet sliding along his torso. My hands buried themselves in his hair, learning the texture of it as he learned the taste and texture of me. He drew his tongue out, dragged it along my labia until he licked at my clit, closed his mouth over that nerve center, and gave me gentle suction. His free hand probed between my thighs. Two fingers, then three, pushed inside me and established a rhythm.

"Matt." I said his name on a low moan, my hips moving in time with the thrusts of his fingers into my sheath. He varied the suction on my clit, harder, softer, and gradually increased the force of his hand moving in me. And it still wasn't enough. I arched my back in an agony of frustration, thrusting my breasts up and my head back in the process. "Matt."

He lifted his head, his blue eyes stricken. "I pushed you too far." He kept his hand between my legs but eased his fingers out. "You can't come for me like this now."

What did he mean, I couldn't come now? I wanted to scream. Instead, I only repeated the litany that thrummed in my blood. "I need to. I need to."

"Chandra." He pressed his hand against my sex. "You need to fuck. You didn't ask me for that, so I have to stop."

I stared at him, struggling to process the words.

"It's all right." David was there beside me, his hand stroking my upper arm in reassurance. "If you need him, it's all right."

I felt tears sting the back of my eyes. "David."

"I'm here."

"Help me."

"Always." He kissed the corner of my mouth. I turned my face toward him until our lips met and clung.

CHAPTER SIXTEEN

DAVID'S MOUTH WAS HOT AND HARD ON MINE. MATT WAITED BETWEEN my open legs for my decision, his hand on my sex keeping me from sliding over some invisible cliff that felt like madness.

This was what they'd meant when they said I'd suffer, I realized. I needed what no human male could ever give me, and in this state I needed more than any one of the Neuri could give. I might really have to give myself to all of them before it ended.

"David." I whispered his name against his lips. "I can't stop." Maybe if we'd stuck to the plan, if Matt had been less generous, less inventive, and gone straight to oral, I could have let him lick me to orgasm to our mutual enjoyment.

Instead, he'd aroused me too far for anything less than full penetration, and he'd attuned my body to him in the process, so now it was his cock I ached to welcome inside me. I wasn't sure I could find relief with any of the others at this point, and without relief I was afraid I'd fall over that cliff. "I can't stop," I repeated on a sob.

"Shh." He speared his fingers into the short strands of my hair and cradled my head in his hands. His dark eyes met mine. "Don't be afraid. Give your body whatever it needs."

"I need him to fuck me." My lips trembled as I said the words.

"Then do it." David gave me another brief, hard kiss before he let me go.

I looked at Matt, saw the tension in his posture, and knew he hadn't meant for this to happen. Neither of us had, but we were past the point of no return. Now I had to show him that I didn't blame him, that I didn't see him as a lesser choice, that I wanted him. Time to let go of everything else, to give myself to the moment and to him.

"Matt." I said his name in a throaty drawl. "I've been very, very bad."

The corners of his eyes crinkled and a small smile tugged at his lips. "Have you?"

"Very." I stared at him, my breath coming hard and fast.

He gave a shake of his head. "Then I'll have to discipline you." He took his hand away and stood up. "Turn over on your belly."

I managed it with every limb trembling and moved into the position David had wanted me in, bent over the ottoman.

Matt cupped his hands over my butt, shaping the curves, squeezing. "Now I'm going to have to warm your bottom."

I drew in a sharp breath. Would he, really?

He put one hand on the lower curve of my spine, just above the swell of my ass. His other hand delivered a stinging smack that made me jolt. Then another. And another. Each time his hand struck, my sex clenched in involuntary response and blood rushed to the point of contact. When he stopped, I had to bite my lip to keep from crying out and begging him to go on.

"There." He ran possessive hands over my butt and the backs of my thighs in light, teasing caresses that served as sharp contrast to the spanking he'd given me. "You'll behave now, won't you?"

"Yes." I would have agreed to anything he said in that moment, if only he'd take what I offered and give me what I needed.

"I'm going to fuck you now." He bent over me, kissed the nape of my neck. "If you give me any trouble, I'll have to punish you some more."

My ragged breathing caught at the sensual threat. His hands closed on my hips, pulled me back toward him until the hard length of his cock nestled in the valley separating the round swells of my buttocks.

"I want you like this, too," Matt told me. "I want to stroke myself back and forth here, with your bottom all pink and hot from a spanking. And then when I'm right on the edge, I want to push between these cheeks and ream you while I come."

I sucked in a breath, caught by his fantasy, even though I needed him inside my sex so badly I was shaking with it. "I might like that."

"I bet you would." He rocked back and forth, riding the cleft that cushioned his erect shaft. "A good, hard ass-fucking would teach a bad girl like you a lesson."

I wanted to explore this possibility later. "What about the knot?"

"If I was already close to coming before I got inside you, it wouldn't take long before I finished and you could get free."

He pressed his chest against my back, covering my body with his. He slid his arms under me, lifted me upright until we knelt together with him supporting me. He cuddled me close and caressed my belly and breasts with gentle hands, dropping the play dominance. "I won't do that to you when I take you now. I won't cheat you by cutting it short."

I almost shook my head at the inverted logic, that keeping his cock buried in me as long as possible was an act of giving, not taking.

Matt ran his hand down until it nestled between my legs. "I want you on your back," he said. "I want to see your face when I make you come."

I shuddered, nodded my acceptance. He eased us both to our feet and helped me stand.

"Where?" I asked. I felt almost mindless with need, unable to pick a spot to accommodate us.

"The cushions in front of the fireplace. Can you walk that far?"

I couldn't see that far. I shook my head, and he bent to catch me behind the knees and cradle me in his arms. "I'll carry you."

They all seemed to be doing that a lot, I thought, but crawling on the floor mewling with need would be even less dignified, so I didn't protest.

Matt lowered me down into the soft nest and then knelt over me for a minute, looking at the picture I made sprawled in naked abandon. "God, you're beautiful," he whispered.

He blanketed me with himself and pushed his legs between mine, forcing them apart. He captured my wrists with his hands, pulled my arms up over my head, and pinned them.

His engorged cock rested between my open thighs now, ready to possess the soft flesh he'd already taken with his mouth and fin-

gers, stroked and laved into readiness until he'd overshot the mark
and sent me into this state.

"My dance, I believe." Matt held my eyes with his while he drove
his body into mine, forcing his way in faster than my sex could stretch
to accommodate him so that I felt every inch of his entry until he
penetrated me completely.

I gasped and trembled under him, struggling to adjust, already
feeling an urgent need to move, to rock my hips and take him deeper.
He swelled inside me, filling my channel even more tightly as the knot
formed.

"Matt." I wrapped my legs around his, the slight change in position opening my body to him a little more and deepening the angle
of penetration. "Fuck me hard."

He did. Over and over, he rammed his cock into me, fucking
me with brutal thrusts that made me gasp, then moan, then scream
in pleasure. He held me down and rode me hard, every powerful
stroke of his shaft into my willing flesh a mix of ecstasy and torment.
Not enough, not enough, no matter how fast and deep he drove.

My legs moved higher, clamped around his waist. My arms
strained with the need to touch him, hold him, urge him on. "Oh,
God, Matt," I half-sobbed, wild with the need for release. "Harder.
Harder."

"I'll hurt you." His voice was thick and guttural, and I knew he
was almost as far gone as I was.

"No." I shook my head from side to side and bucked under him
in frenzied movements. "You'll hurt me if you don't." I started to
cry, tears of desperation and fear that he'd let me fall into a dark
abyss if he didn't slake the wild hunger that possessed me.

The sight of my tears made his face twist. He made a savage sound and released my wrists. He shifted his weight onto his knees, slid his hands under me to cup my butt and lift so that he kept his cock buried deep inside me as he leaned back.

The new position put him upright between my open legs, his hands holding my hips up, my bottom partly resting on his thighs as he knelt on the cushions. My shoulders stayed on the cushions, my torso at an incline.

"If it hurts, stop me," Matt ordered. And then he was fucking me so deep and hard I couldn't move or speak and my breasts bounced from the impact.

The angle sent the head of his cock pounding against my cervix with every thrust, but it didn't hurt. Or if it did, it was a pleasure pain, my body so far gone it couldn't distinguish between the two sensations. He pulled my hips into his pistoning strokes to deepen and intensify each movement, and that brought us both to the brink.

"I'm going to come," he groaned, the pace escalating. "Come for me right now or I'll have to punish you."

The erotic threat pushed me past the breaking point. My body writhed and twisted in the grip of orgasm, and then both of us were coming together, his cock jerking inside me with each ejaculation, my inner muscles clamping hard around his shaft.

"So tight." Matt rocked faster, pumping himself into me. "You're so tight, stuffed full of my cock."

He lowered his body over mine again so that he lay on top of me, crushing me into the cushions, his chest hard and hot against the swollen peaks of my breasts. "I'll keep fucking your tight little pussy until you can't come any more."

He kept his promise, driving into me as we both spent ourselves in waves of violent release that went on and on, until finally I lay under him, still except for the quivering aftershocks that made my inner muscles grip and release his shaft again and again.

"Good?" Matt levered himself up on his elbows to look into my face, his eyes searching.

"Very." I gave him a satisfied, sleepy smile, my body cradling the pleasant weight of his, enjoying the sensation of his thick penis still implanted deep in my flesh.

He lowered his head to settle his lips over mine in a soft, sweet kiss, amends for the frenzy he'd driven me to, homage to the pleasure we'd shared. We kept on kissing in lazy satiation as our bodies unlocked and he withdrew his spent member.

Matt rolled onto his side, bringing me with him so that we lay together facing each other, legs tangled. The tips of our tongues touched, parted, touched again as our mouths meshed.

His hands caressed me, soothing my fevered skin. I snuggled into him with a soft sound of relaxation, touching him back, telling him with my hands and lips that I had no regrets. I felt dreamy and content, the demands of my body satiated for the moment.

I felt a muscular body spoon up behind me, sandwiching me between two males. A hand that wasn't Matt's curved over my hip.

Matt gave me a last, lingering kiss before he raised his head to look over my shoulder. "Wait your turn. I'm not done with her yet."

The tone of his voice made me grin and told me the identity of the body behind mine.

"Hi, Jack."

"Hi." He nuzzled the exposed side of my neck and kissed the spot below my ear. "Don't mind me. Just joining the afterglow."

"Mmm." And checking up on me. I shivered in delight when Jack sent the palm of his hand skimming over my breast. "That feels nice."

"Well then, I must be doing it wrong," Jack said as he thumbed my nipple. "I was trying for naughty."

I exerted myself to roll over, reversing so that Matt's body curved around mine from the back and I faced Jack. "Kiss me."

He complied, drugging my lips with narcotic kisses that sent me deeper into sensual bliss. His hands wandered over my body, skimming the line of my jaw, the upper slope of my breast, the soft skin of my belly.

"She can't take you this soon," Matt informed him from behind me. "I took her too hard."

Jack lifted his mouth from mine to answer, "I'm just here to play doctor."

Something in the way he said that made me stir and start to rise out of the lethargy that claimed me, but he gentled me into settling back into their joint embrace. "Rest."

He kissed me again, and placed his open hand against my belly, below the navel, above the rise of my mound. Heat radiated from his palm and seared my skin, but I was too relaxed to move away, and then I felt warmth penetrating to the muscle and organs beneath. There was a brief, sharp pain, and then only the soothing comfort of Jack's touch.

"There." He kept his hand in place for a moment, then lifted it to stroke the silky skin he'd covered. "All better."

"What did you do to me?"

"You let him bruise your cervix," Jack said. "You won't heal as fast as we do until after your first full change, and you'll need to have sex again before you heal on your own. So I helped you along."

Matt went still behind me. "I told you to stop me if it hurt."

I heard the pain in his voice and knew he was blaming himself, not me. "It hurt less than the alternative," I said, remembering the agonizing need for release.

I met Jack's eyes, certain he wouldn't try to soften the truth when I asked the question, "Is estrus dangerous? It felt like if I didn't have sex with Matt, if he didn't fuck me to orgasm, I'd lose my mind."

"You can't fight the process," Jack said, his face sober. "You can't deny your needs. For you, heat is part of your transformation, merging your animal side and your human side, drawing the wolf out by stages through sexual contact. If you relax and allow what your animal side needs, it can emerge slowly enough to be assimilated with your human mind ascendant."

I stared at him in horror as the penny dropped. "Or I could lose my mind and turn feral." A monster for real.

He pushed his body into mine, a reassuring press of flesh. "We won't let that happen. We'll take care of you. We'll help you through it."

I shuddered. "A bruised cervix seems like a small price to pay."

"Well, don't wait so long next time," Jack scolded. "The longer you wait, the more the need builds up, and the harder it is to satisfy."

My mouth went dry. "It wasn't that long between Zach and Matt."

"It was too long." Jack reached down and gripped my thigh, hooking it over his. He guided his cock to the nest of curls between my legs, still damp from sex. His shaft rode easily along my slick labia and my flesh parted to welcome him.

I clutched at him. "Wait. Zach. David."

"They understand. They both know they can't trade you back and forth between them all day. There's not enough recovery time for them, too much delay for you. They won't risk losing you. And you need to let all of us mark you."

I nestled into him, my body already accepting the inevitable while my mind struggled against it. "I can't just let all of you take a turn between my legs," I whispered, feeling lost.

"You can if it means we bring you safely through this." Jack rolled onto his back and pulled me on top of him. My thighs parted without conscious volition and slid to rest at the outside of his hips. I stared at him, breathing faster as arousal built in me, wanting what he offered.

Matt reached over to stroke my back in reassurance. Then he rested his hand on the curve of my bare butt. "Go on. Let Jack take care of you, or I'll have to give you another spanking."

I let out a soft laugh that ended in a sigh. Matt let his hand fall away but stayed beside us. I stretched my torso on top of Jack's, delighted by the feel of his lean, corded muscles in contrast to Matt's broader build. Jack wrapped his arms around me to hug me close. I raised my hips up until I had the entrance to my body aligned with the head of his cock. My eager flesh, softened from sex, opened at the light pressure so readily that his head entered me without resistance.

"Ready to finish what we started earlier?" I asked him in a throaty murmur.

For an answer, Jack brought his hands down to cup my ass. He used the leverage to pull my body into his, thrusting up at the same time until he was buried balls deep in the welcoming clasp of my snug channel. Warmth radiated from his engorged shaft, soothing me from the inside the way his hand had from the outside. A now-familiar sensation of swelling told me we were joined.

"That feels so good," I sighed. Funny how the very thing I'd been so afraid of at first felt comforting now. I didn't feel trapped by the knot. Just confident that he'd stay with me as long as I needed him to. I rested my cheek against his chest and listened to the thunder of his heart, racing to match mine.

"I'll make it feel better," Jack promised. He arched up into me to gain another fraction of penetration. I adjusted my angle to get the full benefit of the hard, male flesh impaling me. Then we held each other and rocked together in a slow, steady mating that pushed me into a series of climaxes, each one raising me to a higher plateau.

When Jack finally let go and poured himself into me in a deep pulsing that sent a spike of heat through me, I peaked and shattered from the intensity of our joint release. I collapsed on him, eyes shuttered, breathing deepened, half-asleep before he eased our bodies apart and settled me beside him.

"Come here." He tucked me into his side, his arm warm and strong around me, my head pillowed on his shoulder. "I like you like this, all soft and satisfied. I like knowing I made you that way."

"Um." I kissed his throat. "I like knowing it was you, too."

"Just what the doctor ordered, a nice, easy fuck."

I giggled. "Not that easy. You made me do all the work."

"All the work, hell. Half the time you were just hanging on and moaning."

I laughed again, and knew it was going to be okay. This part, at least. Between the eleven of them, they'd get me through today. Tonight, the moon would be full and it would be over. The next day, well, one problem at a time.

CHAPTER SEVENTEEN

MATT WAS STILL WITH US IN THE NEST OF CUSHIONS, A FACT HE RE-
minded me of when he rolled to warm the side of me that wasn't
pressed against Jack.

"This is a brain bender," I said, stretching to luxuriate in the feel
of all that nude male flesh. "I just did both of you and now we're
all cuddling together."

"We like cuddling you." Matt bumped himself against the curve
of my butt and I recognized the unmistakable shape of a recovered
erection. I remembered the desire he'd expressed that we hadn't
explored yet.

"Sure that isn't all you'd like?" I wiggled until I had the length of
him cushioned in the valley between my buttocks.

"Yes, but I've already had you once when it wasn't my turn. I
won't be greedy and selfish."

I savored being held by two lovers, feeling desired and desirable, cared for. Not the rightness I felt in Zach's arms, not the sense of homecoming I felt in David's. Being with Matt and Jack just felt good.

In a way, it was a relief that I didn't respond the same way to all of them. The mental and emotional confusion that would've created I didn't need. I didn't feel owned by Matt despite the rough dominance of our sex play. I'd loved it, I'd been wild for it, responded to him with an intensity my body might never forget. But I didn't feel like I would belong to him forever because of it.

I just hoped I wasn't horrified by my wanton behavior tomorrow, and that this wouldn't ruin our new friendship.

"What's got you thinking so hard?" Jack tousled my hair and hugged me tighter.

"That I want us to still be friends tomorrow," I said.

"We're still friends now," he pointed out.

I reached back to caress Matt and urge him to slide himself along the cleft of my bottom, rocking my hips in invitation and welcome. "That goes for all of us," I said. "You, too, Matt. And it *was* your turn. I asked for you. I wanted you. We didn't plan to get carried away, but you didn't do anything I didn't want you to do."

"Keep squirming like that and I'm going to get carried away again," Matt said, his voice roughened.

"Go ahead." I burrowed into Jack and offered my ass to Matt. "I want to do something just for you." I wanted to show him in some tangible way that he hadn't just been a convenience when my body screamed for sex, that he'd been the one to arouse that level of need and the only one who could satisfy it.

"Don't tempt me." His breathing sounded harsh, and I could feel the tension in him. "You need a chance to rest, drink some more, let us clean you up. Getting my rocks off again isn't taking care of you."

"If not now, when?" I arched my back, moved suggestively, the slide of my bare butt against his tumescence drawing a groan from him. "It's afterplay. I'm already sexually attuned to both of you. And it's penetration, so maybe it'll help me go longer before I have to start all over again. I'll let you both take care of me afterward, but right now I want Jack to hold me while you do it."

"Do it." He let out a short laugh. "Say what you want me to do."

I grinned, even though he couldn't see it. "Matt wants me to talk dirty to him," I informed Jack.

"He's just slow," Jack said. "He needs very specific instructions."

"Oh. See, I thought grinding my butt into his groin after he told me he wanted to give me an ass-fucking made it pretty obvious," I said. I struggled to sound thoughtful and to keep the laughter welling up inside me contained.

"That was your mistake. Maybe I can help." Jack looked at Matt over my head. "She wants an ass-fucking. Give it to her."

"Lube," Matt said, raising his voice. I felt him reach down and begin working the length of his shaft in one hand. His other hand kneaded and stroked the smooth skin of my naked butt.

"Here." It was Nathan who brought it, and I was glad it wasn't Zach or David. Either of them would have distracted me, disturbed the equilibrium I'd established with Matt and Jack. Nathan was neutral.

"Change position?" Jack asked.

"Not yet. I'll just raise her leg over yours, like this." Matt arranged me to his liking. "She'll be at a comfortable angle while I make things easier for her." He coated his fingertips with lubricant, stroked it over my puckered anus. The cooling sensation made a nice contrast to my heated flesh. He repeated the application on his cock, preparing to ease his entry. Then he worked more of the lube inside me, inserting a finger in the process.

"Tight and hot," he murmured.

I did feel warm, now that he mentioned it. I felt his hand moving faster behind me, bringing himself closer to orgasm so the reaming he intended to give me wouldn't last uncomfortably long for delicate tissues unused to that pressure.

He continued to stroke and tease my anus while he readied himself. Each leisurely insertion of his finger sent shivers of delight through me. By the time he guided his penis down and positioned it against that untried entry, I was squirming in anticipation. He probed, testing, and my body gave way for the round swell of his head.

"She's ready," Matt told Jack. "Move her onto her stomach. I want her under me."

Jack brought a hand up to smooth my hair. "Want me to do anything for you?"

"Be with me."

They helped me into position. Jack pulled an extra cushion under my hips, elevating my butt. Matt moved over me.

I closed my eyes as Matt aligned himself and pressed forward, pushing into my anus by inches. The lubricant eased his passage, but there was still a sense of being stretched to capacity that didn't end as he worked his way inside.

"Almost," Matt murmured. His hand moved underneath me to

caress my sex. His fingertip searched out my clit and began to stroke it, coaxing me to respond. "Almost there. Just a little more." He gave another thrust, and then his cock was buried as deep as our position allowed.

Jack soothed me with his hand in my hair, Matt stimulated me with his hand between my legs, and the multitude of sensations staggered me. Sheer hot lust as Matt's hard cock tunneled into my virgin ass. Tenderness and closeness in the way Jack touched me. The slide of Matt's fingertip over my clit until it throbbed in reaction and my hips were moving in restless urgency.

"I want to make you come," Matt said as he rode his cock in and out of my tight passage, each thrust stimulating the sensitive tissue of my anus to an almost unbearable degree. "I want you to come while I'm fucking your ass."

The pressure he exerted between my legs increased, and his hand slid down until his palm pressed against my clit and his fingertips pushed into my sex. The sensation of being dually penetrated by him made me gasp and sigh. I clenched my inner muscles around Matt's invading fingers, first two, then a third filling me, heightening my awareness of the way his cock filled me from behind.

"Come for me." Matt manipulated my sex, drove his fingers deeper into my sheath, rocked his hips harder into the soft cushion of my buttocks. "Come for me, baby. Let go. That's it." He coaxed and encouraged my response as he felt the involuntary movements of my inner muscles signal my impending orgasm.

His thrusts increased, pushing that thick shaft into my anus again and again. I arched my lower back in an effort to take him deeper, loving the primal pleasure he offered me. He played my sex with expert skill, reamed me with relentless strokes, and I couldn't have stopped the orgasm that ripped through me if the roof had fallen in.

Nothing mattered but the hot slide of his cock, the press of his hand, the almost unbearable pleasure as he began to spill himself in me.

"Ah, that feels so good," Matt growled, pushing harder, deeper. "I love the way you take my cock."

"Love the way you give it to me," I panted, hips bucking. "Fuck me harder, Matt."

He did just that while coming in spurts, making me come again with his hand between my legs and sending us both rushing toward a final release. When it was over we stayed locked together for long minutes, his cock buried in my anal passage as deep as he could go, Jack still caressing me while the three of us recovered.

"Don't wait much longer to take your next lover," Jack said, a note of warning in his voice. Matt heard, kissed my shoulder, and withdrew, rolling onto his back to make space around me.

I raised my head to look at Jack. "What you said earlier about marking me, it's scent marking, isn't it?"

"Yes. You've marked all of us. We need to mark you."

No wonder Zach had said I needed to have sexual contact with all of them. The sex organs carried our scent. I'd marked the pack when I'd let all of them touch and taste me before Zach claimed me.

"Stay close?"

"You don't have to ask."

I relaxed, confident that he'd fix it if I managed to hurt myself again. The connection I felt with him and Matt along with the intensity of my need told me I needed more contact with the rest of the pack. It wasn't what I felt for Zach, but something now unified and cemented us. I needed to connect with all of them.

I searched out David's eyes, found them watching me. "David?"

"I'll wait."

And he'd watch everything I did while he waited. The knowledge sent an erotic charge through me.

"Daniel, Roman, Will," I said, raising my voice just enough to be heard.

"Here." They formed a loose ring around me. I rolled onto my back, naked and splayed. Matt got up and left, only to come back a moment later with a cloth he used to sponge me. I thanked him with a kiss, then turned my face toward Will.

Brown-haired Will, youngest, but full of heat and surprises. My eyes moved from him to Daniel, who looked tough even naked and aroused. Then Roman, dark and fierce.

"How do you want us?" he asked.

"All together," I whispered.

We met in a sensual slide of hands and mouths and bodies. I breathed in their scents, explored their shapes, traded kisses with them by turns. I pushed Will onto his back and straddled him, pressing my sex to his while Roman's tongue swept mine. His taste intoxicated me, and I broke the kiss to move my mouth down until I could lick the crown of his penis.

"I guess your ass is mine," Daniel said, running his hands over my cheeks.

I felt a surge of heat at his words, and the accompanying mind picture of three cocks filling all my available orifices. I arched my back and raised my hips up in invitation. Will grabbed them and pulled me back down and I felt the head of him push inside me.

Then his shaft filled me, shorter and wider than average, and I made a low sound of pleasure and satisfaction that was muffled as I drew Roman into my lips. Will's shape made his entry both comfortable and a stretch as I accommodated his width.

Daniel kissed and caressed my back, neck, and buttocks, and I realized he was waiting for me to sate myself with Will before he entered me. I felt his shaft ride between my cheeks as I began to move, and knew he'd be close when he plunged in.

My mouth on Roman grew hungry and demanding. Daniel pleasured himself against my bare ass, and Will kept my hips imprisoned with a grip that stopped just short of bruising, giving me hard, fast thrusts that made me writhe and moan. Daniel's movements sped up, and then I felt him probing my anus, slick with lubricant, his cock already jerking to signal his approaching orgasm.

For a minute, we all shuddered on the brink. Then I was lost in Will's driving rhythm, grinding myself against him, taking Roman deeper while I came. Will began to spurt inside me, and Roman's shaft swelled in my mouth before he spilled himself in a hot rush. I rode Will as I swallowed Roman's semen, licking and sucking his cock with fevered greed.

I was still spasming in the throes of seemingly endless orgasm when Daniel penetrated me from behind. My sex contracted sharply around Will's now-still shaft, and that heightened the sensation as Daniel began fucking his way inside my anal opening.

"My turn," he groaned, pushing deeper as the lubricant eased his way. He took me in a white-hot frenzy, plunging his cock into me, coming with each stroke until he'd spent himself in furious coupling.

I kissed Roman from balls to crown and gave him a last, lingering lick while my body trembled with aftershocks of pleasure. This was what I needed, contact, connection, completion.

Nathan, Aidan, Cam, and Sean surged forward. I felt their hands on me, Cam's on my breasts, Nathan's touching the point where my body joined with Will's. Aidan kissed me with openmouthed heat when I raised my lips from pleasuring Roman. Sean ran his palm over my belly.

Daniel pulled out and kneaded my butt with rough, murmured sounds of praise. Then he moved back to allow the others access. They lifted me clear of Will as the knot released, and carried me to the fainting couch.

Cam and Nathan feasted on my breasts. Aidan ran his hands over my body and kept on kissing me. Sean pushed my thighs apart and buried his fingers in my sex and I nearly came up off the couch in response. I touched all of them, any part of any partner I could reach, learning them, acknowledging them.

When my hips were rocking against Sean's hand between my legs and I was straining to take his fingers deeper, he moved to cover my body with his.

I broke free from Aidan's kiss to utter a guttural, "Yes," spreading wider for Sean as he mounted me. His cock probed my sex. He found his angle and thrust deep. I wrapped my hands around Cam's and Nathan's engorged shafts and began working them in tandem. Aidan rubbed his penis against my lips and I opened wide to take him, falling into the ecstasy we shared.

The bathroom off the library had a tub big enough for two, which was a good thing because left to my own devices I might have drowned. David climbed in with me, and I sat between his legs so I could recline against him and let him support me while he washed me. The protein shake he'd pressed on me had already vanished in thirsty gulps.

"So," I said, watching his hands slick soap over my breasts. "This has been an eventful day. I've had five cocks that weren't yours between my legs. That's past the point where most boyfriends would stomp off, never to return."

David continued to wash me with thorough attention to detail. "Am I your boyfriend?"

I shrugged. "Just saying."

He cupped water in his hands, let it run over my breasts, rinsing away the soap and leaving droplets of water clinging to my pouting nipples. "Most girlfriends don't have your special needs. I care more about your sanity than your sex life."

I sighed. "Until I met you guys, I didn't have a sex life. Now I'm a nympho." Then I perked a little. "Am I *your* girlfriend?"

"You're my lover." He kissed the side of my neck.

"We haven't actually had sex," I pointed out.

"We've slept together." His hands ran down the sides of my body. "I've had my hands on every part of you, kissed you until you would have done anything I asked, stripped you naked, spread your thighs, and made you come with my mouth between your legs."

I had to admit, it added up to an impressive argument when he put it all together. Still . . ."Zach," I said, feeling pensive.

"I know." David wrapped his arms around me and squeezed. "I won't take what's his. I owe him too much. But I'll take what's mine now. You're my lover today. Let tomorrow take care of itself."

I squeezed my eyes closed. "Maybe tomorrow can take care of

itself, but I want to have you as many times in as many ways as possible today." I wanted to store up a lifetime of memories, because no matter how I felt about David, no matter how much I wanted him, Zach owned me.

"I'll give you as much as you want. You deserve that."

I let my muscles relax a stage further, melting in him. "I really don't know what makes me deserving."

"For starters, you're handling this pretty well." David ran his hand down my belly, over my mound.

"Well." I snorted and turned my head to rub my cheek against his chest. "I decided group sex is not a fate worse than death. Or insanity. Or turning into something out of a horror story. Also, let's face it, none of you are exactly ugly."

"And?" he prompted me to go on as he washed me between my legs.

"And if I'm going to be married to a virtual stranger, I've decided I might as well consider this one hell of a bachelorette party."

"So you're okay with what you have to do now." He moved his hand around to nudge my shoulder. "Lean forward so I can scrub your back."

"It's funny." I bent obediently and then nearly purred as his soap-slick hands covered every inch of my back, stirring nerve endings I didn't know I had. "It isn't at all how I thought it would be. You're all comfortable with what you are and what I am. That helps. Also, it's hard to pretend human norms apply when the penis inside you has a knot."

"You looked very comfortable with Jack and Matt." David's fingers dug into the muscles that ran along my spine. The soap acted like a lubricant, intensifying the massage. Bliss.

"Because I didn't want to push them away as soon as I had an orgasm? They deserve better than that." I sobered, remembering the tension in Matt when he thought he'd accidentally forced me into a situation that wasn't my choosing. The lust and the tenderness he'd shown me. "They're people, not body parts."

"Not just playing hide the salami?"

David returned my earlier words as his strong fingers worked away aches I hadn't been aware of until he soothed and released them.

"I was freaking out when I said that." I felt a blush stain my cheeks. "And I didn't get it. I thought I was going to be like some kind of piñata everybody wanted a piece of. But that's not how it is."

I flashed to Matt straining to bring me off, knowing what the price of failure would be. Jack healing me with a touch, then seducing me with gentle insistence because he knew what I needed better than I did. "If I get broken, it'll hurt all of you."

David abandoned washing my back to wrap his arms around me and pull me into his chest again, crushing me in a fierce embrace. "I won't let you get broken."

I turned my head to the side and up to make my mouth accessible to him, inviting a kiss. "I know."

His mouth covered mine. I turned into the pressure, sliding over to face him. He scooted forward so my legs could go around his waist. I rocked into him, loving the way the rough hairs on his chest tantalized my nipples, feeling his engorged shaft press against the cleft of my sex. His hands were hard and bruising on my body, and I found myself hoping he'd leave marks. I wanted to be marked by him in some way.

He broke off the kiss and buried his face in the curve of my neck. "I want you." His voice was low and harsh, his body taut with tension. "I want to be inside you. I want to know you're safe because I'm in you, giving you what you need."

"David." I wasn't burning in the grip of heat just yet, but I'd wanted him before it started, and that hadn't changed. "I want you, too. I wanted you in my apartment. I wanted you upstairs on the couch. I wanted you when you kissed my hand last night."

"You want a mate." His lips explored the hollows of my throat, and my head tipped back to let him.

"The wolf does," I muttered in a thick voice.

"You are the wolf." David nipped at my ear, the edge of his teeth sending a thrill through me. He worked his way back to my mouth. His tongue pushed between my lips, and we stopped talking.

CHAPTER EIGHTEEN

TWO WORDS BEAT IN MY BRAIN, IN MY BLOOD.

David.

Mine.

I pushed up to align our bodies, bring myself to the right angle. He helped, lifting me, rocking back to guide himself to my opening. I gave a wordless cry that his mouth swallowed. A hot shiver ran over my body at the first intimate probing as my flesh gave for the head of his cock.

I broke the kiss to pant out, "Slow. Slow."

His hands flexed on my hips. His breathing sounded ragged. "Sorry. Sore?"

"No." I trembled as I arched closer, struggling to gain a little more of him. "I just want to make it last."

David let out a short, hard laugh. "We're in the tub. If you want slow and lasting, we need to get out."

"Right." My mouth agreed, but my sex gripped his flesh, unwilling to release him. He groaned.

"Sorry." I was breathing faster, harder. "Can't help it. I want you."

David pulled back to break the contact and pulled me back down into his lap so that we pressed together without risk of penetration. "Let me finish washing you. Then we'll take it as slow as you can stand it."

"Okay." I let him rinse me clean, but I didn't want to let go of him, not even to get out of the tub.

He didn't want me to choose him. I had to remember that, had to keep it straight in my head. He didn't want to displace Zach, didn't want to be the leader. But as long as David wanted me, I wanted to have this much of him at least.

In the end, David climbed out first, then helped me stand dripping on the mat while he patted me dry.

"How'd you know to be so careful with the cloth?" I asked, watching his hands blot the excess moisture from my skin.

"You'll be sensitive until after you change." David moved down my body and paused to circle my belly button with the tip of his tongue. My knees weakened and a pulse of desire hit hard.

"David." I said his name on a breath of heat. My hands found his hair, held him, urged him to move lower.

"Want me to lick you dry?" His mouth explored the curve of my belly and I shuddered in reaction.

"Please."

He dropped the towel and stood up. I started to protest, but he cut off the sound when he covered my mouth with his. He turned me, backed me up to the counter, and lifted.

Oh. I caught his intent and settled onto the cool surface, sliding my legs apart while my hands clung to him and my lips opened for his. He licked into my mouth once, then began to move down, trailing fire over my skin everywhere his lips grazed. The curve of my neck, the slope of my breast, the soft skin of my stomach.

"David." I closed my eyes and waited for him to kiss me lower.

He raked my inner thighs with his teeth instead. I gasped and arched my back in an involuntary movement that opened me further and thrust my breasts up.

A soft knock sounded at the door. David shifted to look up at me. I knew my face was flushed and I was breathing in ragged gulps, nipples swollen, my sex pink and pouting for his attention. "Want me to tell whoever that is to go away?"

I shook my head, certainty gripping me. "It's Zach. Let him in."

"I won't stand aside this time." David's gray eyes darkened to the color of a stormy sky.

"I don't want you to." I reached out to lightly trace the shape of his mouth with a fingertip. "If things get out of hand like they did with Matt, I'll take Zach somewhere else. In my mouth, in my ass. If I need him too much to be satisfied with that, you can take turns with me, but it's you I want first."

David's eyes darkened even further until they were nearly black. He put his hands on my hips, flexed his fingers so they dug into me. "Tell him to come in, then." His head lowered. His mouth touched me. And the room tilted.

He kissed me with fierce hunger, lapped at me like a coveted dessert, suckled at my folds, circled my clit with his tongue, thrust his tongue into the flesh I wanted him to claim with another part of himself.

"David." My head fell back as I moved with restless need. "David."

The knock came again. His tongue delved deeper. I struggled for the words I'd meant to say. "Come in."

Zach opened the door and took in the tableau. Me, seated on the counter, legs wide apart. David kneeling between them, his hands on me in a possessive hold, his mouth on my sex.

Zach looked at the whole picture, then focused on my face for a long moment before his gaze slid down to my breasts. He crossed the small distance between us and bent to circle first one aching nipple with his tongue, then the other.

"Zach." I felt a swell of yearning, wanted him closer. "More, please."

He lifted his head and let his lips touch my temple. "That's what I'm here for. More."

I leaned my head against him. "What time is it?"

He stroked my hair, then the curve of my cheek, his thumb tracing the hollow of my cheekbone. "Late afternoon. Almost evening."

So soon? This morning the day had seemed stretched out before me to eternity. I'd wondered how I'd endure it. Now it was slipping away too fast, and I hadn't touched David the way I wanted to, hadn't told him with my lips and hands and all of my being that I craved him, adored him, wanted him.

I hadn't sated my need for Zach, either. Through every erotic encounter, I'd felt an invisible tug and known he was at the other end of it. Our bodies had separated, but something else hadn't. My heart? My soul? I didn't know. I didn't have words for it. But some part of me was tangled up in him now, and I thought it always would be.

"Both of you," I whispered. I reached up to lay my palm over Zach's heart as if I could claim it. "I want to be with both of you, just the two of you, for as long as it lasts. Until it's over."

David lifted his head, and I thought it was rejection. I clutched at him. "Don't leave me."

The desperate plea in my voice would've humiliated me any other time. Maybe tomorrow it would, but now I would say or do anything to keep him here. "David, don't leave me. Please. I need you." Tears slid down my cheeks, unheeded. I was blind with them and too blind with need to care.

"I'm not leaving." David stood, positioned himself between my thighs, and began to fill me in long, slow, steady strokes.

"Oh." The pleasure was so intense it was almost a shock. Our bodies joined, a merging of flesh and something more. A completion. I wound myself around him, pressed my hands against him, buried my face in his neck. I held him to me and breathed his scent. *Mine.* "David."

His hands gripped my hips and he pulled my body into his, deepening the penetration. "Not. Leaving." He growled out the words, drove into me to punctuate them.

I lost all sense of time, all awareness of anything but David inside me, Zach beside me. I knew Zach would take me again when David finished. I wanted him to. I was beyond caring what that made me.

Wild cries echoed in the small room. I didn't know they were mine until David silenced me with a kiss that tasted of salt and musk. I rocked my hips into his, raked him with my nails, urged him to give me more. And he did.

He took me endlessly, and every stroke he ended buried in the

depths of my body was another shock of ecstasy that made me
crave more. My nerve endings sang; my blood ran hot, every cell in
my being aware that David possessed me.

Something began to grow in me, beating in time to the rhythm
of David's flesh driving into mine. It seemed familiar, like the un-
finished urge to give my body over to some unknown need when
David changed forms. Some deep change was taking place below
the surface, some alignment, and then it rose up in me with a sudden surge of power that made me gasp and arch my back.

David pulsed deep inside me, and I convulsed around him, burst-
ing with pleasure and exultation. He poured himself into me, giving,
taking, demanding more of me. It went on and on, and the need built
with each wave of release, until he pushed me to the final peak and
we rushed into oblivion together.

Heartbeat. Mine? His? I couldn't distinguish. Skin to skin, a
press of heat and need. Connection. Bodies fused, melded, the link
unbroken.

"Can you hear me?"

The voice came from far away. Then my awareness shifted focus and it was Zach, his mouth close to my ear.

I licked dry lips, tried to remember what words were and how
to give voice to them. Pieced together fragments. Zach, worried.
David, still locked inside me. I needed to touch Zach, reassure us
both. Him, that I was unhurt. Me, that the invisible thing joining
us still held.

I found the strength to release one hand clamped to David,
fighting the instinct that said to hold, cling, keep every part of me
possible in contact with every part of him. I reached out, shaky on

every level, and put my palm over Zach's heart again. It beat under my hand, harder and faster than I expected.

"Zach," I whispered his name, turned my face toward him, keeping my cheek against David's bare shoulder.

"All right?" Amber eyes searched mine.

"Yes." I smiled, a tiny movement, but the effort was enormous. "The energy rose up. I feel it just under my skin."

"How do you feel?" He cupped one of his hands over mine, trapping it against his chest as if he wanted to hold some part of me close to his heart.

"Like I'm turning into a werewolf." I laughed, a low, soft sound that rippled like liquid. "Does it feel like this all the time? I feel so strong."

"Yes." Zach's hand caressed the back of mine. "Stronger as the full moon approaches."

"I think I could bench-press a Buick," I said. I let my eyelashes flutter down to lie against my cheek. "If I could move," I added. "That was so intense."

"I can't move yet, either," David said. I felt him rest his forehead against my hair.

"That's okay." I luxuriated in the sensation of David against me, in me, the rightness and wonder of it. I didn't want to lose this. I wondered how I'd survive never having this again. Even now, I knew the shock of his body withdrawing from mine would leave me bereft. "Stay."

He gave a low laugh. "Told you I wasn't leaving."

"Mmm." I kissed his shoulder. "Sorry I lost it. Emotions all over the place. I can't remember the last time I cried before today."

"Hormones. Full moon. Heavy combination."

"We have to move somehow," I said. "This counter is hard, and I can't touch Zach the way I want to."

"Want the pile of cushions again?"

I thought about that for a lascivious minute. It seemed like the best option.

"Yes." I grinned, feeling sensual and wicked and desirable. "I want both of you at once. I want Zach inside me and I want you to fill me from behind."

"Sure?" Zach asked the question.

"Sure." My hand on his chest stroked him, loving the texture of his skin, unable to resist exploring it.

"Can you move yet?" That was David.

I unlocked my legs from around his waist and let them slide down. "As long as I don't have to walk."

"I'll carry you," Zach offered.

"We'll support her between us," David returned.

A good plan. I warmed to it. I didn't want David to stop touching me, but I hungered for more contact with Zach. Standing between both of them would feed that dual need for their touch.

David rocked his hips back, pulling out of me in the process. I told the empty ache he left behind that it would be filled. Soon. Zach produced a cloth and proceeded to gently clean the evidence of David's possession from my inner thighs.

The two of them helped me down and helped me stand. Almost instantly I felt more balanced. Grounded. "Better. I think I can make it if you both help me."

They did, although getting through the doorway was awkward, and I started to laugh halfway through.

"Guess you're doing fine," Jack said as we stumbled out, sex drunk and under the influence of the approaching lunar change. His bright blue eyes met mine and I read the deeper question there.

"Yes." I laughed again. "I'm fine. Never better. Kiss me, Jack."

I felt a twin tension from the men bracketing me and ignored it. I was theirs, but Jack was special. I wanted one last kiss.

Jack came toward me and touched his lips to mine in a salute that felt formal, ceremonial.

"Jack," I scolded. "A real kiss."

"I'm not making a challenge."

"Nobody will take it as one," I said.

"I would." Jack's voice deepened and the sound of it sent a thrill of anticipation down my spine. Then his hands were on my waist as he pulled my nude body against his and his mouth took mine. I parted my lips under the pressure of his, touched my tongue to his. My nipples rubbed against his chest and the contact made them tighten. He made a sound in the back of his throat, drew me a fraction closer, kissed me harder. And then it was over and he moved back to put a little space between us. He kept his hands on my waist for a moment before he let them fall away.

"Thank you." I smiled at him, feeling light and happy and pleasantly flushed.

"My pleasure."

"That was obvious," David growled, and I laughed out loud again.

I bumped my hip into him. "He deserved that."

"What about me?"

"You deserve more." I let him see my hunger for his touch, the way I ached for him to take me all over again.

"And me?"

I turned my face to Zach, drawn by the sound of his voice. "You, too." Urgent need flared and laughter vanished. "Hurry."

CHAPTER NINETEEN

THE THREE OF US MOVED TOWARD OUR GOAL IN UNISON. ONCE WE reached the pile of cushions, they sandwiched me between them while we were still standing. Zach facing me, David pressing into my back, both of them framing me with the heat of their bodies.

I ran my hands over Zach, caught by the lines of muscle, the sheer harnessed power in his body. I rubbed myself against David and felt intoxicated by the slide of his skin against mine.

A sudden insecurity struck me and I moved into Zach. "Is it okay?"

"Is what okay? Having an audience again? Letting you be on top this time? Having you between us?"

I shook my head. "Being last."

"Seems fair." Zach's lips brushed against my forehead. "I was first."

First and last. The rightness of it resonated in me.

"Zach." His name trembled on my lips. He bent his head and kissed my voice away. His hands moved down to cup my breasts. David's teeth raked the back of my neck and took a sharp nip at the nape that made my body clench in expectancy.

It was heaven to stand between them, being touched by both of them. And then pleasure twisted into an inferno of need. I took a long, shuddering breath, trying to calm my thundering heart and to draw this out just a little longer.

I wanted to touch them and be touched by them, to take time to kiss and hold one another. My body screamed that it wouldn't be enough. I had to have more. Now.

The conflict showed in my face. Zach let his hands slide down to my waist, a more neutral caress. "What do you need?"

I gave a faint shake of my head. "Too much." *Breathe. Breathe.* "I want to go slow, and I don't think I can. I feel like I'm on a runaway train, rushing forward, and I can't find the brakes."

"It's okay." His hands moved around to my lower back to press me closer.

"I would slow down if I could. I want to touch you everywhere and take you in my mouth. But I can't. I'm being selfish. I'm sorry."

"Not selfish." Zach nuzzled me.

"Zach." I belonged to him. I belonged to both of them, and I needed both of them to take me. "David. Now. Please, now."

They eased me down. David supported me while Zach arranged himself on his back. The two of them lifted me and helped me settle onto Zach, my upper body resting on his, my knees on either side of him. David's hands moved over the round swell of my butt. Zach's stroked my shoulders. I shifted on him, feeling a restless urge to move.

David smoothed something cool and slick over my anus. I let out a soft moan and pushed up, offering myself, inviting more. His lubricated finger slowly penetrated, withdrew, returned, the action readying me and arousing the fever inside of me to an almost unbearable degree.

I slid up until I felt Zach's erect penis align with my entry. The urge to push back and down and sheathe his flesh with mine made me tremble. I needed Zach inside me again, but I needed both of them to enter me together. So I waited and sank my teeth into my lower lip while David positioned himself. I felt the head of his cock, slick with lubrication, make contact and then press forward as if eager to claim another part of me.

"Now." I said it in a low voice, but they heard me. I let them direct this step. Even relaxed and ready, it might be an effort to accept the dual invasion that would join all three of us together.

Zach began to push inside my sheath as David worked into me from behind. Tissue stretched and heightened the sensation of indescribable fullness. They were slow and careful and penetrated me by inches, giving me time to adjust and accept the reality of two cocks thrusting into me. When they were both inside me all the way, I rested on Zach and blinked back the sting of tears.

This was what I wanted. The two of them taking me, claiming me, fucking me. Burning out the fever in my blood.

"All right?" Zach asked the question, his voice rumbling deep in his chest under my ear.

"No." I carefully levered myself up to look into his face. "I'm not all right. You're both too still."

Amber fire leaped in his eyes, but he didn't move. "We don't want to hurt you."

"Hurt me." I lowered myself back down, caressing his chest with my lips. My voice sounded soft and dreamy in contrast to the words that spilled out to inflame them. "Fuck me so hard I can't take it. Make me come screaming from the force of David's cock fucking me from behind while yours fucks me in front."

David let out a guttural groan behind me. His cock pulsed in my anal passage. Zach surged up under me, making me take him even deeper, the head of his cock bumping the opening to my womb.

They began to move and established a rhythm that sent first Zach's swollen shaft as far inside me as I could take it while David pulled back. Then David thrust forward to fill me while Zach stroked out as far as the knot allowed. The pattern repeated endlessly. Both of them taking turns plunging into me while neither ever left me. They thrust slowly at first, then harder and faster as they caught my feverish response.

"Yes. Yes. Like that," I moaned in abandon. "More, Zach. Oh, David. Yes."

"Want you." David's harsh whisper filled my ear as he drove home, burying himself in me with fierce hunger.

"I'll give you more," Zach gritted, and did with a force that made me gasp.

My lovers. For this moment they were mine, and I took them into my body, over and over, welcoming the joint claim they made on me. They were mine, and they made me theirs, and I surrendered myself to both of them. Urgency gripped all three of us, escalating into a frenzied mating. Zach's cock throbbed inside me as orgasm approached. An answering pressure told me David was on the edge, too. Knowing they were both going to spill themselves into me made my inner muscles spasm, and then all of us went together into a white heat.

I lost time somewhere. When I could hear and see and feel again, I was lying on my belly in the pillows, with Zach and David braced on either side of me. Hands stroked my body, smoothed my hair. Bare flesh warmed me. I swallowed hard and raised my head, finding myself eye to eye with David. "Hey."

"Hey." He kissed the tip of my nose.

"What happened?" I asked. Then I blushed dark red as I remembered every explicit word I'd said to them and the porn star performance I'd carried out, and added, "I mean, besides the obvious."

His face was solemn. "Did you know if you come hard enough you can pass out?"

I blinked. "No. Did you?"

"Almost."

Zach stroked the nape of my neck in a caress that sent pleasurable shivers down my spine. "You got the brunt of it since you were in the middle," he said.

I blew out a breath. "You're both just trying to make me feel better about swooning like some Victorian maiden." Of course, any Victorian maiden probably would've swooned just imagining today's events.

It seemed almost like a fever dream now, surreal. Except that I was still naked. With two naked men touching me as if they had the right. I rolled over so I could look at both of them more easily, and that gave me a wider view of the empty library. "Where'd everybody else go?"

"Dining room. Jack ordered in dinner." Zach kissed me, the

warm pressure of his lips on mine sending a very nice zing to my center.

"Is it over?"

"Yes." Zach's hand settled on my belly, caressed, slid lower to cup my mound. David stroked my breasts. My nipples tightened at his touch and my whole body gave a happy sigh of remembered satisfaction.

"I don't want either of you to go, yet."

Zach petted my tender flesh with gentle fingers. "We're not going anywhere. Except to the tub. When you're ready."

"Clean up first, then eat?"

"Yep."

We got to our feet and made our way to the waiting tub. I sank in up to my chin with a groan. "That feels so good."

Now that I wasn't sex crazed I could feel a thousand little aches from all that unaccustomed exertion, and every one of them wanted to be soothed.

"Overdid it, wild thing?" David climbed in and pulled me into his lap.

"Mm, no. Did it just right." I kissed his chin, feeling silly with happiness because he was still there, holding me, touching me.

"Sure?" He ran his hand over the curve of my ass.

"Sure." I snuggled closer. "I think I blew out every pleasure receptor in my brain, but it was worth it."

Zach moved up behind me to kiss my bare shoulder. His quiet voice struck into my heart like Cupid's arrow. "No regrets?"

I felt a pang as that fragile organ felt pierced all over again, buried the reaction, and shook my head. "No."

We all washed, helping one another more than we hindered the process, but with plenty of lingering touches. By the time we dried off, I felt composed enough to face dinner with my eleven lovers.

Somebody had left us clothes. David handed me soft white terry pants with flared legs that rode low on my hips and a matching sleeveless top that left my midriff bare and zipped closed between my breasts.

"No underwear?" I asked him with the shirt gaping open.

"No."

I shrugged. We'd all be naked again soon to change more than our clothes. Going commando would just save time. David took the bottom of my shirt and matched up the zipper, then pulled the tab up, trailing his hand between my breasts in the process.

I drew in a breath. "Thanks."

I felt Zach's arm slide around my waist and leaned into him. The guys were shirtless, wearing loose pants. I reached for David's hand. After a beat of hesitation he gripped my extended fingers, letting me hold his hand while I walked arm in arm with Zach to the dining room.

Zach seated me and stood with his hands on my shoulders until he was sure I would be okay at the opposite end of the table from him. David released my hand as soon as we came into the room as if formally relinquishing any claim on me.

My official choice might as well have been announced already, but as far as I could tell, nobody minded. A celebratory mood filled the room and I found the party atmosphere contagious. There was enough food piled on the table to feed an army.

I looked at my own heaping plate. "I'm supposed to eat all this?" I asked Nathan, since I didn't trust myself to talk to David.

"Yes." He surprised me with his serious expression and the

emphatic tone of his voice. "You have to have enough energy to fuel your transformation."

Oh. Right.

Nathan saw my expression and leaned closer to touch my hand. "It's a little scary the first time, but then it's fun. You'll see." He smiled at me, enthusiasm dancing in his eyes.

Sounded like a description of sex. I took a bite and discovered a voracious appetite. When I found myself staring in disbelief at my empty plate a few minutes later, Nathan just laughed and offered to refill it.

When the plates were cleared away, the conversational volume rose until Zach stood and waved us all to our feet again. But this time we weren't going outside for dancing. The guys started to discard clothing. I swallowed hard, but it wasn't due to the now-familiar sight of nude male flesh. This was it. Time to unleash the beast that prowled eagerly under my skin.

CHAPTER TWENTY

A FINE TENSION TOOK ME AND MADE MY HANDS AWKWARD ON MY ZIP-
per. I managed to get it stuck, so I gave up and pulled the midriff
top off still zipped. Pants next. I wasn't sure what to do, so I folded
the clothes neatly and stacked them on my chair.

The electric hum I'd sensed first when all the wolves were in
one room together intensified. My skin itched and I felt a dull ache
begin in my muscles.

Everybody else had taken a place on the floor, and I remembered David in a sort of modified runner's crouch before he'd shown
me his other shape. Only yesterday. So much change since then, it
felt like a week ago.

I crouched down and concentrated on breathing. I had to stretch,
so I did, and I felt an odd ripple go through me, as if I was trying to
use muscles this shape didn't have. Another stretch failed to provide relief. The ache became a burn, like a muscle fatigued beyond

its limit continuing to work. Tendons and ligaments in my arms lengthened, while my legs contracted. My spine softened and shifted. Hands and feet shrank and re-formed. I closed my eyes, afraid to see myself midway through the transformation, and felt the change in my nose and jaw. My whole body shuddered as the beast burst out, and then I was on four paws, shaking myself.

Excitement rose up. Free! I opened my eyes and looked for my packmates. A black wolf waited beside me. David. An auburn pelt caught my eye and a playful Jack came to crouch in front of me, shoulders down, nose almost to his front paws, then bouncing back up, body language saying, *Isn't this fun?*

I sprang at him to agree, and we tumbled over in a flurry of limbs. Zach padded over and nuzzled me and I sat up, embarrassed that he'd caught us roughhousing inside like a pair of puppies. I let out a soft whine of apology. Zach touched his nose to mine, then stood shoulder to shoulder with me. I felt the readiness in his muscles, and remembered his earlier challenge to race.

Ah. I knew the way out, and I knew this game. I took off and found that my new body cornered with better speed than I expected. Zach kept pace with me easily, then let me take the lead, but I knew the real race would happen outside. I heard running paws behind us, and then we were going through the solarium, over the moon tiles, and out into the night.

The full moon and the glitter of stars made it easy to see obstacles. I also found my night vision sharpened, like I'd gained more shades of gray. It was so pretty, I wanted to sing, so I did, and then we all sang together. Our combined voices sent shivers through me. I felt fierce, exultant, joyful. This was where I belonged.

The song died away. Zach took my right and David my left.

They dared me silently with their eyes. I didn't need any encouragement. My muscles hummed in eagerness to run with them, swift and strong.

I leaped forward. They leaped with me, and we became blurs of speed and grace gilded by moonlight. We reached the woods, and I began to dart between trees, changing the race to a game of catch me if you can. They bounded after me, and I eluded them, all the while laughing inside and knowing sooner or later one of them would leap out at me to tumble me into an undignified heap.

Except before either of them could, a dark shape sleeker than a wolf pounced.

Panther, my mind said. *Invader,* the wolf snarled. *Enemy. Threat. Attack!* I struggled to contain the impulse. Wait for Zach or David, see if there are more of them, call the pack. But the panther wanted to fight, and then I had to dance after all.

I felt a weird disconnect when the wolf mind pointed out new strike zones to aim for instead of human weaknesses. My wolf body seemed to have muscle memory that didn't match the ingrained techniques carried in my human form.

I knew how to fight on two legs. If I tried to direct myself like a human on four legs, this was likely to end badly.

David's words came back to me. *You are the wolf.*

Okay, then. Get out of the way; let the wolf fight as a wolf. Instinct came to my rescue, and I let my body move with the speed and agility that came from muscle and reflex instead of conscious decision.

I didn't want to kill. The panther was a person under the fur, and even if he'd come to kill me, I only wanted to wound or disable. But when my jaws locked on his neck, it was hard to go against the urge to bite down harder. I fought the instinct that had saved me and held him instead. Help couldn't be far off.

Now that we were frozen in a weird tableau, I heard other sounds of fighting in the night and understood why Zach or David hadn't already appeared. They were fighting their own battles. The werepanthers must've picked tonight to invade in force. Why, I couldn't imagine. Unless they thought I'd be more vulnerable in my first change, unaccustomed to my new body, and the men would be distracted and tired because of my presence.

And I hadn't named a new leader yet.

A new thought struck me. Had the werepanther aggression begun after the rogue wolves left the pack? Was there a bastard wolf named Ray behind all this, looking for his chance to seize control?

The idea that he might've been waiting years in the grip of some sick obsession creeped me out. I needed to talk to Zach and David about that.

In the meantime, I had to figure out what to do with the cat I'd bagged. I couldn't hold him forever. If I let him go, he might continue the fight. I didn't want to become a murderer, but I didn't want to die, either.

The solution to my dilemma appeared from a blade of grass. I watched him grow this time and thought from my new perspective that I'd never seen anything more wonderful.

The lord of the forest. He looked like one from animal eyes. If I'd been free to move, I think I would have lain on the ground at his feet and rolled over to expose my throat.

"Now I get to rescue you again." He smiled at me, cheerful as if the prospect entertained him. He turned his attention to the panther, and the beast I had pinned shuddered. "You don't belong here. These are my woods. My wolves."

His voice vibrated with power and command. I felt all the fight go out of the cat.

"Go."

The panther obeyed, almost faster than I could loose him, fleeing into the night.

"This trouble must end." The Leshii came forward and put his hand on my head. "You'd better let the boys finish it, though. I'll tell your alpha I've sent you home. You shouldn't be fighting in your condition."

I turned that one over, puzzled. What condition? First change? Tired from the day's exertions?

The Leshii rubbed one of my ears. "Ah, I see you didn't know. My two red wolves have made a red pup."

I pretty much had instant heart failure. Without four feet to balance me, I might have fallen over from shock. Jack? I was having a baby with Jack? How could I name him as my mate when I knew in my soul I belonged to Zach?

Either the Leshii was a mind reader or furry faces were easy for him to interpret. "You can't choose Jack. Red wolves are special, gifted. In tribal terms, he's the pack's shaman. You can't make him king. He can't abandon his gifts or his responsibilities to take on that role."

Shit. Shit. Shit. Pregnant. Not Zach's, not even David's. Can't marry the father. Can't marry anybody else, but I'd have to name a king or there'd be trouble. Inside the pack, as well as outside the pack.

I trembled under the joint weight of fatigue and an unsolvable dilemma. Distress made my body falter. I collapsed on the ground, curled in a ball, and sometime later realized I was wearing skin again.

"What am I going to do?" I asked the question out loud, not expecting an answer.

"The right thing," the Leshii answered, as if that should have been obvious.

"I don't know what that is." My voice sounded small and hopeless.

"You will. You're special, too."

Special. I wanted to laugh, but it wasn't funny and the laughter would probably turn to hysteria before it ended in tears. And I couldn't summon the energy to have a breakdown just now. Maybe later.

Tomorrow, talk to Zach and David. Name a king. Buy a book of baby names. Think of something to tell my parents. Then I could have a nervous breakdown. Except it might be bad for the baby. *Hell.*

I let the lord of the forest take me home. Nobody else was back yet, and I was relieved. I didn't want to face any of them. I went up to my suite and took a shower, too tired for the tub. Afterward, I looked at myself in the mirror, trying to see if the change in me was obvious.

My own eyes stared back at me, darker than normal but otherwise the same. My face looked chalky, but redheads are always pale. My body didn't look any different.

"You'll do the right thing," I told my reflection. Sure.

I left the bathroom and spotted my purse in the bedroom on the nightstand. Somebody must've brought it up for me. Thoughtful. I opened it and dug out my packet of birth control pills. I could take the rest of the tablets all at once, the college girl's morning-after solution. I threw them in the trash instead.

Bed drew me like a magnet. I climbed in naked, pulled the covers up to my chin, and longed to pull the pillow over my head for good measure.

When I woke up, I was warm and safe and secure and everything felt right. I wasn't alone in the big bed. Zach's body curled around mine from behind, his arm over my rib cage tucking me close.

I rolled over to burrow into him, wrapping my arms around him, sliding one foot over his calf. "Mmm." I nuzzled the curve of his throat. "Good morning. Or is it still night?"

"Does it matter?" Zach's voice held a tone I didn't have to work very hard to interpret. I could feel his penis pressing against my belly, full and thick and eager.

"Not if we don't have to get up." I reached down to close my hand around his shaft, exploring the length and breadth of that part of him, all male heat and hardness and silky smooth skin drawn taut.

His hands moved over me, cupping the bare curve of my butt, stroking the swell of my breast. Our mutual search widened. There were so many planes and angles to discover, so many tastes and textures. He liked it when I stroked the back of his neck with fingers so light they barely made contact, and he growled when I raked my nails over his muscular butt.

His lips settled on mine as he slid a hand between my thighs and cupped my mound. His fingers caressed the hidden folds with a light touch. "How does that feel?"

"Like there should be more," I answered, smiling against his mouth. And then there was. He rolled me onto my back underneath him, covered my body with his, settled his legs between mine. I felt him probe at my soft, slick entry, and gave a low moan of encouragement.

He entered me slowly, pressing home in an unrushed stroke, allowing my sex to stretch and open and accommodate him by degrees until I held all of him.

Not all of him, some corner of me whispered. I shoved the thought away. I had this much of him. I wound myself around Zach, embracing him with arms and legs in addition to the most intimate embrace of flesh that joined us.

The knot swelled, and my breath caught. Zach's mouth claimed mine again. He began to move inside me, gentle, careful strokes, a leisurely lovemaking to make up for yesterday's impatient, aggressive lust. The sweetness of it made my throat ache and my eyes burn.

He took me in a rhythm that was easy to match and follow, his body rocking on mine and driving him deep. He took me with kisses that drew me closer and closer to some invisible brink. He took me with thorough attention to detail that left no part of me unclaimed. Flesh to flesh, heart to heart, breath to breath, he took me, and I surrendered myself to him.

CHAPTER TWENTY-ONE

I DRESSED AND LEFT THE SUITE WHILE ZACH WAS IN THE SHOWER. I HAD an ominous list of people to talk to, but it seemed to me that the first person who ought to know about my little problem should be the one who helped cause it.

This trip down the stairs should've been easy compared to yesterday's, but my feet felt leaden and my heart felt worse. Dread pooled in my stomach. Although at least I knew Jack wouldn't be angry.

He just might be the only wolf who wasn't.

My steps dragged as I made my way through the quiet house and into the peace of the solarium, where he stood looking outside through the glass wall. I stopped a couple of feet behind him.

"Jack." My voice came out hoarse with strain.

He turned, concern darkening the blue of his eyes. "Chandra?" He took in my stiff posture, the defensive way I'd wrapped my

arms around myself, and came to me. His hands settled on my upper arms. "What's wrong?"

So many things. I had no words, so I took one of his hands
and placed it low on my abdomen. If he could read a concussion by
touching my head and bruising on my cervix by touching my stomach, he could read what lay under his palm now.

He drew in a breath. His other hand moved to my waist and
urged me closer. I took a half step forward and rested my head on
his shoulder.

"I can't say I'm sorry." He slid the hand at my waist around to
the small of my back to rub lightly back and forth. His hand over
my belly cupped as if shielding and cradling the little spark of life.

I closed my eyes and felt my throat swell, thickening my words.
"I don't want you to be sorry."

"What do you want?"

I took a long shuddering breath. "I don't know. I can't choose
you. You aren't my mate, and even if you were, you have a position
in the pack nobody else can fill."

"I might not be your mate, but I'm in this with you." He rested
his cheek against the top of my head, still mussed from sleep and
sex. "I'm also your friend. What do you want?"

"I want it." A whisper of sound, choked with the threat of tears.
"I want to keep it, but I don't know how that's going to work."

Jack let go of my abdomen in order to wrap his other arm around
me. "I want it, too. We'll work it out with Zach. I'll help however you
want me to."

One bridge crossed, I thought, and took a deep, calming breath.
The remark from behind us made me blow it out in a rush.

"You look cozy."

David. I attempted to stiffen my resolve, my knees, and my spine. I had to face him sooner or later. I'd just hoped for later. After I'd had time to wash Zach's scent off my body, and preferably not while trying to figure out how to deal with a co-parent who wouldn't be my husband.

"Yep. We're cozy." My tone came out more flippant than I'd intended and I winced.

My discomfort communicated itself to Jack. He ignored David and brought his hands up to frame my face, meeting my eyes with his steady gaze. "I mean it. I'm in this with you."

"I know." His caring, open response took the edge off my tension. I rose up on tiptoes to kiss his cheek in gratitude. "Thank you."

Then I turned to David and almost staggered. Jack caught my elbow to steady me. Good thing. The sight of David hit me like a gut punch, driving the air out of my body. I wanted to drink him in with my eyes, as if he were water in the desert and I was dying of thirst.

It hadn't gone away. So what else hadn't changed since yesterday? I had to know, and I had to know before I said something irrevocable to Zach.

I stumbled toward him. He didn't meet me halfway. He made me cover the full distance between us, and then he didn't reach for me. I heard the soft sound of Jack's exit behind me, leaving us alone together.

"David." I licked dry lips and stared at him, overly aware of the too-rapid rise and fall of my chest and the racing of my heart. He didn't smile. Just stared at me with his face shuttered and his eyes unreadable, his body language closing me out. The silence dragged on, growing increasingly awkward, but I couldn't move away. I had to know.

"If you're waiting for me to give you a kiss and a cuddle like Jack did, you might want to take a bath first. You reek of sex and the alpha."

My face burned and I longed to slap him. Instead, I shot back, "That didn't bother you yesterday."

He didn't blink. "Yesterday you were a bitch in heat. What's your excuse today?"

Good question. I didn't have one. I didn't know how to proceed. I couldn't detect any openings in his guard. If I'd left my bra off, maybe I could've opened my zipper, flashed bare breasts, and then taken advantage of his momentary distraction.

Probably just as well. He might not even have bothered to look. I could hear his cruel, cold voice in my imagination. *Thanks, but I've seen the show.*

I licked my lips again. "You're making this very difficult."

"Really." He stared me down. "Too fucking bad."

"Yeah." I nodded in agreement and resignation. "It really is." Then I brought my knee up to his groin. He blocked me as easily as I'd expected him to, but since kneeing him wasn't my goal, I didn't mind. I moved into him, and where our bodies touched it felt like coming home. I froze, dumbfounded, staring at him with wide eyes.

David froze, too. Then he let out a snarl, caught my arms, turned me, and pinned my back to his chest with my trapped arms crossed in front of me. "You fucked him. Not half an hour ago you had your legs open for him. You fucked him, and now you come to me? Did you think I'd still want you? Did you think you could make me challenge him for you?"

"No." A whisper, but David heard me.

David couldn't possibly be my mate. He didn't want me. He didn't feel what I felt. But I felt it, and now even if Zach was willing to take me pregnant with another man's baby, how could I pledge myself to him?

Even now, even with David's anger and disgust driving daggers through my heart, if he kissed me, I'd be lost. A year from now, ten years from now, if he crooked his finger I'd go to him. I wouldn't be able to stop myself.

I guessed that meant I could add pride to the list of things I'd lost yesterday. Humiliation scorched my skin and tears blurred my eyes.

"No," I whispered again, lips trembling. Reaction set in, making me shiver. "I didn't think you'd still want me." Why would he? "Let me go."

I needed to get out. I needed to escape, run, hide. Most of all, I needed David to never touch me again. Why was he still touching me? He made me burn like fire and left ashes in my mouth.

"Let go!" I fought, twisted, dug my thumb into a convenient nerve point, and broke free when David's hold on me loosened. I was running before he recovered, and by the time I reached the woods I'd far outpaced any potential pursuit. I still found a creek to confuse my trail, splashed through it until my pants were sodden and my legs felt numb with cold, then returned to the sheltering trees.

Run to the woods; woods, won't you hide me?

I laughed at myself and the high, sharp sound sobered me. I stopped, put my hand against a tree to brace myself, and leaned there, panting hard. So David hated me. So what? I had to stop this. Stop acting like a hysterical girl and be a grown-up.

Time to remember I was the monster.

Time to remember I had somebody besides myself to think of.

And then there was Zach. Zach, who would publicly accept me and probably be kind to me in private, too, because he wanted to do the right thing and because he was a decent man. A political marriage didn't have to be one without a shred of common courtesy or warmth. We had an undeniable chemistry, and physical attraction had to count for something. My future could be what I was willing to make of it.

I straightened up and brushed the tears from my cheeks with the back of my hand. Okay, then. I had a plan. Go home, go to Zach, spill my guts about everything, including my unplanned pregnancy and my fatal attraction to David.

I turned around and headed back the way I'd come.

I didn't make it very far, because the panthers surrounded me, and this time my good friends, Rhonda, Wilson, and Miguel had some interesting company. They had a man with them who was old enough to be my father, whose black hair was shot with gray, and who looked at me with the coldest stare I'd ever seen. *He could give a furnace frostbite,* I thought, and resisted the urge to warm myself by rubbing my arms.

I knew with icy certainty who he had to be. Out loud I said, "Hello, Ray."

He looked me over with cold calculation. "You know who I am. You must know what I want." Then he asked me a question that made my flesh crawl. "Have you named a king yet?"

I didn't hesitate. "Yes."

A humorless smile twisted his lips. "The bitch lies."

"That's Queen Bitch. Or Bitch Queen, I'll answer to either."

Rhonda made a choking sound that bore a suspicious resemblance to a laugh.

"Bitch Queen." My father's killer came to me and unzipped my shirt. I said a silent thanks for the impulse that had sent me searching for my sports bra this morning instead of going without. I didn't dare slap his hands away. Not now, not if he just intended to embarrass me by exposing my breasts.

Of course, if he tried to rape me in front of a crowd of witnesses, all bets were off. I'd kill him as swiftly and brutally as I knew how.

He smiled wider as if he could read my thoughts on my face. "She thinks she can fight me." He sounded like I'd given him something to look forward to. He walked around behind me, undid my bra, yanked it off. I stood still, waiting for his next move. "She thinks she can defy me."

Ray caught me by the back of the hair and used the hold to force me down to my knees. He ran his other hand over my breasts in an obscene caress. "She thinks she'll be able to refuse when I order her to name me." His hand moved lower, fisted in the fabric of my pants, pulled down.

He worked the fabric down to my knees, put his knee at the small of my back, and dropped me onto all fours. "When I'm finished, you'll say anything I want to make the pain stop."

I tore free of his grip, flipped onto my back, grabbed his balls, and squeezed with a force I hadn't possessed two days ago. He turned a lovely shade of puce and rained closed-fisted blows down on me, but I refused to let go. Instead, I squeezed harder.

"Were you planning to use this?" I asked him. "I think you should wait for it to grow a little."

The panthers didn't rush forward to help him, and I wondered if they considered this a sort of duel. Maybe they wouldn't interfere. Of course, that didn't mean they'd let me go after I killed him, but one problem at a time.

"I'll kill you slowly for that," he promised me.

I shook my head. "You're saying your lines all wrong. Here's mine: You killed my father. Prepare to die."

The monster under my skin rushed up, grew fangs and powerful jaws that would serve as the weapons of my vengeance, and then the hot taste of blood was spilling in my mouth and Ray fell backward with a gaping hole where his throat used to be.

"Heal that," I snarled, although it came out as a growl, since human speech was beyond me just now. I kicked away the remnants of my clothes and let the change take me. A heartbeat later I stood over Ray's fallen body on four legs. The animal I'd become decided he might not be grievously wounded enough to stay down forever, so I tore open his belly and spilled his intestines into the dirt.

I threw back my head and howled my victory into the air. Then I ran like the wind while the rest of my enemies scrambled to shift and come after me.

CHAPTER TWENTY-TWO

IT OCCURRED TO ME AS I FLED THAT I WAS MAKING A BAD HABIT OF running blind through the trees. I really needed to get a map of the area and learn the landscape. I didn't exactly have the home ground advantage right now, despite being on home ground.

I could hear sounds of pursuit and it sounded like the rush of a thousand paws. How many damn cats were there? I hadn't exactly counted. But I didn't need to count noses to know there were more of them than there were of us, by at least double our number. No wonder they'd been bold enough to come against us.

And there wouldn't just be cats hot on my heels. Ray had left the pack, but he hadn't gone alone. The other rogues would be coming to reclaim their home.

Damned if I'd let them have it. It was mine now.

"You can't stay out of trouble." That cheery voice again. I was making a habit of running into its owner, too.

I kept running. I didn't want to put the brakes on and get a panther up my ass. He plucked me off my feet and dangled me in midair so he could look me in the eye. "You don't listen, either. Didn't I tell you to let the boys finish this?"

I growled. If I was going to be the queen, then the boys could damn well get used to letting a girl play.

"No need to take that tone with me." The Leshii didn't sound offended. The lord of the forest tucked me against his chest like a pet dog and strode toward the house. "You'll get to have your fun."

Yeah, like now, when every shape-shifter in the world overran us and trampled us into the forest floor. I looked over the Leshii's shoulder and wondered why I suddenly heard nothing back there but silence. I looked at him, my eyes full of questions.

"Where'd they go? I sent them to cool off." He smiled and it was positively gleeful. I made a bet with myself that the whole crew had suddenly found themselves someplace very uncomfortable. "You have some time before they regroup and come again. Use it well."

I nodded to show I understood, which felt very strange in this form, and my wolf perplexity at the sensation amused the Leshii all over again. He was still laughing when he deposited me on my doorstep.

Then he sank into the grass to vanish from view, and I nosed open the dog door that let me into the solarium. My nails clicked over the moon tiles. The hair at the back of my neck ruffled when I caught the scent of my fight with David. I skirted around that spot and made my way into the main part of the house.

I listened, and caught voices coming from the library. My paws padded in that direction. Odd sounds punctuated the indistinct speech. I couldn't identify the source of those noises, despite my new and improved hearing. Until I walked into the room and took in the sight of eleven lean, mean fighting machines packing enough heat to finish Armageddon.

They were loading weapons and Zach was yelling at David. Well, not yelling. That quiet angry voice was so much worse than yelling that I had to fight the urge to drop on my belly. "You let her go. You let her leave by herself."

"I didn't let her leave." David bit out the words. "She fights dirty. She got free and bolted, and I lost her scent."

"What were you fighting about in the first place?" Zach looked furious. A good look on him, honestly. Not that I expected David to appreciate that the way I did.

"Nothing." David rammed another cartridge home.

I felt my stomach drop at the sound of that word. "Nothing." The touch of my skin to his that said home to me was nothing to him. The rush of events hit me and I staggered. The fight with David. My idiotic flight. Ray's obscene hands on me, worse than him hitting me. What damage had those fists done?

I gagged and searched the room with frantic eyes. Jack, where was Jack? Jack would touch me and tell me everything was all right.

I found him and lunged forward, and everybody froze except Jack, who knelt down and opened his arms for me to rush into. I buried my nose in his neck, making soft whining sounds, and then I collapsed. When I blinked my eyes open, I was lying naked in his lap.

"Jack." I hardly recognized my own voice. I sounded like I'd been gargling gravel. "Tell me it's all right."

Jack rubbed my tummy and gave me a reassuring smile. "It's all right."

Relief turned my muscles limp. "Oh. Good. That's good."

"What's good?" Zach appeared in my field of vision, his eyes searching mine.

"The baby isn't hurt."

Behind me, David dropped something that landed with a solid thunk.

Zach bent to lift me into his arms. "Is that what you and David fought about?" he asked.

"No." I curled an arm around Zach's neck. "Not directly, at least. David didn't know until just now."

"Okay." Zach's worried gaze searched mine. "You had blood on your muzzle. What's happened?"

I started to shake with reaction. "Can't talk about it now. Need a shower." I burrowed into him. "Is it too late to take you up on that offer?"

"No. It's not too late." His arms tightened around me. "Are you hurt?"

I shook my head. "I'm okay." I turned my head to look at David. I wanted to kick him in the balls right now, but he was our soldier and I'd vowed to be an adult. To put the pack ahead of personal feelings. "It's a good thing you're ready. The panthers are coming and they've teamed up with the rogue wolves."

David didn't blink. "They're coming now?"

"No. The Leshii sent them away, but he said they'd be back."

"We'll be ready for them." David looked like grim death as he spoke. Good. He could go fight the bad guys and leave me alone.

Shivers wracked me and I clutched at Zach. "Cold," I muttered. "Shower, please. I want to be clean." I wanted the touch of my father's killer washed away.

"I'll get you clean and warm," Zach promised. He carried me all the way up the stairs to my suite and didn't put me down until he set me in the shower. He stripped and climbed in with me, then pulled me into his arms so I could lean on him while the water streamed over us. He lathered as much of me as he could reach, then turned me so that my back rested against him while he washed my front.

His hands felt so good on me. So right. I put my hands over his and guided them to cup my breasts. "There," I said, my voice just audible over the sound of the water. "He touched me there. I want you to touch me until I can't feel any hands but yours."

Zach went very still. "Chandra. Where else did he touch you? Were you raped?"

I shook my head. I reached out to turn off the water and said into the sudden silence, "I killed him."

Zach turned me around to face him. "Who?"

"Ray. It was Ray." I took a deep breath and went on, "I need to tell you everything, but I can't do it standing up."

Zach slid an arm around me, supported me as he helped me out of the shower and followed me. He wrapped a towel around me like a sarong and another around his waist. Then he led me to the bed.

"Here." He stacked pillows against the headboard, then used them to support his back while I sat between his legs, supported by his chest. His arms wrapped around my waist. "Comfortable?"

I nodded. I put my hand on his arm and felt the warmth and strength in him. Touching him made me feel like everything would be all right. And maybe it would be. Honesty was a good place to start.

"I shouldn't have had sex with you this morning," I blurted out. "I knew I was pregnant last night, and I didn't tell you. That was wrong. This morning I'd just woken up. I was distracted." I left unsaid *by your body and the way you make me feel*. "I wasn't thinking, but that's no excuse."

Zach gave me a gentle squeeze. "Is this why you snuck off afterward?"

"Yes." I felt a light blush sting my cheeks, but "snuck off" pretty well described it. "It's not yours. Jack's the father. I told him first because I thought he deserved to know. David saw me with him in the solarium, and . . . I think he misunderstood what he saw."

"So you fought."

"Not exactly over that, but yes." My fingers traced the line from his wrist to his elbow. "We'll come back to David in a minute. About Jack, he isn't my mate. He knows that, and he accepts that you are." *There. More out in the open. Keep going.* "I want the baby, Zach. I didn't plan it, I didn't expect it, but it's here and I'm keeping it. You should know that before you agree to take me as your mate."

Zach leaned forward to slide an arm under my knees, lift me, and turn me sideways on his lap so he could look into my face. "Did you think I'd tell you to get rid of it? To choose between your child and me?"

"I didn't know what to think, Zach." I dropped my gaze to his shoulder. "I'm having another man's baby. I'd understand if that changed things for you. If it did, I'd rather know before we make a formal announcement."

And now things got harder. I steeled myself to go on. "You might be willing to take me just for the good of the pack, to present a strong, unified front to our enemies. I'd understand if that was your only reason, but you should know . . ."

Oh, God. I couldn't say it. My tongue stuck and my throat closed off my voice.

"Chandra?" Zach stroked my cheek, his touch so gentle I wanted to cry. "What should I know?"

Coward, coward. Say it.

"I love you." The words burst out in an agonized rush. I took a deep, shuddering breath. "I feel good when I'm with you. Right. Safe. Warm. I want to be with you. The first time—" My voice choked and I had to swallow hard before I could go on. "The first time we had sex, I knew I'd belong to you forever. The knot let me go, but I knew I'd never be free."

"Do you want to be free? You said you didn't want a mate."

I put my hand over his heart. "I want you. I want to be with you. I think if I couldn't be, it would break something inside me."

The way I felt broken from David's harsh rejection. I didn't know how I'd stand it if Zach rejected me, too, but if he was going to accept me as I was, he had to know it all. "There's more."

"More? No wonder you ran off," Zach muttered. His hands moved on me, stroking, soothing. "You had all this bottled up."

I let out a half laugh, half sob. "It's been an intense couple of days."

"You got dropped in at the deep end. You've handled it, too. You just reached your limit." The admiration in Zach's voice warmed me. "Tell me everything you need to. Get it off your chest."

I curled into him. "This may be the thing that makes you kick me out of your bed," I warned him.

"Would that matter? We've been sleeping in your bed."

I shook my head, my throat tight. "Don't joke. I killed a man today, but this is worse."

"I doubt it." Zach kissed my hair. "And I'm still waiting for you to tell me that story."

I shuddered at the memory of blood in my mouth. Ray's fallen body. The smell of death. "I'm getting there. I thought I'd deal with everything internal to the pack first, and then the outside problems. Not that Ray's a problem anymore."

"So what else is internal?" Zach rubbed my back, and I felt the tension in my body ease a degree. "Is this where you get back to the fight with David?"

"Yes."

I was quiet for a while, trying to find the right words. And then they came, halting and awkward, but honest. "Yesterday, I told you I'd want David even if he hated me." My fingers dug into Zach, clinging. Holding on to him helped steady me and gave me the strength to go on. "He does, and I do."

Zach went still. "Want, how?"

I let out a shaky breath. "I look at him and I want to touch him. I touch him and it's like being home. It didn't go away. I thought it would go away after we gave in to it, burned out with the heat, but I saw him this morning and it hit me all over again. I touched him and there it was."

"There what was?" Zach didn't sound cool, exactly, just very controlled.

What, indeed. Obsession? Infatuation?

"He thinks I'm a whore." I said the ugly word out loud, feeling so cold inside I thought I might never be warm again. "He's right. I belong to you and I'm pregnant with another man's baby, and it doesn't matter. Any time, anywhere, if he touched me, I'd spread my legs and beg him to fuck me again, because I'm his whore."

I didn't realize I was crying until Zach brushed away the tears.

"Shhh." He rocked me in his lap. "Shhh, it's all right."

"I couldn't deal with that on top of everything else, so I ran," I said. "I stopped because I realized I was being stupid. But it was too late. All the panthers surrounded me, and Ray was with them. He wanted to rape me, and I think he planned to beat me until I named him king. He didn't get very detailed, but his plans apparently involved a lot of pain. He tore off my clothes and got me down on all fours. I turned over, grew fangs, and tore his throat out."

I was shuddering and sobbing now. "He fell. I tore his stomach open, too, so he'd stay dead. And then I ran and the panthers all shifted and ran after me, until the forest lord showed up and sent them away. He said they'd be back, but we'd have some time."

I huddled into Zach and clung to him like he was the only solid thing left in the world. I cried until I had no more tears left, just a dull, empty ache. "I thought I wanted to know who I was," I said when I could speak again. "I wanted to know who my real parents were, because I thought that would tell me what I am. Well, now I know."

Monster. Whore. Murderer. God, how could I be a mother, too?

"Shhh." Zach shifted us, turning and stretching out so that we were lying down on our sides, facing each other. He held me in a tight embrace. "It's all right."

I shook my head. "It's not all right. But we have other problems to deal with. I think the rogues teamed up with the panthers so they could overrun us. They want to take the pack back. They'll try to make me name one of them king."

"Let me worry about that."

"Okay. You worry." My eyes drooped as exhaustion hit me.

"You're tired." Zach pulled the comforter over me and tucked it securely around me. "Rest."

I didn't so much fall asleep as shut off, too overwhelmed to cope with anything else, retreating into healing oblivion.

And when I woke up, David was the one who held me.

CHAPTER TWENTY-THREE

"LET GO OF ME." I SHOULD'VE HAD THE STRENGTH TO MOVE AWAY ON my own, but I felt too numb inside, too drained. I lacked the will to break free of the touch that was heaven and hell all in one.

"Make me."

I closed my eyes. Maybe it would be better if I couldn't see him. "Don't, David. Unless Zach kicks me out and throws me to the panthers, we're packmates. We have to deal with each other. That would be easier if you didn't torture me."

"This is torture?"

"Yes. I didn't think you were a sadist."

"Tell me." He moved into me, pressing his body against mine. "Tell me how this tortures you."

Oh, let me count the ways. "You don't want me, so putting your hands on me is just mean. I can stand it if you don't touch me, but if you do, I can't help wanting you. I hate myself for it, but that doesn't make it stop, so you have to. Stop. Just stop, and don't ever touch me."

I ended on a high-pitched note of desperation. Heat curled through me and my body trembled with the unfulfilled urge to get closer, to tear away the towel that covered me, push away the comforter, and press my naked flesh against his.

"I like touching you." His hands shaped my breasts. I sucked in a breath. The fabric separating us wasn't thick enough to ward off the sharp sword of desire that had me at the pointy end.

"Stop." But my body was moving in invitation, back arching to offer my breasts to his touch, nipples tightening.

"You don't want me to." He pulled down the comforter, tugged away the questionable protection of my towel. I couldn't move. I just lay there while he looked at my naked body, aching for him to touch me again, praying for him not to.

"Why are you doing this? What did I ever do to you?"

"What did you do to me?" His face darkened. "You made me want you. You made me burn for something I can't have. I don't want to want you." He pushed me onto my back and rose over me, and I realized he was naked when he settled on top of me. My heart pounded. He felt so good. Too good.

"I don't want to want you, either." The words came out soft and throaty. I sounded as sex drugged as I felt. If he didn't let me up, this was going to end with him inside me. "Why are you doing this, David?"

His body rocked on mine, and I moved in response, breath catching as we aligned. His hard shaft probed between my legs. So close. His answer came in a low growl. "Zach thinks I may be your mate."

Zach. He'd done this to me? Set me up, left me defenseless against my own body's craving? Betrayal pierced me. I'd never expected Zach to love me back. I'd said the words; he hadn't. I still would've sworn he wouldn't betray me like this.

"No." Tears stung my eyes. "Zach said it was a choice of heart, not hormones."

"Is that all this is? Hormones?" David shifted, and the ridge of his head pressed into me.

I couldn't stand it. I wanted him. I needed him inside me. In another heartbeat, he would be. I had to stop this now. "Yes. No. How the hell should I know?" I shouted the words as I tried to twist away. "Don't do this to me, David."

"Don't do what? Make you face what you feel?" He rolled to the side and I thought it was a respite, but then his hand was between my legs.

"Lust. I feel lust." I closed my eyes, wanting to shut him out even as his fingers slid in, my slick and swollen sex offering no resistance.

"Nothing else?" He lowered his head to draw a nipple into his mouth. He tongued and suckled while his fingers pushed deeper into me and I wanted every tormenting sensation his hands and mouth could give me.

"Self-loathing." I couldn't stop myself, and I couldn't stop him, either. "Betrayal." Zach had given me to David like I was an impulse purchase and he had buyer's remorse. I'd told him I loved him, poured my heart out to him, and he'd sent David to fuck me.

David released my nipple and raked the curve of my breast with his teeth, making me gasp. "Get over it."

Oh, if only I could. "It's not your baby, if that's what this is about."

"I know. Zach told me." He kissed the slope of my other breast. "I wouldn't have pinned you this morning if I'd known. That won't happen again."

I didn't know if I wanted to laugh or cry. "You think that hurt me? That was nothing. You treated me like I was garbage. You said you didn't want me anymore."

"I never said that." David's mouth burned a path up to the curve of my neck.

"You called me a bitch in heat. You threw what I did yesterday back in my face." The pain of that hit me all over again. "How dare you put me down for that when you were standing in line to take your turn?" I rolled away, dislodging his hand in the process, turning my back to him. I curled into a protective ball. "Go away, David. Go chase a cat."

"The only pussy I want is right here." David spooned behind me, his body curving around mine. His cock probed between my legs and I drew in a sharp breath. "We're going to settle this."

"Settle what?"

"You. Me." His lips caressed the back of my neck and his hand played my breast with expert skill. "If you're not my mate, you won't let me roll you over onto your knees. If you're not my mate, you won't spread your thighs and raise your sweet ass in the air for me. If you're not my mate, you won't love the way I take you and you won't moan and beg for more until I make you come."

His words and his hands did their job. I didn't resist when he pushed me up on my knees. He stroked the upraised curve of my butt, and when his hand dipped lower I parted my thighs and deepened the arch of my lower back, offering myself to him.

"This doesn't prove anything," I said as he guided his head to my willing entry. "You'll still hate me when it's over, and you still won't want to be king of the wolves."

"I don't hate you." David trailed kisses down my spine. He began to press forward. My eager flesh opened to accept him.

Since I couldn't push him away with my traitorous body, I tried to do it with words. "I fucked Zach in this bed this morning. I loved it. I love him."

"Maybe you love us both." David thrust all the way inside me. When the knot swelled to lock us together, I wanted to cry in relief because it was what I needed, what I wanted, what I ached for.

"I can't love you both. Wolves are monogamous and they mate for life." But if I didn't love him, why did he have so much power to hurt me? Why had his rejection cut so deep that I still felt like I was bleeding from it?

"Red wolves are special." David's torso covered my back, a protective gesture. His arms wrapped around me, holding me close while he took me with forceful thrusts. "There's never been a red queen before. Maybe you have two mates."

"You said you didn't want to want me," I reminded him as my body moved in counterrhythm to deepen each stroke he gave me.

"I don't." His teeth grazed my neck. "I don't want to need you so much that I'd share you with another man because I can't give you up." His tempo increased, his cock driving into me with relentless insistence. "You're mine. But you're his, too, and if I challenge him for you it would tear you apart."

I caught my breath at his words, then lost it again as he moved deep inside me, hard and hot, claiming every inch of me.

"I don't like it. I don't like knowing you want him, too, knowing he's going to have you again and again, and you'll love it every time he fucks you." David pulled me up onto my hands and knees, gripped my waist, and hammered into me. "I don't like any of that. I'm jealous as hell."

"David." I didn't have any other words. He took me higher with each stroke, need and heat spiraling into an orgasm that swept us both away.

"Love me, too," he said in a rough whisper, our spent bodies still joined together. "I know you love him, but love me, too."

I opened my eyes and brought the world back into focus. "I do. I love you, David."

He pulled out of me, leaving me empty and hollow. "Roll over."

I did, turning onto my back to look up at him. His eyes were almost black, his face taut. "I'm sorry," he said. "Sorry I shut you out. Sorry we fought. Sorry I said all those words that hurt you."

I licked dry lips and stared up at him. All my defenses were down and I knew my heart was in my eyes. "You can't ever do that again," I whispered. "I love you, but you can't hurt me like that again." If he did, I wasn't sure I'd survive it.

He bent and kissed me, a long and thorough exchange. When it ended, he rested his forehead against mine. "I will never give you cause to run from me again. Zach told us all what happened. It's my fault you were in danger today. My fault Ray almost got you. For the rest of our lives, I'll be the one you run to and I promise to keep you safe."

I shook my head. "It took two of us to be that stupid," I said. "I put myself in danger. I won't do that again, either."

David settled beside me and pulled me close. His hands stroked and caressed me, as if he needed to keep touching me after the passion was spent. "How are you feeling?"

"Fine." I snuggled into him. "If you mean the baby, it's too early to notice anything different."

"Not quite what I meant." David rested his hand over my abdomen. "Jack's happy. Are you?"

"It's all sort of mixed up and overwhelming." I put my hand over his, a tentative effort to reach out. "I want it, and I'm glad Jack does, too. I don't know how everybody else will feel. You and Zach. The rest of the pack. It complicates things."

"I don't think you need to worry." David stroked the soft skin of my belly. "They're all arguing about where to put the nursery."

I let out a little laugh. "Lots of doting uncles. This kid will be so spoiled." Then I sobered. "And three dads. That's going to lead to some interesting questions."

"One dad, two especially devoted uncles. We won't try to displace Jack." His hand ran up to cup my breast. He rubbed his thumb over the nipple and I made a soft sound of pleasure, loving the feel of his body pressed close to mine and the way he touched me.

"I thought at first Zach sent you up here because he didn't want me anymore," I said. "Passing me on like some kind of hand-me-down."

David frowned at me. "Hand-me-down. Piñata. I can't decide if it's us or yourself you have a low opinion of."

"I'm adopted. Maybe I have abandonment issues." I reached out to touch him back, delighted that I could. "You said you'd share me with him. Is that what he wants, too?"

"He wants you to be happy." David moved his hand up to stroke my hair. "So do I. So does Jack. What do you want?"

I rolled to lie on top of him so I could have all of my body pressed against his. "Besides world peace and a good story to tell my adoptive parents?"

"Besides that." His arms enclosed me and his lips touched my forehead.

"I want the three of us to talk about it." I kissed the curve of his shoulder, infatuated with every line and plane of his body. "How we think it's going to work. I don't want to announce to the whole pack that you're both my mates only to have to admit we can't handle what that means."

David slid his hands down to cup my bare butt. "You already know what it's like to have sex with both of us together."

I shook my head. "I know what it was like in special circumstances. When I was in heat. When both of you were willing to share me because it was what I needed at the time and neither of you had a claim on me. It's not the same as knowing you're both going to be my lovers for the rest of our lives. Neither of you ever expected to have to share your mate."

"Well, neither of us will step aside." His hands flexed, digging into my flesh. The possessive gesture underscored my concern. "Even if one of us could let you go, I think the pain of losing a mate would crush you. Zach thinks so, too. And we're not going to test that theory."

I processed that while I absorbed David through my pores, drawing in strength and comfort. I'd felt so broken without him. Touching him healed my heart. I didn't even want to contemplate what it would feel like to lose Zach.

I couldn't give either of them up. I needed both of them. I loved both of them. I couldn't deny the truth, but it made my head hurt all the same.

"It's not just the two of you that have to accept this three-way arrangement," I said. "I have to figure out how to deal with loving you both. And then there's the pack. They'll have to support our arrangement, too. I don't want to cause resentment or a split, especially now."

A chill went through me, thinking about the combined forces of werepanthers and rogue werewolves descending on us. "That's another thing. We're outnumbered, David. If we aren't all solidly together, we're going to lose. Even if we are solidly together, we might lose."

"We have the home ground advantage. We're also expecting them. And the Leshii keeps showing up to defend you."

"He saved my butt today." I burrowed into David. "I don't think I could've kept outrunning all of them."

He held me tighter. "And you wonder why you need two mates. It's going to take two of us to keep you safe."

I couldn't argue that. The night before the full moon I'd fought off a werepanther. The next night, I'd fought another. Today I'd been surrounded by the whole brigade. I might have killed Ray, but I wouldn't have escaped the rest if the Leshii hadn't stepped in.

"Two mates," I said, trying to wrap my brain around it. "We need to see Zach. And we need to figure out our next step."

"I'll call him. You stay put." David stood up and tucked the comforter around me.

I rolled my eyes at him. "I'm about two minutes pregnant. It's not like I need to take to my bed."

"You'll stay put. You haven't had a chance to recover from your first change and you're running all over the woods fighting like a badass." He flashed a smile that made me suck in my breath because it was like seeing the sun for the first time. "Besides, I want to think of you waiting for me like this."

"Oh. Okay." I stared at him, blinded by the afterimage burned on my retinas. In the few days I'd known him, I'd seen him fierce, watchful, sexual, angry, amused, quiet. I hadn't seen David happy. I watched him walk out of the bedroom feeling dazed.

Maybe this could really work. Maybe the three of us could make one another happy. Of course, we still had to figure out how a marriage with two husbands could function. I pictured moving back and forth between their bedrooms like in an adult version of shared custody. I made a face, hating the idea. No. Not happening. Maybe they'd be the ones who moved back and forth, alternating nights with me. But they'd probably hate that, too.

All three of us sleeping together, me in the middle? I liked that. A lot. I'd joked about abandonment issues, but it felt like the un-covered edge of a buried truth. Maybe I really did need two mates.

CHAPTER TWENTY-FOUR

"YOU STAYED PUT." DAVID SAT ON THE EDGE OF THE BED AND BENT
over to kiss me in a way that thoroughly expressed his appreciation. Then he helped me sit up and Zach handed me a protein shake.
I groaned out loud.

"Oh, come on. If you want to get calories into me, can't I have
a pizza?"

"Sure. Later." Zach claimed the space on my other side and took
my hand. He laced our fingers together. The gesture made me feel
like a teenager in the throes of a mad crush. *He held my hand! We're
going steady!* I drank the protein shake and hoped it would restore
my brain.

When I finished, David took the empty glass and set it on the
bedside table. I looked from one of them to the other. "So," I finally said. "Three of us."

"Yes." Zach turned our joined hands over and looked serious.

"David said you thought I was giving you away by sending him up here. I owe you an apology for that. I thought it would be easier for the two of you to work it out if I wasn't in the same room."

I squeezed his hand. "I expected you to dump me for telling the truth. This is . . . unexpected."

"Unprecedented." Zach brought our hands up and kissed my knuckles. "But it was the only explanation that fit."

I nodded. It did fit. I'd been drawn to both of them from the first, before going into heat complicated everything. In retrospect, I shouldn't have been surprised that my feelings for David didn't go away when things went back to what now passed for normal in my life.

"Any news on the kitty problem?" I asked.

"Yes. A group of people were arrested for indecent exposure after being caught swimming nude at the beach."

That startled a laugh from me. "Well, the Leshii did say he'd sent them to cool off. Wonder how long it'll take them to fight free of the paperwork and pay the fines?"

"Until tonight, best guess." David took my other hand and held it between his. "That gives us some time."

"Right." Time. How little of it had we spent together? "This is so weird. We've just met. How can we be sure this will last? What if one of you wakes up in a week or a month or a year and the feeling's just gone away?"

"Mating forms a bond that doesn't go away. It's for life." Zach's free hand stroked my hair, a comforting gesture. "You'll have to take our word for it, but there's never been an exception in our history."

"This seems like an exception," I pointed out.

"Expecting it to vanish?" David gave me a sharp look. "Sooner or later, you're going to have to trust us."

"In the meantime, accept it as a working hypothesis," Zach suggested in a dry voice. "We do. We're in this for life."

"Okay, then. The pack might swallow me having two mates, but I don't see two leaders going over. Zach, I think you still have to be king," I said. "David doesn't want it, and even if he did, you're better suited to the job. Do you both agree?"

"God, yes," David muttered.

I stifled a giggle at his tone.

"I agree," Zach said. "The pack will be more likely to accept our relationship if we don't try to change the rules of leadership at the same time. When the renegade wolves are at the door, we need everybody focused on the real problem, not a change in tradition."

"Also, the bad guys will be looking for any weakness they can capitalize on. Wrong time to switch leaders." I settled back between them and thought, *Well, that was easy.* "What about, you know, accommodations?"

"I think the house will accommodate anything you want," Zach said. "If it doesn't, we'll remodel."

I felt myself turning pink. "I mean sleeping together. What about the three of us sleeping together? How often? Not just, you know, sex. But maybe we need to think about that, too."

"She's blushing," David said.

"It's cute. Also hot." Zach teased the upper slope of my breast. "I think we're going to have sex pretty often. How about if you just tell us when you're too tired?"

My skin burned darker red. "Are you both going to sleep with me? Or take turns? Or what?"

"I think we should all share rooms." David looked at Zach when he said it, not me. "If we're both with her, she's twice as safe. We can work out whatever we need to for individual time, but we should both stay with her."

"Agreed."

"That sounds ominous," I muttered.

"We take our role as your mates seriously," Zach said. "Get used to it. You're newly transformed, you're a red queen with unknown special abilities, and you're pregnant. You can swear at us for being overprotective, but we're not letting you out of our sight."

Considering how much trouble I got into every time I was out of their sight, they probably had a point. "Okay," I said. Then I frowned. "What do you mean, unknown abilities?"

"You haven't had a chance to discover them," David said. "Jack learned he could diagnose and heal with his touch by accident, shortly after his first change. He can also do astral projection. We don't know what you can do yet."

"Oh." With my luck, my superpower was probably excessive blushing. Then a thought struck me. "There might be one thing. When I changed shape the first time, I did it the same as David. But today, with Ray, just my face shifted. Then I changed all the way. Is that unusual?"

"Yes." Zach met David's eyes over me. "Partial shifting isn't unheard of, but it's a rare ability. Useful in a fight, as you discovered."

"So we know what I can do."

"No." David shook his head. "We know one thing. Don't assume there won't be more."

I blew out a breath. "It'd be nice if this werewolf thing came with a manual."

Zach grinned at my tone. "Well, no relationship comes with a manual, so we'd have to write our own anyway. Back to accommodations, we put you in this suite for security reasons and if you don't object, we'll all share it. We can knock down the adjacent wall if we need more space."

"I don't object." I looked at Zach, then David, feeling unaccountably shy. "I want you both with me."

"I'll want solo time," David said. "Time when you're mine alone and I don't have to share you. This will be our shared space, but either Zach or I should be able to arrange some time alone with you when we need it."

"Not a whole night," I said. "I don't want either of you kicked out of your own bedroom. But we should be able to agree on privacy for an hour or two."

"I'll want you all to myself once in a while, too," Zach agreed. "We're possessive and territorial by nature. Let's not strain that quality by not allowing for it."

I nodded. "I can live with that. I like being with both of you together, but I like being with you individually, too. We can find a balance that suits all of us."

"Any other concerns?" Zach asked.

Yes. You haven't told me you love me. Either of you. I couldn't bring myself to say that, so I said instead, "Aside from both of you losing all desire for me when I blow up like a balloon?"

The two of them exchanged a purely male look. Then they each cupped one of my bare breasts. "You do know these are going to get bigger, right?"

"More sensitive, too," David murmured. He teased my nipple until I squirmed in reaction.

"And I'm going to blow up like a balloon," I reminded them. "You're really okay with that?"

"We're kind of hoping you'll be willing to do it again," Zach said. "Not with Jack. With us."

"Oh." I blinked at the thought. "It's probably going to happen even if we're not trying. But I think for the short term we all have enough to get used to."

"We don't plan to keep you barefoot and pregnant in the kitchen," David said. "But you should know we both want children."

This was making my head spin. If I had one with each, my three children would all have separate fathers. "Is it a deal breaker?" I asked.

"There is no deal breaker." Zach bent his head to kiss the curve of my shoulder. "You get us. That's the deal. The rest is details."

"Oh," I said again, trying to absorb that. Nothing that would make either of them walk away from me. They might not have said they loved me, but they sure as hell were committed.

"So how do we do this?" I asked Zach. "Is there something we do or say, something formal?"

"It's already done." He looked surprised. "You acknowledged us both. Now we make an announcement."

Already done. Mated. Twice. I slid down on the bed, needing to be horizontal to take that one in. They came with me, and we shifted into a comfortable arrangement on our sides with David spooning me and Zach facing me, both of them holding me.

"You realize we can't get away with no ceremony at all," I said when I thought I could string words together coherently. "I have human friends and family who are going to expect a wedding."

"So we'll have a wedding." Zach's lips covered mine in a long, deep kiss. The sensation seemed multiplied by David's presence. *Double the pleasure, double the fun,* I thought, feeling a little giddy. Then reality took me down a notch.

"Yeah, about that." I put my hand over David's on my breast, pressing him closer while I looked at Zach. "Only one of you can be the groom."

It was David who said, "Zach. He gets all the formal titles. That way it's consistent."

"And it won't bother you?" I turned my head to kiss his upper arm as I asked the question.

"You're my mate. I don't need any other acknowledgment." His hand moved on my breast, sending a wave of heat through me. "As long as we all get the wedding night."

"Okay with you?" I asked Zach, knowing my lips were puffy from kissing him and my face was flushed from what David was doing to me.

"He'll stand up with us," Zach said, watching me relax into David's hold and surrender to the pleasure of his touch. "Best man. But the three of us will know the vows are for all of us."

I smiled. "I like that." Then I sobered again. "We'll have to wait awhile. We'll have to think of some explanation for all this, too."

"Why wait? You're already ours," David growled, burying his face in the curve of my neck.

I rolled my eyes, even though he couldn't see my face. "I can't tell the people who loved me and raised me from infancy that I'm marrying a guy I met less than a week ago, but it's okay because we have a mystical bond. Oh, and on the way to the altar I slept with somebody else who is the father of their future grandchild."

Zach laughed. "At least the baby will have red hair. Nobody's going to question where that came from."

I scowled. "It's not funny." Although it sort of was.

He kissed me once more, and that combined with David nuzzling my neck and teasing my nipple made me forget everything else for a minute. When Zach started talking again, I had to force myself to focus on the words.

"Tell your friends and parents we've been serious for a while but kept it quiet because we wanted to be sure. We're going public now because you're pregnant and you're moving in with me. Set a wedding date six months out. That will give everybody time to get used to the idea and not feel like you're rushing into something you might regret."

I blinked. "That sounds so smart and adult. No wonder you're in charge." It was a good cover story, too, believable and completely omitting the outlandish truths nobody would swallow. It would even cover my pre-transformation hibernation and explain why I'd been avoiding everybody.

He touched my lips. "I told you we could make things work with your human friends and family. I'd rather ease into it and get their acceptance than alienate people who matter to you."

"Thank you." I stared at him for a minute, lost in wonder. I could almost see our wedding day.

A garden wedding, early summer. Dancing first with Zach and then with David by the large fountain where we'd all danced for the first time. My white dress floating over the grass and a string quartet playing in the background. All twelve of my handsome men in their tuxedoes making Michelle drool.

"Look at that," I told Zach when David brought me back to

him. "My maid of honor's giving Matt the eye, and he's eyeing her back."

We watched them watching each other and I thought how right it would be if the two of them got together. So he grew fur once a month; no guy was perfect. And he'd rock her world in bed. Then I gasped at a sudden sharp sensation and put a hand on my stomach.

"Okay?" It was Zach who spoke, but both Zach and David moved closer, hands going to my round belly in reflexive response.

"Yes. I think Junior wants to dance, too." We stood in a circle of three, feeling the baby kick, our eyes meeting, and it was a moment so beautiful, so perfect, I thought my heart couldn't contain my happiness.

"Chandra? Jack's coming."

I blinked. I was lying on my back, looking up at Zach and David. Their faces were drawn with alarm. The music and the scent of summer garden went away.

"What happened?" I asked.

Zach answered me. "You stared off into space and stopped responding. You couldn't hear us and didn't blink or follow anything with your eyes. David called Jack to see what's wrong."

Oh. I licked my lips. "I think another unknown ability just manifested. I was at our wedding."

CHAPTER TWENTY-FIVE

"YOU WERE AT OUR WEDDING?" ZACH STROKED MY FOREHEAD, AND I wasn't sure if he was trying to soothe me or check for fever.

"Yes." I frowned in concentration, going over the details in my head. "It was here, outside in the gardens, by the big fountain. About six months from now, like you said. All of you guys were in tuxes, and my friend Michelle was my maid of honor. I danced with both of you, and then we all felt the baby kicking."

I bit my lip in sudden worry as another thought struck me. "Or maybe I only saw a potential future. Like it could happen that way, but only if we don't screw up."

"Then we don't screw up," David stated in a flat voice.

I nodded. Good plan. I didn't want to screw up. I wanted to dance with my two mates at our wedding, to celebrate with my old family and my new family. We all had too much to lose. So we wouldn't.

Not to mention, I had an almost gleeful desire to see Michelle dating Matt. I missed her. I missed all my friends, but I'd been surrounded by testosterone at Wolf Manor and some girlfriend time was going to be long overdue.

"Girlfriend time," I said out loud, feeling thunderstruck. Then I looked at Zach. "I have an idea."

But before I could run it past him, we were interrupted.

"Hey." Jack came into the bedroom and made his way over to me. "How're you doing?"

"Fine." I beamed at him. "Good news. We make it through the first two trimesters without major problems."

Zach pulled the sheet up over me and I realized I'd forgotten I was naked. Oops. Oh, well, I didn't have anything Jack hadn't seen already.

"That is good news." He was studying my eyes, not my body. I wondered if my pupils looked funny. "And you know this how?"

"I visited the future. Not physically. My body stayed right here. It must've looked like I was having some sort of seizure."

Jack nodded and put his hand on my forehead. I felt it grow warm above and between my eyes. "Your third eye is active," he informed me. "The spiritual eye. Did you ever have visions before you changed?"

I thought back to my dream of running over the moon tiles in the solarium with the pack. "Not exactly. I had some dreams. And, you know, everybody has intuition. Instincts. But not like this. This was like being there. Sounds, smells, everything."

"Well, fortune-teller, I think you're just fine." Jack took his hand away and dropped a light kiss on the spot that had warmed under his touch. "You're a little fatigued and showing signs of stress, but that's normal, all things considered. Your body's still adapting to the change and you haven't exactly been taking it easy."

I made a face. "It's not my fault. Stuff just keeps happening."

"No, it's not your fault." He tousled my hair and moved back to give way to my mates. "You two should try to keep her in bed for the afternoon. By whatever means necessary. Doctor's orders."

"Like that'll be restful," I muttered. But it might be interesting. And wasn't physical exertion good for stress?

Jack left and I held up a pre-emptive hand before Zach and David could make me forget what I'd been about to say. "Wait. No nookie until you tell me what you think of this."

"Think of what?" David moved up beside me and trailed his hand down my bare spine. "Talk fast."

"Girlfriend time," I repeated, catching Zach's eye. "The panthers tried to grab me, right? So what if we turned the tables on them? Took their queen and had a little heart-to-heart chat with her? Maybe we could settle things with diplomacy."

Zach's lips twitched. "Diplomacy at gunpoint?"

"Whatever works." I shrugged. "They won't go against their queen, will they? If she agrees to a truce with us, they have to go along with it. It's not like they can replace her. That just leaves the rogue wolves to sort out, and I don't think they know the Leshii's returned. They wouldn't go against him. I'm not sure they could." I remembered the compulsion to go down on my belly before the lord of the forest and the way the panther had run at his command. "But no matter what, we're younger, stronger, and we can beat them. We just can't keep fighting all of them combined or they'll wear us down with sheer numbers."

"This is a good idea." Zach looked at David. "What's the easiest place to get to her?"

"When she comes out of the police station after paying her fine," David said without hesitation. "Or if there's no opportunity, follow her and wait for the right chance."

"If Jack can astrally project, maybe he can spot when she's vulnerable and pass on the information," I suggested. "Then Matt or somebody grabs her."

"I like it." Zach pulled the sheet back and gave me a caress that made me melt. "I'll go tell our guys the plan. You two, don't get too carried away without me."

"Wouldn't dream of it." I caught him by the shirt and drew him down for a kiss. "Hurry back."

As he left, David scooped me into his lap. I curled into him and said, "One of us has too many clothes on."

"Must be me." He ran his hand over me, breast to belly, then lower. "You don't have any."

"Not a stitch." I grinned at him, feeling light and flirtatious.

"Stop trying to get me to knot you again before Zach gets back." David settled his hand between my legs, cupped my mound, and squeezed. "We just finished agreeing to share our toys."

"Am I your toy?" I wiggled my hips, inviting him to do more.

"You're my mate." His palm pressed into my sex and my body hummed in delight. Then his lips took mine, and he showed me what that meant.

"Told you not to get too far without me," Zach said from behind us.

I blinked, feeling blind and dumb. "Didn't you just leave?"

"Fifteen minutes ago." He raised a brow at me. Then he started stripping.

I watched. Then I looked up at David. "Shouldn't you be doing that? I think I mentioned you had on too many clothes."

"If I hadn't left them on, I'd be inside you already." He plunged a finger into my sheath to demonstrate his meaning. I groaned.

"Get naked, both of you, and hurry."

"She's so demanding." David plunked me onto the mattress, stood, and took off the clothes I'd objected to.

"I know." Zach nodded. The two of them stood over me, looking down at my sprawled body. "We should teach her a lesson, or she'll be like that for the rest of our lives."

"Yeah." David gave me a look that could've scorched the sheets. "Maybe she should learn to be careful what she wishes for."

"Um." My belly fluttered as the two of them climbed onto the bed and headed toward me, twin predatory expressions on their faces. "What are you going to do to me?"

"Everything we want to."

I gulped. Then giggled when Zach scooped me up and nuzzled my stomach before blowing a raspberry on my bare skin. "Hey. That tickles."

"Good." He carried me toward the bathroom while he grinned at me. "You needed a tension breaker. Speaking of which, I think it's time for a nice, relaxing bath."

I looped my arms around his neck and hung on. "As long as you both fit in the tub with me."

"It's a large tub." Zach reached it, kissed my nose, and stood me on my feet. David was already there, turning on the water and adjusting the temperature. He sprinkled some bath salts in, then held his hand out to me. I took it and let him help me in.

I settled back and looked up at them. "Well?"

"How's your skin sensitivity now?" David asked.

I hadn't thought about it, but now that he brought it to my attention, the overreaction to cloth and friction from yesterday was gone. "Fine."

"Want a loofah, then?" He brought out a mitt and slid his hand into it, and I realized he planned to do it for me.

"You're bathing me like a kid?"

"No. I'm bathing you like my mate who's been overdoing it and needs pampering."

Zach slid into the tub with me and arranged us so that I rested my back against his chest. David wet the loofah, added some gel, and began a very gentle massage on the bottoms of my feet. He worked up to the heels and ankles, calves, and as much of my thighs as he could reach with me sitting. Then Zach lifted one of my arms and supported the weight while David gave my hand, arm, and shoulder the same treatment before switching sides.

I relaxed and gave myself up to the novel experience of being attended to in the bath by two lovers. Residual tension melted away. The loofah felt just rough enough to stimulate my skin without irritating. The bath salts softened the water, and when each thoroughly stimulated limb returned to soak, the soothing submersion made me sigh out loud.

Zach leaned me forward so David could scrub my back. I rested my cheek on my knees, eyes closed in bliss, savoring the slow strokes David made up and down my spine, along my shoulder blades, then switching to tiny circles that erased all hints of strain in my neck.

I got lowered into the water to rinse my back, and wet my hair before Zach drew me back against his chest and began to massage shampoo into my scalp. His fingers moved from the front of my head back, working my neck again, then the sides. He finished with a temple rub that wiped out all memory of the headache the day's dilemmas had built.

Back into the water, floating while Zach's fingers rinsed away the shampoo. I felt like I was drifting in a dream. A sensual dream that drugged my responses and seemed to slow time down. Hands moved over me, following the curves and dips of my body. Shaping and cupping my breasts, tracing the hollows of my throat, the line of my rib cage, the swell of my hips.

One pair of hands stroked my thighs, first outer, then inner, ending with a gentle petting of my sex. Another pair caressed my breasts and teased my nipples, circling them, squeezing, tugging.

I didn't resist when my legs were hooked over David's shoulders. Zach lifted me until my hips rested on the edge of the tub and held me while wandering lips replaced hands. David kissed the swells of my breasts, the dip of my belly, then moved lower. He traced my labia with his tongue but didn't thrust it inside me or lap at the sensitive bud of my clitoris.

"David," I whispered. I lifted heavy lids halfway to look at him. His eyes met mine with the expanse of my naked torso between us.

"Mmm?" He planted another kiss between my legs, then drew back.

"I'm glad you're here." My throat constricted for a moment. I reached my hand out, slid my fingers through his hair. "I thought I'd never touch you again after yesterday." Having both of them with me now seemed like a miracle, all the more precious for being so unexpected.

"Same."

The two of them helped me all the way out of the tub, and David wrapped me in a towel. Zach dried my hair. Between them they cocooned me in comfort and blotted away the excess moisture before Zach took the damp towels to hang while David carried me back to bed.

"I love you," I whispered, turning my face into his neck.

"My mate." He cradled me close, then lowered me to the bed. Both of them joined me, bracketing me between two male bodies that tantalized and mesmerized me. I wanted to wallow in the sheer joy of unhurried contact.

"I didn't get to do this yesterday," I told Zach, running my hands over him. "I wanted to do so much for you, and I couldn't."

"You have time now." He pulled me into a kiss that seared my senses. "We have the rest of our lives."

"Mmm." I kissed my way down his chin, his neck, his chest, explored his sculpted abs, then touched my tongue to the tip of his penis. I tasted salt and male musk, savored the silky texture of the skin pulled tight over his engorged organ.

I drew him into my mouth and closed my lips just below the ridge of his head. He groaned and settled his hands into my hair. I explored him with my lips and tongue, felt him tighten as I rode his length in and out of my mouth.

"Stop, or you'll make me come," he muttered in a voice gone thick with desire.

I worked my way back up to his head, let him slide free of my mouth with a tiny sigh of regret, then traced his length with the tip of my tongue. "You say that like it would be a bad thing," I murmured.

"It would be. I want to come buried deep inside you." The explicit words drew a visceral response, making my inner muscles clench in anticipation.

I turned my head to look at David and found him watching me. I smiled at him and moved to give him the same treatment.

"I want to touch you both everywhere. I never want to stop," I said as my lips touched his flat male nipples and my fingers traced his biceps, his shoulders, lost in discovery and wonder.

I took David into my mouth and felt Zach's hands move over me, stroking the curves of my buttocks, smoothing the backs of my thighs, sliding between to tease and tempt me before one finger pushed inside my sex.

I shifted to encourage him and drew David deeper, licking him like some exotic candy, loving him with my lips. Zach pushed a second finger into me, and began to work me with leisurely deliberation that built until I had to release David to draw in air.

"Zach. That feels so good."

"It's going to feel better," he promised.

He shifted onto his back and pulled me on top of him. Our mouths met and our tongues tangled in a deep, demanding kiss that sent heat curling through me and made my heart pound in my chest.

Zach's strength and warmth under me was a heady delight. David's hands replaced Zach's, caressing my butt and moving lower, but then I felt something cool and slick stroke over my anus and realized what he intended.

They were going to have me between them again.

While Zach seduced me with kisses and relieved the ache in my breasts by crushing them against his chest, David prepared me to take him. He worked two lubricated fingers into me and scissored them inside in a gentle stretching. The action pressed my sex against Zach's, and I forgot to breathe, head spinning with the rush from that intimate contact.

They shifted my hips up, and then Zach's cock probed my labia, aligned, and thrust deep inside.

David withdrew his fingers, positioned himself, and I felt the head of him press into my anus, the lubricant easing that tight entry. He moved forward by stages until I'd accepted all of him and both of them filled me.

Our bodies glided and rocked, met and retreated, moving together in a pattern that became a dance of pleasure. The pace quickened gradually, hearts racing, breath coming faster. Soft sounds, hoarse moans. *More. Yes.*

They took me and I gave myself to them, each stroke claiming me until there was nothing more. There was tender possession and rough lust and heat that built to an inevitable peak. We spent ourselves, and when release came it came with unexpected force.

I collapsed on Zach, feeling David's body sheltering my back while both of them remained locked inside me. "Zach," I whispered his name, kissed his chest. "Thank you."

His hand found my hair, caressed. "For what?"

"For giving me this." I stroked his shoulder, the only part of him I could reach without moving. "For seeing what I couldn't. For sending David to me, because you knew I needed him, too."

"You cried for him like your heart was broken," Zach said, his voice low and rough. "I knew you were mine. I could have kept you to myself. But if it was in my power to take away your pain, how could I do anything else? I'm your mate."

I blinked away moisture. "I don't deserve you."

"Yes, you do." He stroked my hair, cupped my head against his chest. I listened to the steady rhythm of his heart.

David kissed my shoulder, then carefully withdrew. Zach lifted me off of him and onto the mattress. I sank into it with a soft sound of pleasure. They settled me between the protective shelter of their bodies, both of them holding me close. I clung to them as I slid into sleep, not wanting to let go ever again.

CHAPTER TWENTY-SIX

"ALMOST PARTY TIME." ZACH'S VOICE BROKE INTO THE DREAMY HAZE I was drifting in, dozing but not really awake or asleep.

"Mmm." I stroked his arm and snuggled closer. "Time to get up?"

"Yes."

Damn. But then, the sooner we settled all of our problems, the sooner we could all go back to bed. I reached for David and frowned when I found the space on my other side empty.

"Where'd he go?" I asked, blinking sleepy eyes at Zach. The sight of him temporarily made me forget everything else. His eyes glowed golden and his face showed the excitement of the hunt. A predator ready to pounce.

"To get ready for our guest." Zach flashed a wicked grin at me. "She's on her way. We want to welcome her properly."

I laughed. "You're evil."

"You thought of it."

"Yeah." I bumped my body into his. "I'm highly motivated to resolve the cat problem. It's interfering with my sex life."

"Is that a complaint? Because the way you came screaming the last time, there, I didn't think your sex life was suffering."

"My sex life is fantastic." I smiled wide, glowing with remembered satisfaction. "Which is why I resent all these damn interruptions. Just once, I want to dance outside or run in the woods with you and David and not have some belligerent panther crashing our party."

"You sound a little belligerent yourself." Zach tweaked my nipple, teasing and playful.

"It's my territory they're invading and my sex life they're screwing with."

"Well, let's go screw with them."

"Call me payback," I said to Zach, jumping out of bed.

He got the joke and laughed, then laughed harder when he saw my consternation at finding no clothes.

"Why don't I have anything to wear?" I asked him. "I live here now. I should have clothes. That's another thing all these crises are keeping me from taking care of. I don't have time to run back to my apartment and pack."

"You have clothes for today." Zach padded naked and barefoot into the sitting room and came back with a shopping bag. "Here."

"My hero." I kissed him, and it wasn't good enough so I did it again. Then I took the bag and drew back from the lure of his mouth before I got carried away.

"Am I?"

The serious note in his voice made my head snap up. "What? Yes." I dropped the bag and wrapped my arms around his waist, leaning in close to press my body against his. His arms came around me to hold me there.

"You helped me when the transition was burning my body up and I had no idea what was happening to me. You helped me understand a world I didn't know existed. You brought another man into our relationship because you saw that I'd bonded to you both, that I needed him, too."

His arms tightened around me. "Chandra. I'm a selfish bastard who dragged you into the middle of a shape-shifter war."

"The panthers and rogue wolves are not your fault," I pointed out. "You didn't cause the problem, but we're going to solve it. And what would have happened to me if you hadn't had the pack watching me? David wouldn't have been there to bring me to you when I collapsed. If I'd gone through heat and my first change alone, would I have even lived through it?"

I pulled back to look into his eyes. "Zach, you saved me. You and David both."

"I wanted you for the pack at first," he said, his face tight. "Because you belonged with us, and we needed you. Then I got close to you at the mall, and I just wanted you. I wanted you for myself. I wanted you so much I may have influenced your choice when you should have been David's alone."

I felt my jaw drop. "Zach, is that really what you think? You think I don't know my own mind, my own heart? You think I couldn't tell the difference between compulsion and willing submission?" I shook my head in amazement. "I surrendered to you. I acknowledged you. I gave myself to you. That was my choice."

He bent his head to brush his lips over mine. "My mate."

The way he said the words warmed me. "You bet." I rubbed my nose against his. "This is a macho thing, isn't it? You think you're not doing a good enough job protecting the little woman from the dangerous world."

"I'm not." The stark declaration boggled me.

"Zach, I killed a man this morning." Saying it made me cold inside all over again. "The world is dangerous, but so are we. And we have something that makes braving the danger worthwhile."

We held each other for a long moment. It was hard to let go to dress, but we could both feel the clock ticking. We needed to announce our unconventional status to the pack, get their backing, and deal with an angry cat queen in hopes of gaining an end to the territorial fighting.

The shopping bag held jeans and a soft red sweater that I had to stop and pet because it was cashmere. Socks, underwear, and bra were also in the bag. Whoever had been sent shopping had been thorough. I took everything into the bathroom.

When I came out clean and dressed, I found Zach dressed and looking mouthwatering in the sitting room. He held his hand out to mine and crooked a smile at me. "Ready?"

"Ready." I squared my shoulders, placed my hand in his, and we went down together to face the pack. David joined us in the hall.

"Everybody's in the library," he said.

"Is our guest here yet?" Zach asked him.

"Here and secure."

"How do we do this?" I asked them both.

"We stand with you, and you declare your choice."

I took a deep breath. "Then what?"

"Then they either stand with us or they stand against us," Zach stated in an even tone.

Crap. My stomach knotted. "Does anybody already know besides Jack?"

David shook his head. "We've been upstairs, but it's understandable that I'd stay close to you during a crisis. The general assumption we all made last night was that you'd made your choice and it was only a matter of formality to acknowledge Zach."

"Zach plus one," I said brightly, trying to stay positive. "Almost what they're expecting."

We filed into the library, David first, maybe to make sure it was safe for us to follow, then me, then Zach.

It looked different from the militant atmosphere of this morning in some subtle way. Maybe because the readied weapons were now being kept out of sight.

The pack waited in various positions around the room with serious faces. I tried to get a feel for the mood of the moment. Not the carnal atmosphere of yesterday, when they'd all welcomed me as potential mates in openly sexual competition, and more sober than the celebratory tone at dinner before we'd all changed together and gone out to sing to the moon.

That party had gotten crashed in a big way, and I felt a twinge of regret for that. My first full moon with the pack, and we hadn't spent it running and hunting together. We'd spent it defending our turf.

I took my position by the fireplace, and Zach and David moved to stand a little behind me to my left and right.

I looked around for Jack and indicated with a hand gesture that I wanted him to come forward. He did, and I took his arm. Partly I wanted the support, but partly I wanted a visual statement of unity.

"Hi," I said to the assembled wolves. "Before I announce my choice, I'd like to announce something else. Last night, the lord of the forest gave me some interesting news. You already know from this morning that a child was conceived in this room yesterday."

I paused and waited a minute before I continued, "Jack is not my mate, but he's my co-parent and we plan to share the happiness and the responsibility this new life brings to the pack. Our baby is loved and wanted by us, and we hope another red wolf will be welcomed by all of you."

There was an uproar of congratulations as they all came to hug me, pat my tummy, shake Jack's hand or punch him in the shoulder. Relief rushed through me. So far, so good. And having them on my side in one thing made it more likely they'd at least give my unconventional choice a receptive hearing.

When the room quieted down, I kissed Jack on the cheek and let him go. "Thank you. I hope you'll be equally pleased that I'm formally recognizing Zach as our alpha and king."

A general cheer sounded, but when they started to come to stand with us, I held up my hand. "I have one other thing to say. Zach is my mate, but he recognized the truth before I did. It's unprecedented and we've spent the day trying to come to terms with it before we asked you to do the same." *Deep breath. Deep breath.* "I bonded with two mates. If you accept us, Zach will remain alpha and leader and David will remain second in command, but all three of us are mated."

Dead silence. Jack came to stand with us again. I stepped back to take my two mates by their hands. And the room fell away. I had time to recognize what was happening and think, *Ah, shit, not now,* and then I was in the woods with the rogue werewolves.

"I say we hit them now," one was saying. "Don't wait for the panthers to arrive. Let them be the second wave."

"Ray's dead," another stated. "They know what we're planning."

I scanned the scene, trying to find some clue to the time of day. Was this now, an hour from now, near evening? It wasn't dark, but I couldn't gauge the position of the sun from inside the thick forest.

"Do you want to run with them?"

The voice to my side startled me. I turned to the Leshii and blinked. His skin glowed like white marble and his eyes shone with green fire. I wondered if I was seeing his true form. "What do you mean?"

"It's not a rhetorical question." He nodded to the renegades who'd left our pack years before. "Do you feel an urge to run with them?"

"No." I bared my teeth. "I don't feel pack. I see invaders."

"It's your pack now. Defend it."

Then he disappeared and so did everything else. I blinked back to awareness in the library and found myself supported between both of my mates.

"I'm back," I said, struggling to stand on my own. "Crap, that's annoying. Is that going to just happen all the time without warning? I'll never be able to get behind the wheel of a car again."

Then I blinked again and saw that we were surrounded by worried faces, all the wolves pressing close.

"Sorry." I waved an apologetic hand. "Just a little visit to the future. We're about to be attacked by the rogue wolves. They don't want to wait for the panthers. They'll hit us as the first wave and the cats will come second, unless we can stop them by making a truce with Rhonda."

I dropped that bombshell on top of my last and waited to see what they'd do. Then I saw they were doing it already. Standing with us, united.

They each dropped to one knee, fisted hand over heart, the way they'd first greeted me. "Our queen."

I felt my eyes sting at the sight and blinked furiously. They were mine, and I was theirs. Pack. They weren't strangers to me now, not one of them. We'd eaten together, danced together, shared the sexual intensity of estrus where we'd all given and taken pleasure. We'd changed forms together, sung to the moon together, and fought for what was ours.

Defend, the Leshii had said. Do the right thing. He'd given me a clue to my awakening abilities. In order to do the right thing, I needed to know what that was. Now I had a new window on the world to help me see what was right.

The pack was my family and my home, and the rightness of that resonated through my soul.

There would be more cause for celebration in the future. We needed life, growth, hope. We needed an end to the territorial struggle.

The pack rose to their feet again and I felt the power of our unity. I'd joked about mystical bonds with Zach and David earlier, but I felt it here and it was real. All of us were linked, and together we were strong.

Time to have a chat with a cat. I took a deep breath. "Okay, guys. Let's do some diplomacy."

CHAPTER TWENTY-SEVEN

"RHONDA." I BEAMED AT HER, FEELING FIERCE BEHIND THE SMILE, AND took a seat opposite. Zach stood at my back. The rest of the pack waited outside the windowless room she'd been stashed in. "So good to see you."

She glared at me through narrowed eyes. The phrase *mad as a wet cat* went through my mind. She'd had time to dry off after the dunking she'd gotten, but she still looked pissed.

"So I have you to thank for this." Rhonda nodded at her body, which was thoroughly tied to a chair. It might not keep her from shifting, but it would at least slow her down.

"You mean your stunning new look?" I eyed the rope. "That wasn't my idea, but you know, a lot of guys are really into the bondage thing. If you want to try it out at home, you can keep the props."

She hissed at me, "Bitch."

"That's right." I nodded, smiling. "I never did answer your question at the mall, although you actually asked Zach, not me. But just to be clear, yes, I am his bitch."

"You're going to be sorry you did this." She jerked sideways, trying to loosen the knots, but whoever tied her knew how to do it right and it was a wasted effort.

I wondered if David had done it. If so, there was a game I wanted to play with him later. But for now, no happy distractions. Focus.

"I doubt it." I leaned back and crossed one knee over the other, letting my top lower leg swing in a deliberately careless pose. "See, I was thinking, we female shape-shifters are rare. And you showed such an interest in me. I thought I should give us girls a chance to talk. It seemed only right."

"We have nothing to talk about." Rhonda glared at me, and I wondered at the depth of her animosity. I mean, really, was I the one who'd been causing trouble?

"Are you sure? Because I have to believe you want something." I tapped my chin. "I wonder what it could be? I don't think it's about real estate. Until the rogue werewolves confused things, our two groups had a relatively peaceable history. Maybe the occasional fight, but you know, boys will be boys."

"I'm not playing this game with you."

I shook my head. "Oh, Rhonda. It isn't a game. If you didn't know that before, watching me disembowel Ray should've given you a clue."

Something flashed in her eyes. What, I wasn't sure. Not fear, but something.

Acting on instinct, I went on, "Speaking of Ray, I was rude to run off this morning without saying thank you. You kept your cats from interfering in a pack matter." I put my feet flat on the floor and leaned forward a little. "I do have you to thank for that, don't I?"

She didn't say anything, but she didn't tell me I was wrong, either. *Hmm.*

I tilted my head to look up at Zach. "Can you give us a minute alone?"

He didn't like it. I saw it in his eyes, the tight muscle in his jaw, the firm line of his lips, and the set of his shoulders. But he nodded. "I'll be right outside."

I smiled, just for him, loving that he trusted me to handle this and to take care of myself. "Thank you."

Zach left the room and the door closed behind him. I watched him go, then turned back to my guest. "Now it's just us girls," I said. "You want something. So do we. We want to get on with our lives without cats dropping out of trees unexpectedly. We want our territory undisturbed. Your turn to share. What do you want, Rhonda?"

She gave me a long look. Finally she said, "You're serious."

"Serious as a heart attack. I want a truce. If we can accommodate what you want in exchange, it's yours."

Rhonda's eyes took on an interesting mix of lust and fear. Whatever she wanted, she wanted it bad and she didn't think I'd give it to her. Her next words confirmed that. "You won't give us this."

After a long silence, Rhonda gave me a thoughtful look. "Okay. You want me to ask? I'll ask. We want the red wolf. Not you. The other one."

My eyes widened in surprise. "Now that I didn't expect," I said. "If you wanted Jack, why were you after me?"

"We weren't. The wolves wanted you. They wanted to take

back your pack." Rhonda shrugged. "What's it to us how you work out your internal problems? But if we got you for the renegades, they promised to give us the red wolf in exchange."

"Ah." That made a certain sort of sense. But still, why Jack? "I can't give you Jack. He's my friend. He's my packmate. He's also my baby daddy, so he's really not replaceable."

Her face froze and for a moment genuine hatred showed in her eyes. Oh. I hit a hot button there.

"Why do you want him?" I leaned forward, looking for clues in her reactions. "Do you want to kill him? Keep him? Or did you maybe just need to borrow him?"

Rhonda stayed stubbornly silent. My brain kept racing, trying to solve the puzzle. Turning pieces this way and that. What fit?

Red wolves were special, but the panthers didn't want just any red wolf. They wanted Jack, who could diagnose and heal with a touch. Rhonda had started to warm up to me . . . until I called Jack my baby daddy. She was the queen, she had no shortage of strong, virile males around her, and unlike wolves, cats did not mate for life.

So why weren't there any little kittens tumbling around?

"You're infertile," I said as the pieces fell into place. "And human fertility experts can't help you. But Jack can. At least, you think he can. I can't promise his abilities work on your species."

Her face told me I'd nailed it.

I shook my head. "No wonder you were all willing to invade our territory in force. No wonder you were willing to hand me over to Ray." I stood up. "I can't promise he'll solve your problem, but I can promise he'll try. For whatever it's worth, I conceived right after he used his healing touch on me. If you'll give your word to declare a truce with us, I'll go get him."

"My word." Rhonda gave me an unreadable look.

"Yes. Your word." I stared back at her and waited for her answer.

She finally nodded. "Okay. If your red wolf agrees to help me, we'll declare a truce."

"Try," I clarified. "He'll try to help. If he can't, it's because his gift doesn't cover everything. And if he can't give you what you want, further attacks against us serve no purpose."

Rhonda looked at me, then down at the rope and back up. "Done. And since you offered, I do want to keep the props."

"Okay," I said, once I'd gotten out of the room without cracking up over the visual of a naked Rhonda trussed up to play naughty kitty. "Here's the deal. Rhonda needs a supernatural fertility clinic. Since no such thing exists, she's desperate. The panthers know about Jack. They were never after me, except as a means to getting Jack. The renegade wolves wanted me and agreed to trade."

While everybody absorbed that, I waited, then searched out Jack's eyes. "I promised you'd try to help her, in exchange for a truce. I did make it clear that your gift might have limits and we couldn't promise success. Jack, will you?"

He studied my face. "She stood by while Ray tried to rape you."

"She also stood by while I tore him apart," I pointed out. "And she told the other panthers not to interfere."

"So you think this is fair?"

I blew out a breath. "What's fair? We want a truce. She wants help only you can give her. Am I tempted to hold a grudge? Hell, yes, but I want peace more than I want revenge."

Jack grinned at me. "I think you're going to be a good queen. Lead me to my patient."

I grinned back at him and took his arm to introduce him to the newly cooperative panther queen.

"Rhonda, Jack. Jack, Rhonda." They looked at each other. I let go of Jack's arm and took my chair again.

"Chandra explained the situation," Jack said. "I'll need to touch you. That's how it works."

Rhonda nodded. Now that she had what she wanted, she looked tense.

"It doesn't hurt," I volunteered. "He's done it twice to me. It feels hot, and then it just feels good."

"I'm not afraid," she snapped.

"She's afraid to get her hopes up again," Jack said.

His insight made my brows raise. He really did clown to cover a serious core.

I watched while he untied her. She didn't try anything. In fact, she seemed unnaturally still, as if she feared any wrong move would make Jack back off. Once the rope was out of the way, he crouched in front of her and placed his hand over her abdomen.

Rhonda sucked in a sharp breath, and I guessed she'd just experienced that penetrating heat I remembered. I watched him work and saw the concentration it took.

That made me wonder if I could get better at controlling my prescient ability. It would make my new life easier if I could focus and learn to do it on purpose instead of falling into it by accident, when it might not be convenient. Maybe Jack could help me practice. We had different abilities, but it seemed likely that the way they worked might have something in common.

Rhonda's face relaxed, softening as Jack's healing warmth spread through her. When he finished, he moved his hand from side to side as if checking to be sure there was nothing more, then looked into her eyes.

"Your fertile cycle is coming up. I'd recommend you have sex as often as possible, with as many partners as possible, for the next two weeks."

I blinked. "Geez, Jack."

"She might be fertile with some partners, but not with others," he explained. "Since there's no way to know which, that's the best way to maximize the odds. And don't bathe or urinate directly afterward."

Too much information. I wanted to cover my face or maybe my ears, but Rhonda didn't blanch over his icky medical advice. "Will you check me again after that?"

Jack nodded. "I can tell you if it succeeded and, if not, when the best time will be to try again."

"Thank you." Rhonda stood and gathered up the rope. Jack shot me a questioning look and I mouthed, *Later*.

We all walked out, and David escorted Rhonda to a phone so she could inform the werepanthers we now had a truce, and possibly tell them to get ready for a kinky sex marathon.

I shot Jack a look after they left the room. "As many as possible, as often as possible?"

He shrugged. "It's true that she'll be more likely to conceive with some partners than others."

"Also a very convenient way to keep them all busy and out of our hair."

He grinned. "Make love, not war. So what was the deal with the rope?"

"I told her some guys were into that, and offered to let her keep it for immoral purposes."

We both laughed, and then I went to Zach to see if there'd been any developments on the rogue-wolf front. He watched me come to him with a gleam in his amber eyes that made my breath hitch.

"Hi," I said, trying not to drool at the sight of him. The unbelievable truth that he was mine hit me all over again. I wanted to fling myself into his arms, so I stopped about a foot away from him. That seemed like a safe distance. "How goes the war?"

Zach gave me a crooked smile. "So far you've cooked up a plan to negotiate a truce with the werepanthers, pulled it off, and given us advance warning of the rogue-wolf invasion. I should be asking you."

"I figured I should handle the girl talk while you focused on the other side of things." I gave him a shy smile and added, "Thank you for trusting me to do that."

He reached out to cup my cheek. "You knew what you were doing."

The open admiration in his voice made me want to blush and scuff my toes. I cleared my throat. "So no sign of them yet?"

"Not yet. We're ready for them, though." His face grew serious. "I want you to stay out of this fight. They'll be focused on you, and I don't want to give them a target."

"You don't want the good guys distracted by trying to protect me instead of fighting, either."

"True," Zach agreed. "Keeping you safe is our priority. Let us finish this."

I nodded. The logic was sound. "I'll stay inside like a good girl."

"I thought you'd be harder to persuade." He arched a brow at me. "I was prepared to offer you bribes."

"The last thing I want to do is lower our odds in a fight. I want this over." I gave him my best attempt at a sultry look. "I'm open to bribes, though."

"Good to know." Zach slipped his hand around to the back of my head, stepped closer, and claimed my lips in a heated kiss that promised many naughty things later. Before either of us could be tempted to take it further, before he could tell me what sort of bribe I could look forward to as my reward for cooperation, an alarm sounded.

Zach broke away and produced a gun from behind his back. He pressed it into my hand. "Go to your suite; lock the door; stay there until one of us comes for you. Do you know how to use this?"

I looked down and saw I was holding a .357 SIG. I aimed the gun at the floor, thumbed off the safety, checked the slide, and found a bullet ready in the chamber. I popped out the clip, found it full, pushed it back in. "Point and click," I said.

"I'd kiss you again for that, but I have to take a rain check. It's got jacketed hollow points, so you can aim to wound and he'll stop and drop." He waved me toward the stairs. "Go."

I went, running in a low crouch, heart thumping. I didn't slow down until I'd locked the door behind me. Then I went through the suite, checking for unwanted guests. Behind doors. Under furniture. Any place big enough for a dog to hide, because they might not be in human form.

Once I was sure it was clear, I picked the walk-in closet as the most protected spot and the easiest to defend. I took a position that let me cover the door.

Then I waited. This was the worst part, and it wore on my nerves from two directions. I didn't know where the enemy was or what was happening. I didn't know where my people were, if they were safe. I didn't know what David and Zach were doing.

Zach had trusted me to do my part. Now it was my turn and I had to do the same. Stay out of the way and let him prove that alpha was more than a title.

Still, a tiny corner of my mind chanted over and over again, *Be safe. Be safe. Be safe.*

I wanted to be in Zach's arms. I wanted David. I wanted my mates and the reassurance of physical contact. I wanted to know in my cells that they were with me, mine, and unharmed. I wanted them both to say the words my heart ached to hear, but as I sat there waiting I decided I'd willingly forego that for the rest of my life if I could just be held between them again.

The gun grew heavy, so I held it in a double-handed grip and rested my arms on my upraised knees from my position on the floor. I kept my eyes moving so I'd see any warning glimpse of motion or shadow. I listened for any sound and heard nothing but my own measured breathing.

Then a muffled noise stopped my heart. The sound of a door opening and closing.

CHAPTER TWENTY-EIGHT

MY DOOR? I COULDN'T TELL. IF NOT, IT WAS NEARBY. BUT WHOEVER IT was, they were on two legs, not four. Werewolves couldn't turn doorknobs.

I looked at the gun Zach had given me and wondered if it held silver-injected bullets or if the regular kind would do the job.

I quieted my breathing and stayed motionless. I didn't want to give away my presence. The silence stretched out while I strained to hear another telltale noise. If the door had been opened by one of the good guys, he would have come in calling my name and telling me it was safe. Whoever was nearby was being very quiet.

Wait, I told myself. *Listen. Don't panic.*

When a man's shape appeared in the closet door, it still startled me, even though I'd been expecting the intruder to reveal himself. I aimed for the shoulder and my finger was tightening on the trigger when a blood-chilling snarl came from behind the renegade wolf. Help was here. Relief flooded me.

"That would be your warning to stop, lie facedown on the floor, and put your hands on your head," I said.

He froze.

"There's a wolf behind you ready to hamstring you, and I have a gun pointed at you, so I strongly suggest you do what you're told."

I kept the gun steady, not sure if he'd prefer to take his chances or he'd surrender. He chose surrender, but I kept the gun trained on him all the same, even after he was on the floor. Once he was down, I could see the black wolf his body had blocked from my view. David.

The wolf gave me an approving look and shifted back to human form. He held his hand out for the gun. I gave it to him. He cold-cocked our prisoner on the back of the head with the butt of the weapon and turned back to me. I was already running to him, and his arms closed around me in a solid clasp that promised home.

"You're safe," he said in a rough voice. "God, I thought I might not catch up to him in time."

A little laugh escaped me. "Hey. I'm not the helpless female. I'm the monster in the closet."

He laughed, too, a hard, surprised sound, and then neither of us made any sound at all for a long minute. When he broke off the kiss, I held on to him for balance, my knees watery for a reason besides relief.

"Where's Zach?" I asked when I caught my breath. "What's happening?"

"In the woods. It's over. This straggler slipped free, and I came after him, but we got the rest of them. We're safe."

Over. Safe. I closed my eyes, overwhelmed by gratitude for those two words. I wasn't sure I'd believe it in my bones until I could see and touch Zach for myself, but it was really over. Somewhere ahead, the bright summer waited for us.

David left me guarding the prisoner while he found more rope, secured the renegade, and then hauled him off to rejoin the others.

I went downstairs to wait in the solarium for the pack's return, straining my eyes for a glimpse of curling hair and familiar shoulders.

When Zach finally came into view, I bolted out the door, raced across the lawn, and threw myself at him.

"Where are they?" I asked after a minute.

"Gone."

"Gone how? Dead? Ran away, possibly planning to regroup later?"

"Neither. They all surrendered, and then the Leshii appeared and sent them somewhere. He said they wouldn't be back."

That surprised me. "Sent them somewhere else? Maybe another forest, far, far away." I liked that solution. I especially liked that it hadn't involved more death, ours or anybody else's.

I'd had enough fighting, enough trouble. I wanted my mates and my pack nearby, camaraderie and comfort and closeness. I hugged Zach hard, so glad to be with him I had no words.

"Come on. Let's get you inside." Zach swung me up in his arms. I looped mine around his neck and hung on, and the rest of the pack followed us into the house.

"David said you had a bead on our straggler," he said as he carried me up to my suite. *Ours now,* I corrected myself. Mine and Zach's and David's.

"Yeah." I leaned my head against his shoulder. "I'm so glad I didn't have to pull the trigger. David was right behind him, so he was trapped between us. He gave up at that point."

"I'm glad you didn't have to shoot, too, and sorry it came that close. You shouldn't have been in danger."

"Not your fault," I said, picking up on that tone in his voice. "You sent me to safety and armed me as a precaution. Good thing, as it turned out."

Zach's mouth covered mine, and I wrapped myself around him in surrender and abandon. The sound of the door opening and closing meant David had joined us. When I felt hands settle on my hips from behind me and lips brushing the sensitive nape of my neck, I smiled against Zach's mouth.

"David."

"Mmm." His teeth grazed the curve of my neck and shoulder, sending a very pleasurable shiver through me.

My men. My mates. My future. I nestled between them and absorbed their warmth, soothed by their nearness, intoxicated by the electric dance of awareness they sent skittering over my skin. Zach's kiss deepened until the taste of him filled my senses. David's hands moved over my hips while he nipped and kissed the sides of my neck and teased the lobes of my ears. My pulse leaped, and low in my body heat coiled.

I was wearing too many clothes. We all were. I ran impatient hands over Zach, tugging at fabric, searching out bare skin. I felt starved for contact, and stroking my palms over his bare back fed my hunger for him.

I needed this. I needed them. I needed to know we were really all right. Zach and David both caught the hem of my sweater and pulled it up from the front and back simultaneously, undressing me together. Cool air touched my skin in the places where they didn't, the contrast sharpening my awareness of our bodies meeting.

Zach broke off the kiss long enough for them to draw my sweater over my head and toss it aside. David's fingers went to work on the back clasp of my bra while Zach's found the snap and zipper on my jeans. He opened them and knelt down in front of me to kiss the skin he'd bared, his lips tracing the elastic waistband of my panties.

My bra undone, David slid the straps down my arms, his warm fingers caressing sensitive points along the way. I sighed as he seduced me with a touch on the insides of elbows and wrists. Then my bra followed my sweater, and David's hands moved up my ribs until he cupped my breasts.

His hands squeezed and stroked, evoking a sweet ache for more. More touch, more pressure. My nipples tightened as if pouting for attention, and he gave it. His fingers circled, pinched, tugged, released, and every action sent a reaction through my lower body.

My sex swelled in anticipation. My inner muscles tightened in involuntary flutters. I held my breath, waiting for Zach to work my jeans down my hips, but he wasn't in a hurry. He covered my abdomen with butterfly kisses, then slid his fingertip under the elastic of my panties to touch lower, until he teased the pubic curls covering my mound.

"Zach," I whispered. I wove the fingers of one hand into his hair, reached behind me with the other to press my palm against David's hip. My head lolled back on David's shoulder, exposing the curve of my throat. He bent to trail kisses there while his hands played over my breasts.

Zach gave in to my silent urging and pulled my jeans down to my ankles. I stepped out of first one leg, then the other, and those were gone, too, leaving only the thin fabric of my underwear between me and full nudity. David just wore jeans, pulled on after he'd changed back to human form, and the heated expanse of his skin against my bare back was a pleasure all its own. I could feel the rasp of his jeans against my panties, the hard length of his cock undisguised by the layers between us.

Zach began to undress while I watched him with heavy-lidded eyes. He discarded his shirt first, and I admired his sculpted torso and shoulders while his fingers went to the snap of his jeans. The muscles of his arms worked as he undid the pants and finished stripping. The sheer masculine beauty of sinew and tendon stole my breath.

Then he was naked and my focus went to his thick, fully engorged cock.

"What big eyes you have," David murmured by my ear, noticing my reaction.

I smiled and rubbed against him. "Good thing. I wouldn't want to miss seeing any of this."

Zach came close again, and his arms went around my waist to pull my body into his. His hands moved down to grip the curve of my butt and press us more tightly together. Behind me, David went to work on getting his pants off. I pressed my face against Zach, nuzzled his shoulder, kissed the pulse point at the base of his throat. Then he turned me around, and his hands explored me while I watched David finish getting naked.

"My eyes are not all that's big around here," I said, giving David a wicked look.

He met it and crooked a finger at me. "Come here, Red." I laughed and slipped free of Zach's loose hold to close the short distance between us. I dropped to my knees and traced the length of him with my lips, kissing all the way down to the base of his cock, licking my way back up before I circled his head with my tongue.

"Stop," he muttered. His hands closed on my shoulders and urged me up. We moved to the bed, and laughter faded into sighs and kisses. We touched and clung and rolled, reassuring ourselves and one another that all was well.

I ended on my back under David, holding Zach's hand while he sheathed himself in my willing flesh. The slight bend in David's penis put pressure on a sensitive point deep inside me, stroking my G-spot as our bodies rocked together. I wound my legs around his and urged him to take me faster, but he kept a steady rhythm that drew out the building pleasure. He rode me with leisurely strokes, as if luxuriating in the feel of me under him, wrapped around him.

"David," I protested, my hips rising up to meet his thrusts and straining for more.

"Want something?" He levered himself up to look down at me, his gray eyes dark with desire.

"You."

He picked up the tempo, and a rush of sensation and emotion sent me hurtling toward an invisible peak. When I hit it and shattered, I felt Zach's lips on my knuckles. Knowing he shared the moment with us made it brighter and better.

When the knot released, David came to rest beside me, kissing me with languorous heat while Zach moved between my legs and over me. He pushed the thick length of his cock inside me while David filled my mouth with his tongue. David ended the kiss and

Zach took over, taking my lips while he claimed my pussy. The two of them taking me by turns sent my senses spinning, and the heat built to a flash point all over again.

Zach was utterly unrestrained, rough and urgent, fucking me with animal ferocity. I welcomed his dominant possession of my body and made my own claim on his, raking him with my nails and teeth. He came hard, pumping himself into me in a violent spending that went on and on, and I took it all. Then my own orgasm overwhelmed me and I rocketed to the climax, my inner muscles milking Zach's penis as he drove balls deep into me and spurted a last, liquid burst.

Afterward I cuddled between them, exchanging kisses and caresses, delighting in the slide of masculine legs against mine, the press of bodies, the sense of safety and completion I felt with them.

"I love you," I said, tracing the curve of Zach's face with a besotted finger. I drank in the glowing amber warmth of his eyes. "I don't know how I can love you both the way I do, but I love you. I don't care anymore if you don't love me back. I just want to be with you, both of you, for the rest of our lives."

Zach blinked at me, a frown tightening the relaxed lines of his face. "What?"

I rested my hand against his cheek. "I said I don't care anymore if you don't love me back. It's enough that I love you and we're together."

David rose up behind me to peer down into my face. "Not love you?" He stared at me, then at Zach. "She actually means it."

They pushed me onto my back and both of them leaned over me, propped up on their arms, bracketing me.

"She has abandonment issues," David informed Zach.

"Apparently. Why do you think we don't love you?" Zach asked me.

I felt a little defensive under their twin frowns. "Well, neither of you ever said it. I assumed."

"Assume makes an ass of you and me," David said. "I admit I've been an ass, but I thought I made it clear that it won't happen again."

"You're our mate," Zach added. "What do you think that means?"

I shrugged. "I don't know. Mystical werewolf bond. Lifelong commitment. Needing to be together."

"It means I love you." Zach bent his head and kissed me, slow, sweet, deep, and lingering. "It's a choice of heart, remember? You have my heart. You are my heart."

Oh. I stared up at him, hardly daring to believe.

"I love you," David said, his voice low and rough. "I died a thousand deaths today running up those stairs, thinking I might be too late."

I blinked, feeling tears stinging the back of my eyes. My throat ached with a swell of emotion. David kissed me, hard, fierce, hungry, hot.

Loving.

This was love, and it stole my breath.

When David raised his head, I looked from his face to Zach's, feeling dazed and awed. "You love me."

"Yes." Zach grinned at me, then turned to David. "I think she gets it now."

"Well, maybe." David gave me a doubtful glance. "She might need more convincing."

"She might." They exchanged masculine smiles, then turned them on me. Their smiles widened with sexual intent, and none of us did any more talking for a long time.

A week later, I arranged a bouquet of flowers on my birth parents' joint burial plot. I traced their names on the headstone, the dates, my personal history carved in marble, then sat back to look at the splash of life and color the blossoms made against the winter grass.

So many questions finally answered. The mystery of my identity solved. I knew who I was now. A work in progress, like I'd told Rhonda, but a work I liked. I hoped they'd be proud of me. I sat there for a minute, saying hello and good-bye. Then I looked up to see David and Zach waiting in the distance.

The past could rest now. I saw my future.

I stood up and walked toward it.

READ ON FOR A PREVIEW OF CHARLENE TEGLIA'S UPCOMING

EROTIC ROMANCE

Claimed by the Wolf: A Shadow Guardians Novel

AVAILABLE FROM ST. MARTIN'S GRIFFIN IN SUMMER 2009

*They guard humanity against supernatural threats from the five gateways
into the world. The Shadow Guardians: a vampire, a werewolf, a demon, a
dragon, and a fae are united in brotherhood—and war.*

*Shadow Guardian Kenric is an alpha werewolf forever in his prime.
When Sybil, a beautiful apprentice witch, unknowingly opens a realm to
the otherworld, there is a sudden influx of demons—and it's up to Kenric
to help her stop them. Soon their passion flares, and Kenric desires Sybil
as his mate. But to form their union, Sybil faces the ultimate test: she
must bind herself to the Shadow Guardians by sharing herself with all
five warriors.*

PROLOGUE

KENRIC WOULD HAVE CURSED WHEN THE DEMON HE PURSUED EVADED him, but in his wolf form he could only snarl. The sound of a wolf on the hunt denied its prey was more chilling than any curse he could have uttered, but the demon wasn't there to be intimidated by it. How could the creature have escaped him?

Frustrated fury drove him to cover the ground again, and the trail ended in the same place: a gate. The creature had fled through it to its home in the shadow realms, where Kenric could not follow. The sounds of battle forced him to turn away and abandon his hunt. This demon had fled, but the others still fought.

Kenric's pack boasted a hundred warriors at full strength. The allied forces of werewolves, witches, dragons, sidhe, vampires, and one rebel breed of demon had gathered in this ancient valley that had been home to Akkadians before the Sumerians and then Babylonians ruled. Here they made their stand against the invaders from the shadow realms.

The fight had been evenly matched when he ran after the demon. He returned to a slaughter. He understood why the tide had turned against them when he saw a witch strike down the last of his wolves while he was still too far away to assist.

Betrayed. The witches had changed their allegiance and now fought for the demons, turning on those who had trusted them enough to turn their backs.

The strike had clearly been well planned and executed. The demon he'd pursued had lured him away until it was too late. Now his pack lay butchered.

Kenric felt his muscles gather, tensing to spring. His eyes fixed on the coven's leader. Kill her and see how well her sister witches fared.

His strength carried him through the air. His fury found its target, and he brought the woman down. He saw then the reason for her perfidy, the price of the coven's loyalty. The witch clutched a spell parchment scribed with demon markings. Her desperate grasp became eternal as her life's blood soaked into the thirsty ground.

An unmistakable scent caught his attention. The piece of writing wasn't just inscribed by a demon; it held a demon embodied. Kenric bit at the papyrus, determined to destroy it along with her, but it eluded him, vanishing before his jaws could close around it. The witch's now empty hand still formed a claw, as if reaching after what she had traded their world for even in death.

Death took him next.

He opened his eyes to see a woman in full battle dress, heavily armed, wings extended behind her. A star shone on her forehead.

He knew who he faced. He'd seen her likeness depicted often enough.

"Inanna," he said. "What dream is this?"

"No dream." The goddess regarded him with eyes that burned with power. "You fought well."

"Not well enough."

"I am the judge of that."

Kenric supposed she was. Men forgot Inanna's other aspects when they celebrated her as the goddess of sexual drives. She was also a warrior goddess.

"Would you continue?"

The question made Kenric bare his teeth. "I would continue from death and beyond. I would continue for all of eternity."

"Fierce warrior." Inanna gave him an approving smile. "You choose the same fate as your fellow captains of battle."

"They all fell?" Kenric asked the question automatically, realizing as he spoke that of course they had. The slaughter had been too complete.

"They did. And like you, they choose to fight on. You will wear my star and defend the world's five gates against the shadow realms. Werewolf, demon, dragon, vampire, and sidhe, you are now my chosen immortal warriors, my Shadow Guardians."

As she named him, Kenric felt fingers of fire drawing on his chest. He looked down to see her sign burned into the skin over his heart, an eight-pointed star.

CHAPTER ONE

SYBIL AMES WAS ON HER WAY HOME FROM WORK WHEN SHE SAW THE estate sale sign. The radio began to blast out Ace of Base's "I Saw the Sign" simultaneously, and it struck her as synchronicity. Estate sales had all sorts of things mixed together, trash and treasure. Lured by the possibility of a real find, she put on her blinker and pulled into the drive.

The house wasn't one of the new McMansions that seemed to be all subdivisions produced anymore. It was rickety and gloomy and more than a little surly, slanting on a hill with an aggressive tilt. If any neighborhood covenants and restrictions applied, the home-owners association was either too apathetic or too intimidated to enforce them.

A prime location for a ghost. Sybil perked up at the possibility. She'd never encountered a real ghost. Or anything very interesting, for that matter. Her apprentice witch status pretty much made her

the coven's errand girl, and everything exciting remained shrouded
in secrecy. It was like being a kid who constantly heard a chorus of
"You'll understand when you're older" from the adults, but a whole
lot more frustrating since she was an adult herself.

The scattered items out in the driveway were either thoroughly
picked over already, or the estate hadn't had much to offer to begin
with.

Picked over, Sybil decided, eyeing a piece of dark walnut furniture that had started off quality before it wound up on the wrong
side of entropy. Antique dealers tended to hit sales early and buy
up anything valuable to resell.

Still, that one piece gave her hope that something else had been
discarded or passed up. Her hotel bland apartment really needed a
touch of gothic. A stone gargoyle was just the sort of thing she
might trip over here.

The passed-up, sagging armoire demanded closer inspection,
so Sybil tried the doors and drawers, half-expecting a bat to fly out
in the process. Instead, she found one drawer stuck tight. She pulled
harder, and it came loose in a rush that almost sent her backwards.
Her desperate flailing for balance wasn't graceful, but it saved her
from falling on her ass. Sybil peered into the armoire to see what
caused the drawer to stick and spotted the book.

The leather binding was cracked and dirty. She pried it out carefully and opened it up. It looked like a personal diary of some
sort. It wasn't. The faded words crowded the pages in a cramped,
back-slanting, and almost illegible style, but the content was unmistakable.

She'd found a grimoire.

Interesting. Sybil turned the brittle pages with care, slowly deciphering handwriting for which the nuns at her Catholic school would've threatened the author with hell. Not that witches believed in hell, so the handwriting atrocities would've continued with the sinner unrepentant. Sybil still found a grim satisfaction in imagining the hand responsible for her straining eyes clutching the pen with bloody knuckles.

She should put it back. She held onto it anyway, reluctant to put it down.

It looked like it contained pretty advanced magic. If she could do a spell or two out of this book successfully, on her own, without a senior witch overseeing every step of the ritual and the coven approving her experiment in advance, maybe she'd finally prove she was ready for more than sweeping up spilled salt and washing away used pentagrams.

Maybe she could finally get a familiar of her own. Maybe she could finally start learning something useful. Some real magic.

She opened the book again, deliberating, and let out a startled curse when she got a paper cut on her index finger. A drop of blood fell on the book, making the decision for her. She'd damaged it, although she could argue that the book had damaged her first. Either way, she'd have to buy it now.

She tucked it under her arm and carried it with her while she poked through the remains of the estate sale. It was a disappointment, overall. No leering stone gargoyles. No buried treasure. Just trash, except for the little handwritten leather book.

Sybil made her way to the disinterested woman in charge. "How much for this?"

The woman frowned, pulled out a pair of reading glasses, and consulted a list. "Books are two dollars," she said.

Sybil paid and carted her booty home. Home was a ground-floor apartment in Oakton, Virginia, modern and comfortable and lacking in essential character. Although considering the character the estate sale house demonstrated, maybe there was something to be said for bland. At least her apartment wouldn't attract a ghost. Then again, a poltergeist would liven the place up.

"I need a familiar," Sybil told the book. "This place needs more than a makeover. It needs life."

She put the grimoire down on her altar. It seemed like the right place for it. She felt a little shock jump from the altar's surface to her hand and let out a hiss of surprise at the static discharge.

It's just a book of shadows written in really bad cursive, Sybil told herself. The altar isn't rejecting it.

Except she had cut her finger on it, and if the drop of blood had activated some long-dormant magic . . . a chill went through her, and she took a step back. Her retreat came too late. The book opened, pages rifling as if turned by unseen fingers. Words glowed as if written in fire.

Sybil wanted nothing more than to shut the book. Instead, she found herself running her cut finger along the burning words, speaking the written words out loud. She couldn't even identify the type of spell she was compelled to recite, but the power of it was unmistakable, and it held her trapped. With each syllable, the sensation of power built. Unfortunately, it wasn't power that was hers to command. Just the opposite.

She'd wanted real magic. She realized, too late, that she should have been more specific. This was very real, and she wasn't its master. She was at its mercy.

ABOUT THE AUTHOR

Charlene Teglia made her first novel sale in 2004. Since then her books have garnered several honors, including Romantic Times Reviewer's Choice Award for Best Erotic Novel, two CAPA nominations for Best Erotic Anthology, and Romantic Times Top Pick. When she's not writing, she can be found hiking around the Olympic Peninsula with her family or opening and closing doors for cats.

To learn more, visit her on the Web at www.charleneteglia.com.